GW00503475

ROMANCE COLLECTION

RJ SCOTT

Love Lane Books

Romance Collection - Copyright

For a Rainy Afternoon Copyright ©2015 RJ Scott

Spirit Bear Copyright ©2015 RJ Scott

Child Of The Storm Copyright ©2012 RJ Scott

Valentine 2525 Copyright ©2015 RJ Scott

Three Copyright ©2016 RJ Scott

Cover design by RJ Scott

Published by Love Lane Books Ltd

ISBN - 9781076089465

Dedication

Always for my family

For a Rainy Afternoon

Maybe it's not just Robbie and Jason that can have the greatest love story ever told.

Robbie runs a small Post Office made from a converted Station House in a village northwest of London, England. He is stunned when a close friend dies and leaves him half of her estate. The only proviso is that it is to be shared equally with an American stranger, Jason, who has recently moved to the village.

The sealed box that they jointly inherit includes several rare first editions and an old cookery book. Only when the secrets of the ingredients in a particular recipe are finally revealed does everything begin to make sense... and a love story that began seventy years ago can finally be celebrated.

Chapter One

"At least you tried, Robbie." Doris patted my hand gently in her usual reassuring way.

I didn't need reassurance. I needed the damn cake to bloody work. I mean, how difficult could it be to not fuck up something when I had the recipe sitting in front of me?

I poked what was left of the applesauce cake with a fork. The mess let out an audible "bleurgh" as it collapsed in on itself around the massive hole that had somehow appeared during the cooking of it.

"I followed the recipe." And I *had* followed it, to the letter. Every single cup of flour and tablespoon of butter, every teaspoon of nutmeg, and I'd even performed algebra to work out what two-thirds of a cup was compared to a whole cup. Doris patted my hand again and nodded in her most reassuring fashion.

"Maggie made this cake for nearly ninety years. You're not supposed to be able to get it right the first time." With a shrug and another smile she left but not before the casual use of Maggie's name made my chest tighten in grief.

Maggie Simmons had been the reason I'd stayed in this village. When all my friends had left for the city or even the next town over, I was the one who had come home with a degree in art and no idea what to do with it, then stayed. Three years of study and a first in my degree and I was lost. Maggie had cornered me by the phone box one Monday morning, talking *at* me about her cairn terrier who had curled in and out of my legs as Maggie spoke, the leather of the lead wrapping around my legs. I can remember that day so clearly as the single moment when my life changed:

"I've bought the old station house," she'd explained that day. I must have said something very polite in return. I was always polite, and I liked Maggie. After all, not only was she a fixture in Burton Hartshorn, she was also an indomitable force of nature and had a mean throwing arm. If I was honest, she'd scared me just a little bit. I remember getting rotten fruit thrown at me with pinpoint accuracy when she caught me and two friends trying to steal apples from her small orchard. The phantom ache of an apple to the face had me pressing my fingers on my cheekbone and wincing inwardly.

"Great," I said, because she was evidently waiting for an answer and I didn't know what else to say.

"I'm building a library," she added.

"Where?" Surely not here in Burton Hartshorn, population three hundred and off the beaten track? Why would we need a library when we could just as well get over to Buckingham to use the library there? I remembered the excitement of the library trip out with my dad in his shiny Ford Mondeo. Libraries are big sprawling rows of shelves of every conceivable book possible; they're not tiny places in the back end of nowhere.

"Not really a library," she confided to me on that summer's day. "We could move the post office, and there would be tables, with tea and coffee from a small counter, and a reading area with big comfy sofas. We could run a book-swap program and maybe advertise with the local school." I recall the wistful expression on her face. Even then, ten years back, she was old. Well, as old as any person in their seventies and eighties appears to someone fresh out of university.

"Sounds lovely." I felt then that I was damning her with faint praise, and maybe I was. What she proposed did sound lovely. I was never happier than with my nose in a book, tea next to me, and maybe a couple of chocolate chip cookies on a plate. Add in rain against the window and I was in heaven. Of course a boyfriend next to me, with his head in my lap, would be the icing on the cake. Abruptly whatever Maggie was saying to me mixed in with a recent break up of a university romance.

"Well, I wanted to talk to you," she continued and punctuated each word with a tug on her dog's leash until the tangling around my legs was enough so I would never be able to move. "You're back now, and I need someone to run this place. Not much money, mind you, but there's rooms on the top floor, and you could do what you wanted with them."

"Pardon me?" I asked, stupefied.

"I like your mother," she said, slightly impatient. "She said to me you were rootless, and that building something around books and history and family would be an excellent idea. She suggested a small gallery area for your paintings, which I think is a lovely idea."

I wish I could have concentrated on the good parts in that sentence, but at the time all I could think was that I was angry my mum thought I was rootless. Just because I was lying longer in bed in the mornings and was becoming obsessed with daytime TV didn't mean I was rootless. Just because I wasn't painting at the moment didn't mean I couldn't if I wanted to. Right?

With a final tug of the leash, I was free from the leather confines, but I didn't move. Maggie was teasing me about a job. She had to be. I glanced around me to see if anyone was watching. My gaze caught on the beautiful old station house. L-shaped, it sat close to the deep cutting where the Great Central Main Line used to run steam trains from London to Manchester. Mothballed in the sixties, the station house had fallen into disrepair until a brewery tried to turn it into a pub. How in the hell they thought they would have anything in the way of clientele given the Red Lion was at the other end of the village, I don't know. It didn't last long, and for the last ten years or so, the station house had been a rental property with a high turnover.

"It's a beautiful place." Maggie sounded wistful.

The thatched roof needed fixing, the white windows lacked new paint, and the dark blue door was three different shades in peeled-off layers. And the garden was wild. Not just wild with weeds, but with a glorious display of autumn greens and golds that never failed to make me stop and look. Not that I am into flowers so much, but the whole effect, with the thatch and the small leaded windows and the general air of neglect, somehow captured my imagination.

"Very beautiful."

"So, I inherited money and I bought it. You should know that. It's mine, permanent, some small place that you could make a home." She spoke so carefully and stared right at me with determination in her expression.

"You want me to run the post office?" Real life caught up with my wild imaginings in which I single-handedly restored the former station house into exactly what Maggie wanted. Large oaks shaded the garden to the rear, and ivy spread from the main house to a small seventies extension with roof lights. I imagined tearing back enough of the ivy to expose the beautiful original brickwork of the unique station house.

"Not just the post office," she continued. "Stamps, parcels and post, and a small shop stocking the essentials. Like tea bags, milk, mustard, and marmite."

I didn't flinch at the strange combination of what Maggie thought were essentials. Although I did hate it when I ran out and my toast remained bereft of marmite. "Mustard. Marmite. Okay."

"And the café," she added. "With a small library, good books, and lots of romances. Maybe some DVDs. When could you start?"

I stood there for the longest time and even crouched down to pet the small dog just to give myself time to think. No one knew how much money Maggie had, but she clearly had enough to think of buying the old house that had once been the station on this old line. She wasn't reclusive with money out of sight, but she wasn't flashy either, and no one knew a lot about her. She was the very solid and focused backbone of this village while somehow remaining private. Her own cottage, the aptly named Apple Tree Cottage with its fruit orchard, was right at the center of village life just opposite the duck pond and the village green. The cottage itself dated back three hundred years, and when I was young, rumors said that Maggie was the same age.

"I have an interview at the hospital in patient records. Tomorrow." I needed her to realize I had options.

She nodded. "Good, good. Not your thing, though, is it?"

Me? Stuck in an office with computers? No, it wasn't my thing, but it was good money and there was a staff canteen with discounts. Rent to my mum, fuel in my car, enough money to buy beer and art supplies, and I would be happy. Apart from sacrificing eight hours a day, five days a week to the evil day job, that was.

What prompted me to agree I didn't know. But the endless stretch of long summer days with no idea of what I wanted to do lay before me, and I didn't really want to take the admin job. I wanted time to paint and live and do something special.

"No," I answered then. "I can start now." The small addition made her smile, and just making this decision was the best thing I'd ever done.

That was then, and now, nearly ten years had passed in which I had been the person in this special place. Pulling back ivy to reveal history was the easy part. Stocking, maintenance work, fundraising, those had been the difficult bits. And every Thursday morning, Maggie would come with her friends, all of whom she had known forever, and they would sit and talk and drink tea, and swap books, and make everything right in my world.

My art was good—I'd even sold some of the pieces and made enough to save some money after buying myself a car. What I was saving for, I don't know. Probably that same nebulous future I had always been searching for.

Then last month happened. When the end came, it was sudden. Maggie didn't come to her Thursday tea and cake meet-up, but she'd visited on Friday, told me point-blank her time was up, and that at ninety-one, she'd done her bit. After all, she'd left the station house and bequeathed it in some kind of weird estate contract for the future, and that legacy was just as important as her children.

I'd listened to her talk, and every word had knotted inside my heart in an impossible ball of grief, and that was exactly how it had remained. The day we laid Maggie Simmons to rest had been bright and sunny. The four weeks since had been the strangest of my life. I didn't have a boyfriend at that moment. In fact, if I was really honest with myself, I hadn't had a real boyfriend in over a year. The last of them, Josh, short, blond, and devious, had been the one who put me off men for the longest time. His ability to fuck up everything had left me wary and tired of the scene, of nights out, of drinking and dancing and being on view. I just wanted peace, I wanted my village in the Buckinghamshire countryside, and I wanted to lick my wounds and find Mr. Right.

"Are you okay?" Mrs. Patterson asked gently. I snapped back to the here and now and refocused my gaze on the cake. Applesauce cake was one of Maggie's most requested bakes in the small café. Alongside an ancient whistling kettle and beautiful mismatched china cups and saucers, the cake was like part of Maggie and the shop. The cake was moist, flecks of apple and a vein of cinnamon in each bite—always perfect. She'd scrawled down a recipe for me from memory, but clearly something must've been wrong with it.

"I just wanted to do something nice." This was the first Thursday since the funeral that everyone had met up again. Five instead of six now, there had been some tears and laughter over remembered times. This was the way that Maggie would want to be honored by the five women who called themselves friends.

"And we love you for that," Mrs. Patterson said. "Maggie would have laughed," she added with a cheeky wink. Mrs. Patterson was definitely one for the whole flirting business. One or two of the knots inside me unraveled gently, and I relaxed the breath that had caught in my chest. They were here talking about Maggie, remembering her, and even though my attempt at doing the same had failed miserably, it didn't matter. Somehow during the making of a damn apple cake, I had crossed over from grief to acceptance for the loss of the woman I looked on as fondly as my own grandmother.

"Yes." I poked at it again, and it deflated even further. "She would have."

When they left it was nearly five, and I cleared up and washed the crockery and cutlery. Each piece of china had its place in the small kitchen, and only when everything was put away did I actually relax. I probably needed to get out of the house for the evening. Make my way over to

Northampton maybe, meet up with Tim or Jack, friends from uni, or even Anna from the village, who had been my partner in crime when we were young kids with the freedom of every day after school to be filled with fun.

I tipped away the water remaining in the kettle and placed it back on the stove. Somehow I misjudged it and the edge of it clanked on the iron of the hob, the vibration of the clash traveling up my arm.

"Fuck it," I snapped, because that is what a person did when inanimate objects screwed around with them. No one asked what was wrong, no one would. "Sad fucking bastard, talking to yourself," I muttered.

Then with conviction that this evening would improve with beer and friends, I climbed up to my large open bedroom with its views over acres of green fields. I was going out, and I was going to celebrate Maggie's life my way: by getting completely pissed and talking crap with anyone who would listen.

By the time I'd showered, had exchanged numerous texts with Jack about which pub was better, and had decided what to wear, it was nearly seven. Wallet and keys found, I locked up the station house and crossed to my car, noting that some bastard of a bird had seen fit to christen the polished silver doors.

"Story of my life."

Chapter Two

"*E*xcuse me," a voice came from behind, and I pivoted to face the owner of it.

Pretty.

That was all I could think in my super-startled what-the-fuck-is-someone-like-that-doing-here shock. Taller and broader than me, he had the curliest near-black hair. The man stood uncertainly by the drive to the house and shifted the weight of a flight bag from one shoulder to the other. He appeared tired, and I caught him glancing behind at a retreating car, which I assumed was a taxi. Who would dump tall, dark, and sexy in my driveway?

Courtesy won over curiosity. "Can I help you?"

"I'm trying to locate Apple Tree Cottage," the man said, an American from the way he kind of drawled the words he was reading from a piece of paper. He placed his flight bag down next to the rest of his luggage and rolled his shoulders while staring at me expectantly. The name of Maggie's place was enough to perk my interest. Should I just do the polite thing and point him in the right direction? That is what I normally did. When people got lost, they would come in and ask at the post office. *Am I on the right road for Northampton? Which way is London?* That kind of thing.

"It's empty," I blurted out. Then I realized I shouldn't have said a thing. Maybe this guy was just some kind of salesman and the last thing that he should know was that the house was empty.

"I know," he said with a hesitant smile. Then he held out his hand. "Jason Young," he introduced himself.

"Robbie MacIntyre," I said in response while shaking his hand firmly. He had the most incredible clear gray eyes and at least a few days of stubble darkening his face. His grip was sure and strong, and I felt bereft when he released the handshake.

"Can you point me in the right direction? The cab driver said he had no idea and that all the cottages were called the same thing around here." I really wanted to hear him talk again because he had one hell of a sexy voice.

I pointed away and up the incline of the village to the green. "Keep going this way and you can't miss it. The front lawn butts up to the duck pond."

"Thank you," Jason said before picking up his bags and attempting to grab at two suitcases on wheels all at the same time. I could stand there just watching, or I could get with the plan and help the guy. He really did seem dead on his feet.

"Let me help," I said in my most helpful non-stalkery tone. I took one of the heavy bags and a suitcase and waited for him to gather himself to follow me. We started out on the path, but paths in this village aren't exactly straight or wide enough and we both ended up by silent agreement walking on the road. I wanted to ask him why he needed to find Apple Tree Cottage and how he knew it was empty, but my damn reserve was making it difficult to form questions.

"I only found out last week," Jason interrupted my thoughts. He sounded almost apologetic.

"What about?"

"About Maggie. She's my great-gran's sister, but we weren't close." Again with the apology. "Then I got the letter."

"Someone in the village wrote to you and told you Maggie had passed away?"

"My Uncle Bill did."

Like that explained everything. Who the hell was Bill? I wracked my brains for any Bill in the village, and despite the fact it was a common name, I was coming up empty.

Jason let out a hollow laugh. "You don't know him," he apologized. "Bill is my uncle, and he knows quite a bit about when my great-grandfather was stationed near here in the Second World War."

I stumbled in one of the cursed potholes left after a pretty dramatic winter of snow and rain. The council had promised to fix them, but I imagine a village was low on the list of road prioritizing. Still, I should have remembered that one was there. Jason reached a hand to steady me, and I flashed him a grateful smile.

"At RAF Chelveston?" I hazarded a guess. There was

nothing left of the once-large airbase that housed a small part of the US Air Force in the nineteen forties. Given that Jason was American, I made the assumption that his great-great-whatever was also American.

"Hmmm." Jason skirted another hole as we bumped over the green and toward the cottage. "Came over for two years, went back after the war, and we didn't know anything except he lost his twin brother in a bombing raid over Germany. My great-grandfather received a medal of honor. It's a long story, and I still don't understand all the connections, but the upshot of it is that the cottage is mine." I think he was a little embarrassed he had shared even that, and I didn't press for more. Considering I was English and therefore didn't by nature share a lot with strangers, it was odd that I had even been told this much. Seemed to me that unspoken was the question from Jason as to why he was the one to inherit, almost like he was justifying even being here.

We stopped at the low iron gate emblazoned with the name Apple Tree Cottage, and I felt immediate guilt that I hadn't come up here and at least mowed the lawn in the last few weeks.

Maggie had always used a gardener, but clearly he'd not been called in to work on the beautiful garden since she'd died. Anyway, who would have called him? All I knew was that he was someone from Steeple Aniston or somewhere else close by. It should have been me up here because Maggie loved this garden, and I abruptly felt like I had abandoned Maggie in some way by not keeping it nice.

"Jeez," Jason said with a whistle. "This is like everything England all wrapped up in one tidy package. How old is this place, three hundred years old?"

"Seventeen eleven. That is when it was built," I said. I knew because at the rear of the cottage, the part facing the main through road, the numbers 1, 7, 1, and 1 were built into the brickwork. And I only remembered it because the school bus stop was right by the cottage and I stared at the numbers for years while I was waiting for the bus.

"That's old."

We stood in silence for a brief moment, and he watched me expectantly. I didn't quite understand my role in this conversation, but habit had me talking. "I guess you have a key?" That was my not-so-subtle way of checking that he was actually somehow allowed inside Maggie's house.

He dropped his bag and fumbled in the side pocket before pulling out a silver house key. "From the executor," he said by way of explanation. For a second he held it out to me, and I wasn't sure what I was meant to do. Did he want me to open the door? Or was he just asking me to acknowledge he had a key?

"Good," I said. That seemed to be enough because he closed his fist around the small item. I could see the white of his knuckles at the pressure he was exerting.

I wanted to ask why he was here. Why now? Was he going to be the one responsible for emptying the cottage, then putting it on the market? I didn't ask, because I didn't want to be impolite or come across as weird. What I wanted was to find out how his uncle knew Maggie and what Jason was going to do with the cottage. I helped him to the door, then stepped back out of his way and watched him try to turn the key. I'd watched Maggie do this so many times. She would wait until I closed the post office and ask me to walk her home. I'd learned a lot about Maggie, all except how in the hell she was connected to the man cursing under his breath as he attempted to turn the key.

"Let me." I took the key from him. "You need to push it in, wiggle it a bit until you hear that click. Did you hear that?" I could clearly make out the little click that indicated the worn key and lock had connected. Evidently he hadn't, and as he leaned in to listen, I got a much closer look at those gray eyes that were actually tinged green in this light. They were really beautiful eyes, and I could write lines in songs about them and Jason's lips, which were soft and full and oh so inviting. I pulled the key out and repeated the exercise. This time he must have realized what he needed to know, and he nodded with a very serious expression on his face. "I've lost count of the times I've seen Maggie do this," I added. Then realized I had my tenses all mixed up. I *had* seen her. I wouldn't see her again because she wasn't there anymore.

"Were you close?" Jason asked me. He looked stricken, and I wanted to do my best to reassure him, but no words actually formed in my head. Instead I nodded wordlessly. Jason patted my arm in the same way Mrs. Patterson had patted my hand, concerned and reassuring at the same time.

"I'm sorry for your loss." His words were so gentle, and that accent with the melting gray eyes had me unable to push the grief down where I had it trapped. I blinked, the feelings tumbling inside me causing me to become a hundred types of upset, and instead focused on the damn key in my damn hand.

"Just turn it once all the way around to release the deadlock, then half again and the door will open." I coughed back the emotion and waited for the door to swing open. A rush of air from inside hit me, a combination of lavender and polish, but no stale air. None at all. The house might have been empty and locked, but it had never been completely airtight. It was too old to keep in the warm and keep out the cold. The inside was dark, and instinctively I reached for the light switch, but there was no response. For a few moments I found myself troubleshooting the problem, but then it hit me. "The cottage will have been cut off."

"Yeah, I know. My dad is talking it all through with them, getting everything back on for the interim, but I couldn't wait, I had to get here."

Why? I really wanted to know. The mystery in this gorgeous man was enough for any armchair Sherlock to want to solve.

"Okay, so, if you... okay." I faltered over the words. I was going to offer him my help, but the whole mystery of Jason being here was wrapped up in losing Maggie, and the strangeness of the whole thing made me wary.

"Thank you..." Jason began.

"Robbie," I reminded him. After all, considering how exhausted he was, I wasn't expecting him to recall my name.

He half smiled in the hallway, with the light of the late

evening casting an eerie glow like a halo around him. "I remember your name, Robbie MacIntyre."

I backed out then and half ran down the hill to my car before I said or did something stupid. Hell, I really needed a drink.

"And he legitimately had a reason to go inside the cottage?" Jack asked again. He reworded it each time, like I would answer differently, and he spoke slowly as if I was a small child who didn't really understand what I had done.

The soft beer buzz I had going on was enough to make the repeated questions funny rather than irritating. I'd agreed to leave my car at Jack's and get a taxi the twenty miles back to the village, and even though I had work the next day, I was going to use my car-free time well. Four beers and I was still second-guessing just why I had shown Jason how to get in the house.

"He had a key," I explained. "What else could I do?"

"He's probably some homeless guy," Jack pointed out.

Well, I guess that was a step up from his last comment where Jason was actually an international terrorist using Burton Hartshorn as his base of operations. Seemed to me that Jack was making more sense the drunker he became.

"He had posh suitcases and carry bags, and he was

smart but tired." Smooth and gorgeous, and for a second I stared into the distance recalling the small frisson of excitement at seeing Jason. Something of my thoughts must have been telegraphed on my face, and Jack interrupted them with a snort.

"Which one you checking out now?" He gestured at the guys in the bar. This was the Queen's Head, one of the quieter bars in this town and one where all kinds of mixed groups clustered on mild evenings. The back of the pub opened wide on grass that banked gently down to the riverside, and people spilled outside in small gatherings. Jack clearly thought he'd caught me eyeing up one of the many gay guys we had both spotted. Jack was straight, but he loved picking out men for me—the more overtly gay the better. He had known me twenty years, and he still didn't get it. I preferred quiet, clever, someone who appreciated art and reading and good tea, and evidently I had now added American to the list.

Thinking about Jason had to be because of the connection, whatever that was, to Maggie. But if I was really honest, it was because he had the appearance of a damn movie star and we didn't get many of those in Burton Hartshorn.

"None of them," I said as one of the guys in the group separated from the herd and began to wend his way over to our table. I immediately shifted in my chair to make it obvious I wasn't wanting to talk and that I was with Jack. Evidently Jack appeared completely straight, and therefore young goth-gay must have felt I was vulnerable, like a wounded gazelle at a drinking hole surrounded by lions.

"I love your hair," goth-gay said. He pouted at me and waved a hand at my head.

"Thank you," I answered politely before taking another swig of my beer. Why did nearly all of the conversations with me always start with some comment about my hair? Why not my tattoos or my eyes? Or the fact I kept myself in shape? Parts of my tattoos were obvious in the short T-shirt, the tail of one dragon, anyway, and a few musical notes rendered in black. And my eyes were pretty cool, kind of a brown but dark and velvety if you cared to look close enough.

But no, my hair. Always my hair. Dark auburn, reddish-gold, ginger—all kinds of red shades had been ascribed to my hair. My dad was a Welsh brunet, which explained the dragon on my left arm, my mum a willowy pale blonde, hence the rose on my right arm with its trail of thorns up my bicep. I liked to think I was a mix of strength and passion; but add in the love of music and red hair from my gran, I was uniquely me.

It seemed, though, that inheriting red hair from my gran meant I was destined to be defined by my hair color. I'd heard all the jokes about being a ginger and easily rationalized them as "things could be worse." At least Prince Harry had the same color hair, if a bit brighter, which made it cool. Of course, unlike Harry, I was cursed with accompanying freckles, but at least I wasn't an entire stereotype as my eyes refused to adhere to the expected green.

"I've never kissed a ginger before."

I groaned inwardly. Was it just me or did chat-up lines get more cheesy and stupid the older I got? If goth-gay was thinking that his declaration of interest meant I was immediately going to offer him a kiss, he was mistaken.

"Not going to happen," I said firmly. I expected him to move away back to his friends at the bar.

He sprawled across our table to reach me, soaking up the beer he'd spilled and crushing Jack's cigarettes. Jack made a lunge for the packet with a curse of disappointment, I sat back in my chair in surprise at the whole lunging thing, and goth-gay ended up rolling onto the floor. There was no way that shit wasn't funny, and I couldn't help the snort of laughter that left me.

"How old are you?" Jack snapped at the poor boy, who hadn't moved and looked like he'd landed badly.

"Eighteen," goth-gay said as he pushed himself to stand and winced. He then limped back toward his friends and punched the closest on the arm. Likely enough the other boy was teasing him.

Sighing at the inconvenience of beer trickling onto my jeans, I realized just how tired I was and all I wanted was a shower and bed. "Fuck, were we ever that young?"

I watched Jack straighten his cigarettes and push them into his shirt pocket. He considered the question as carefully as someone with two beers and four whiskey chasers in them could.

"Maybe. But that stupid?" He grinned at me, and I just knew that he was going to make a joke at my expense. It was what we did. "'Course I would never have acted like that. No way would I kiss a ginger." He backed off enough for me not to be able to smack him, but I couldn't stop myself from laughing as I stepped forward and leaned into him. We moved on after that, had hot vinegary chips by the taxi stand, and then I was on my way home.

The taxi rounded the top bend of the village and passed the pond in a wide sweep on the potholed road. I imagined Jason inside Maggie's house and wondered what he was doing in there. Was he an international spy? A vagrant? Or the last suggestion made by Jack, some kind of movie star out to hide from his adoring public? Jason was certainly sexy enough to rock a bad-boy Hollywood style. All I could think as I let myself into my place and switched on the hall lights was that I needed an excuse to go knock on his door tomorrow. It hit me with sudden clarity as I turned out my bedside light and turned on my side to sleep. If Jason had somehow inherited Maggie's cottage, did that mean he owned the station house as well? To lose the place now, after ten years where each corner of it was part of me, was something that snagged me as sharply as the grief I felt at Maggie's passing.

I'd find out more tomorrow. There was nothing I could do tonight, and even with the nagging doubts about my position at the station house, I forced myself to drift off to sleep.

THE VILLAGE was quiet at 6:00 a.m., and the final leg of my run accidentally on purpose took me past Apple Tree Cottage. For the longest time I stood on the green under the oak tree and stretched out my heated muscles. From this angle I could see the cottage and imagine the person behind the door. When I had awakened, the worries I'd pushed to one side were front and center. Maggie had bought the building, which meant it must now be part of her estate? Why hadn't I ever asked? In the last few years, I had felt less a staff member and more a partner, and I'd had plenty of opportunity to ask her outright.

The only time I'd mentioned the future, she'd laughed it off. As if the future didn't matter, as if she had a plan that only she was privy to, and I'd never pushed it.

"Hey."

I stiffened at the call. Jason had been completely exhausted last night, how come he was up this early? I sketched a wave, but he was obviously waiting for me judging by the way he leaned against the gate. There was nothing for it. I needed to acknowledge the hello with words of my own. I crossed the green and finally ended up at the gate, with Jason sitting on a bench on the other side. He had a mug in his hand, coffee probably. He looked good in spite of his eyes that were heavy with a need for sleep. Maybe he hoped the caffeine would work to keep him awake.

Offering him a smile, I leaned on the gate. "Morning, how was the cottage?"

"Dark, cold, and I couldn't find bedding, so I slept on the chair in the front room." He ended his explanation with a small huff and a shrug of his broad shoulders. "But my clock is all fucked up." He added the last morosely and ran his free hand through his dark hair until it stood up on end in unruly dropped curls around his head. "You want orange juice? I'd offer coffee, but first off, I have no coffee, and second, I have no electricity."

I didn't want coffee, but I did want to spend a bit of time with Jason because I had questions for him. Like who he was, and how he had a key to Maggie's place, and what did he know about the station house?

"Come down to mine," I offered without hesitation. "I have electricity."

I have electricity? Why did my brain focus on that?

"And coffee?" Jason asked with hope in his voice.

"A machine."

He visibly brightened at the words and stood up. "I'll be down in ten minutes," he said. He smiled at me and the upbeat start to the day I had been enjoying was suddenly even shinier. I didn't bother explaining how to find me again; Burton Hartshorn was little more than twenty houses in a small cluster around the old station and pond, and he'd find me quickly. As I half jogged down the hill, I tried to work out if I had time for a shower and realized with sudden clarity that a shower wasn't really the priority. Getting the coffee machine turned on and up and running was step one. A shower, no shave, and pulling on clean jeans and a fresh pale green T-shirt was step two.

Taking the time to psych myself up in the mirror was something I had to do. My stubble was blond, my eyes a little bloodshot from the late night and the beer, but at least when my hair was wet it lay flat. I was okay, presentable, and I glanced at the tattoos on my arms, wondering if Jason had noticed them and whether he was the kind of guy who admired them or sniffed at them as a scar on skin.

Whoa.... I reined myself in. My gaydar was crappy to say the least, and a smile that reached beautiful eyes probably meant nothing that I was hoping it did.

He wants a coffee. Just a coffee. And I am a sad lonely

guy sliding into my thirties with nothing but the chance of losing my home on the horizon.

The knock on the door heralded his arrival, and I took the small narrow stairs three at a time, landing as gracefully as I could in the small hall that separated my home from the business. Pausing for a second, I centered myself and practiced a smile before opening the main door and letting him in. He was carrying a box and he'd clearly run gel through his hair as the curls were tamed. The tinge of disappointment was very real; I liked the randomness of the bed curls he'd had before.

"Okay?" He spoke, and I realized the question probably had a lot to do with me standing in the doorway staring.

"Sorry, come in. The machine we have isn't all that fancy, but the coffee is okay. Well, it's okay for me, but I'm guessing you would want it stronger being an American and all." I was babbling and deliberately stopped talking as soon as I realized. Jason was bemused, but he placed the box on the table and pushed it over to me.

"Any caffeine is fine, and this is for you. I think."

"Was it outside?" Parcels were dropped at the back door on a frequent basis for one reason or another. Mostly catalog delivery returns or charity sacks for the monthly run I do to Oxfam.

"From the house." He pointed at a label where my name was scrawled in black pen across the card. *For Robbie MacIntyre from Maggie Simmons.* "I assume you're the Robbie MacIntyre on here, and we probably have to talk."

He took the proffered mug from me and inhaled the scent of the coffee before sipping cautiously and wincing at the heat of it on his lips. I couldn't bring myself to comment, because my chest was suddenly tight. This was it. He was somehow responsible for Maggie's estate and this was my notice to evict. I couldn't help feeling dramatic; this place was my life and I loved it here. Energy left my body rapidly, and I slumped in the nearest chair, not even caring that my mug of tea was out of reach at the other end of the large solid table.

"Okay. I'm listening."

"Open the box first."

"You tell me what you want to say first."

"No, that's not how she wanted it done." Jason frowned and gestured at the box. "You need to open it."

Chapter Four

The tape was loose enough for me to push a finger underneath it and to pull it until it split away from the unmarked box. Cautiously I lifted back the lid and peered inside. Books. Maybe ten or fifteen books. A couple of hardbacks and a whole pile of dog-eared paperbacks. I lifted out the top one. *A Crime at Allstairs*, by Monroe Kitchener.

"Maggie's favorite author," I whispered as I thumbed the pages. There were penciled words in the margin and a couple of the pages had been turned down at the corners in a fashion Maggie normally frowned on. The box had the air of age and when I lifted out a couple more I realized that they were mostly Monroe Kitchener books. Old copies of books that I had read and reread—murders and crime in the middle of the English countryside dating back to the mid-thirties and forties. Under the paperbacks there was a large folder bulging with paper, then a couple of hardbacks and some notebooks. "And these are for me?"

Jason cleared his throat as he pulled out an envelope and placed it on the table. The address on the front was in New York, and it had been opened hastily, given the jagged edge. "So there I am, twenty-seven, tied up in a job I hate and I get this letter. It arrived last weekend, and I thought it was junk mail, only it clearly wasn't. My dad had a similar letter, but inside his was all this legal information about inheritance and wills. It's a long story and one I am trying to pick apart, but the upshot of it is that I own Apple Tree Cottage and you own the station house and Maggie's money is split fifty-fifty. Also that she specifically bequeathed a bureau to me and the books that are yours."

I heard every word that Jason said, that the station house was mine, that somehow I had become a homeowner and the beneficiary of someone who I was close to but to whom I wasn't even related. But shock had me silent.

"Are you going to say something?" Jason asked. He sounded concerned and stood to rummage in the box. "Here," he said softly. "This is your letter."

I took it from him and slit it open without finesse, desperate to see what was inside. Legalese in the form of a will and whole bunch of terms I wasn't familiar with. Then, there, under what appeared to be a will, was a handwritten letter, very simple in tone and few in words.

Dearest Robbie,

I'm hoping that this letter finds you well and not too shocked by what has happened. I also hope that sitting opposite you is Jason Young. He's a relative of mine, an aspiring author and an American over here for the first

time. I would like you to take care of him for as long as it
takes him to decide what to do with the cottage. Please
reread the enclosed books, and you may realize that just
like you, I was once someone who dreamed of sharing my
art with other people. In fact, there is a lot more I have in
common with our American friend than you first may
imagine. My love to you.

   Maggie

"Oh" was all I could manage. I deflated a little because somehow none of this seemed real. Glancing at the clock confirmed that it was half seven and only ninety minutes had passed in my new day, yet everything had changed to the point where I didn't recognize my life. I owned the station house, a box of books, and a folder of papers. And somehow my life was inextricably linked to Jason Young, from America.

"I had the same reaction. Like someone was punking me, pranking me.... You know what I mean."

A snort of a laugh threatened to leave me, and I forced it back. I was actually still in shock. "So you're Maggie's grandnephew or something like that?" Being related to Maggie would explain why Jason was getting the cottage. But I wasn't related to Maggie, and there was still no real explanation as to why I'd been given a huge amount of money in the form of bricks and mortar. None of this made sense. To my knowledge Maggie had never married or had children, although in one of her quieter moments she had admitted to a love that had died young. I wish I had asked her more at the time.

Jason shrugged. "Kind of I guess, if she was Great-Grandmother's sister." He paused and stared up at the ceiling as he counted off generations on his fingers. "I think that's right. Anyway my uncle's digging into all of this, and he's going to ask some questions. I'll let you know when I find out anything." He stood and saluted with his mug before placing it in the butler sink. It clinked as it hit the porcelain, and I spotted him wincing. He evidently didn't know how robust these old kitchen sinks were. "Thank you for the coffee."

I didn't have the control over myself to say anything, so I just waved as he left. I only briefly stared at Jason's firm arse in the snug-fitting jeans because he was at eye level, and then my attention was back on the box. I placed the folder flat on the table and carefully tapped at it to line up all the pages inside. There was a distinct lump in the middle, and when I pulled the papers out, it was the notebook that caught my attention.

The cover had words on it, but they had dimmed with age and I had to peer closely to see them. *Recipes for the Heart: Mystical Meals and Dangerous Desserts*, by Granny B. I wondered who Granny B was. I know Maggie didn't marry or have kids, so she wasn't a granny as such. The pages were loose-leaf and held together with a variety of clips and string. I opened to the first page and realized the writing inside the first page was Maggie's long, flowery script, with curls and flourishes that I often teased her about. She blamed being a child of the twenties. I just thought she loved the way all the curls appeared on the paper. With my finger I traced the words she wrote.

For Robbie and our rainy afternoons.

Emotion choked my throat. We'd done that together. Sitting at the café table staring out at the rain on the road, against the windows, wondering how short summer would be, and whether the rain would go. She had admitted to me that rain against the glass reminded her of someone, but she never explained who and I had never pushed.

I turned another page, and realization hit me as I saw a list of titles. This was an organized handwritten notebook of recipes. The handwriting of the main recipes wasn't Maggie's, but the notes in the margins were. Well, at least some of them. Against a few of the recipes more than one hand had made amendments. The recipes were organized in sections with some pretty unusual titles. This was the kind of document a mother might have passed to her daughter. A bible of failsafe recipes. Under each one was a qualification for the right time to use the recipe. Under Chocolate Slab it said "for sad times." Then there was Meatloaf with Mushroom Gravy—for finding what was lost along the way—and Zucchini Bread— for inspiring passion. I smiled at the notes next to Roast Pork and all the Trimmings. Clearly Maggie's attempt at this had been thwarted by the temperature in her range being too high. There was a note to put the pork in the oven on high for ten minutes, then turn it down for a further.... I peered closer, but I couldn't see how long per pound of meat. What seemed to be a grease stain had made the paper thin and see-through. Notes picked up farther down the page. Something about applesauce, but most of it was illegible. Shame.

The rest of the folder was paperwork to do with the station house, copies of deeds held in the bank along with statements of every penny that passed through the account. The station house didn't make a lot of money, but there was enough to cover outgoings and the statements showed that. I'd never seen the level of information that was in here. An accountant's card clipped some of the statements together; farther down the pile there was the name for a bank manager, a lawyer, in fact, contact details for everyone down to the thatcher who had worked on the roof of the old part of the place six years before. I closed the folder and shuffled everything back into place. The post office was officially open at nine, and a check on the time had me startled that over an hour had passed as I'd flicked through the paperwork.

I dressed in my work uniform of neat jeans and a short-sleeved shirt and made my way out to the main post office. Half of me was hoping that Jason would be standing outside the door waiting for me to open up just so we could talk about what was going on here. Reception wasn't good in the shop, but I managed to pull up a web page on my phone and I googled: Jason Young, Writer. There were some matches. But the Internet was so slow at rendering each page I gave up.

The morning was treacle slow, and I just wanted it over. People from the village came in and did what they usually did: bought stamps, posted mail, gave me parcels from catalogs to return. Conversation ranged from the weather to the birth of Eva's granddaughter. Hell, I even managed to appear I was fully invested in a three-way talk about the chances of Manchester United, and that is saying something as I am more a Formula One fan than a follower of football. The only person who noticed this weird fugue-like state I was in was one of Maggie's friends, Sylvie, who nodded in greeting and said nothing at all. She simply patted my hand and left with a soft smile. Somehow she knew my thoughts were utterly focused on something other than the press and pull of small village commerce and the signings at Man U.

By 5:00 p.m. the unusual day had become more mundane, and even though the excitement of the news I had received had trickled past shock and straight on to a weird state of *holy shit*, I was still able to cash up, tidy away coffee mugs, and restock the chocolate display before locking up and pulling the small blinds at the leaded windows. The knock on the door wasn't unexpected. The station house stocked the essentials and out here it felt like people ran out of things just as I was about to shut. I opened the door with a patient welcoming smile pasted on my face that literally melted away in an instant when I was faced with the last thing I was expecting.

Jason. Not just Jason. Wet Jason. Soaked to the skin, his white shirt so see-through I could make out the cinnamon nipples on his chest. His hair was spiky and wet as well, and I peered past him just to check that the heavens hadn't opened in the last ten minutes. A major rainstorm might well explain the fact Jason, who was very all damp and scowly, stood at my door near drowned.

"I didn't know who else to ask. I don't have reception on my phone," he began in explanation. I realized I was staring and that I had very deliberately checked out every inch of this new-look Jason, and the flush of scarlet had to be obvious on my cheeks. "We got the electric turned on, and I was running a bath and all this water came down through the ceiling. The tank has split. Do you have maybe a plumber or a builder who knows a plumber or I don't know...." He ran his hand through his hair, and I noticed scrapes and bruises on his forearm. Two years of first aid practice at uni and I was able to snap into caring mode quite easily. I gestured him in and through the shop into the back kitchen.

Chapter Five

"Is it still flooding?" I asked, because this was really the first priority. Maybe the water could be turned off at the stopcock or something.

Jason shook his head. "I went up and stuffed a watering can in the hole, then taped it up with this silver stuff. I didn't know what else to do, but for now the water level is lower than the hole. Shit. The water's gone straight through the bedroom and into the kitchen and hall." He was absolutely horrified at what had happened, and I imagined Maggie's perfect home destroyed. The thought of it upset me as well. Her house was an old person's house, all lace doilies and chintz, with wallpaper that defied time, but still, it had been the sum of her years in that place. Another part of her lost to the world. There it was again, that drama gene that seemed so strong in me at the moment. *Focus.*

"I'll call Andy," I explained as I picked up the phone. "He's Maggie's friend's son, a plumber. His brother's an electrician. We can get them out to see what's up."

Andy agreed to meet Jason at the house in thirty minutes.

"What did he say?" Jason asked as soon as I dropped the call.

"That the damage is likely already done," I admitted. Sugarcoating the situation would just cause more angst down the road.

Desolation passed over Jason's face. "And just like that, it's all fucked up," he muttered as he slumped in his chair.

"Go shower here. I'll leave some sweats and a tee outside the door. Leave your wet stuff outside, and I'll run it through the machine. Then we'll go see what happened."

Jason nodded gratefully and loped up the narrow stairs two at a time. Only after he'd disappeared from view did I wrack my brains as to what I could possibly have left out to embarrass myself. I couldn't think of anything off the top of my head, everything that could prove really awkward was locked down. I followed him up after a couple of minutes and found the clothes I'd promised, switching them for the soaked-through shirt, jeans, and underwear he'd left for me. The machine was washing when Jason came down the stairs with a sheepish expression on his face.

"I panicked. I'm sorry," he said immediately upon seeing me sitting at the table.

"No worries. Sit, have a coffee, and then we'll get up to the cottage."

He sat and picked up the mug and spent the longest time simply inhaling the steam. He looked good in my sweatpants, which were just about the right length as they were a little long on me. But the green T-shirt was just this side of too small for him and did all kinds of sexy things to the contours of his body. Add in the nipple evidence from earlier, and I was back to staring again. From the knowing expression in his eyes, he had spotted me.

"Thanks for the clothes," he said. Then he sipped at the coffee, and I could see the tension slip away. Someone was helping him with his problems, and he lost that wide-eyed horrified look in his eyes that he'd arrived with.

"You're welcome. Finished?" I gestured to the coffee, and he passed me the empty mug to put in the sink next to mine. Finally I locked up, and we began to walk up the incline toward the cottage. We didn't say anything; I wanted to start a conversation, but nothing seemed right when the tension grew in Jason as we got closer.

From the outside, the cottage was the same, as if no drama had happened inside. But when Jason pushed open the front door, it was easy to see the damage. From the hall I could see into the front room where half the ceiling was hanging from a huge hole and water still dripped around the edges. The wooden floor was slick with a sheen of water, which went through the hall and into the kitchen. No ceiling damage in there, but water trickled from the light sockets.

I let out a low whistle and did a complete three-sixty, checking out the damage. As I turned to the door, Andy arrived with a bag of tools and a grim expression on his face. That was part and parcel for Andy. He was the harbinger of doom where plumbing was concerned. He tutted in the front room, sighed in the kitchen, and took the stairs carefully up to the bedroom. More tutting and a "fucking hell" came from upstairs, and Jason went from anxious to miserable again.

"One day," he said to no one. "One freaking day and I fuck it all up."

"I don't think you can be blamed for a broken water tank," I reasoned. He didn't answer, and we stood quietly with our shoes in shallow water and waited for Andy's assessment. After banging and crashing and a few more colorful curses, Andy came back down the stairs.

"Tank's broken," he summarized gruffly.

"I know," Jason said. He wasn't being sarcastic, more just a little bit broken himself. I had this impulse to put my arm around his shoulders and pull him in for a hug. I didn't have absolute proof of his orientation, but even a hetero guy needed a hug every so often. I didn't, though, even after he glanced sideways at me with sadness in his beautiful gray eyes. "What now?" he asked.

"It's not safe in here," Andy pointed out. He was gesturing with a wrench and tapping at the old wall. "Water's in the ceilings, the walls. The tank's got rusty and when you ran the water, it just gave way. You'll need to get a team in to fix it. It'll cost you a pretty penny."

My heart sank. That was going to be shitty news for anyone to hear, let alone some visitor from another country who was expecting an English idyll and ended up with a cottage trying to kill him.

"Money's not the issue," Jason said immediately. "Can you recommend someone to do the work?"

Andy glanced from Jason to me and back again. "Reckon I can do the plumbing," he said. "My brother's an electrician, so we have that. Still, you'll need an expert in these old houses for the walls and ceilings."

"But you know someone?"

"My cousin," Andy offered. I kept back the laugh. No one had work done in the thirty or so scattered and small villages around here without one of Andy's family being somehow involved.

"When can you start?"

"I'll get a quote to you by the end of the week."

"Don't bother with a quote," Jason said. "Seriously, just get on and fix the place up. If Robbie says you're the best, then I trust you."

I winced internally. That was a lot of responsibility to put on me given Jason didn't really know me. Good job Andy actually *was* one of the best, or I'd be opening Jason up to all sorts of shitty craftsmanship.

"Okay, I'll get back to you with a date," Andy offered. Then he tapped the wall again with the wrench. "Seems like I was only up in the roof a few months back, don't recall the tank being rusted then. Damn old houses." He left after giving Jason a card, and then it was just me and a very quiet American standing in the hallway.

"Fuck," Jason said, breaking the awkward silence. Then in a flurry of motion, he dived into the front room kicking up water in his wake. He reappeared with a faint smile on his face, a laptop bag in his hand, and his suitcase pulling along behind him. "The rest is wrecked, the stuff I unpacked, but this is all okay."

"Okay, so let's mop up what we can, spread some towels or something." I galvanized us into action, and we mopped and tipped until the wood was dry. There was still dripping, so we placed a couple of buckets and saucepans under the worst of it and stood back to survey it all.

"Can I ask a favor?" He reached into his pocket and pulled out a sadly soggy iPhone. "Can I use your phone to call a cab?"

My immediate reaction was to reach into my own jeans and pull out my older Nokia with its buttons instead of a bright touch screen, but my hand stayed as I realized what he'd asked.

"You can stay at mine," I offered.

"I couldn't—"

"No sense in driving into town now." I glanced at my watch and saw it was already past nine. I was hungry and tired and had a perfectly good spare room that I used as a junk room. There was even a bed he could use. "You can stay until you get your head around what you're doing." I used my best insistent voice, the one where no one argued. I could see a need for discussion in his eyes, but it deflated in the face of my stubborn statement.

"Thank you, Robbie."

"Any friend of Maggie's...," I began, then trailed away.

"I never actually knew Maggie."

I huffed a laugh as I took the key out of his hand and locked the door. "That's mere details. Just don't murder me in my bed." I turned to face him and realized he hadn't moved that far away, in fact he was right- the-fuck-there, and this close up I could see his eyes darkened to a near-black outer ring. This close up I could also smell the scent of him, the tea tree shampoo he'd used in my shower, and the deodorant I also recognized as mine. He smelled good, he looked good, and I swayed a little. Just a few inches closer and we could've kissed. Nothing hot and heavy, just a taste to see if I liked it.

The moment broke when Jason cleared his throat, then stepped away and down to the gate, his suitcase rolling over the uneven path and his laptop bag around his shoulder. I had a black sack of water-soaked clothes to carry and the bag of toiletries we'd rescued from the bathroom. Together we made our way back down the hill, again in silence. Only when we got inside did I feel like I wanted to talk. I had a lot of questions. Why wasn't money a problem? Why did Maggie choose to leave the cottage to him and not to another branch of her long-lost family? What kind of things did he write? He yawned widely behind his hand, and I saw the exhaustion that ringed his eyes.

"Jet lag." He gave a rueful smile.

"This way." I led him up the stairs and tried to remember the last time I'd had someone stay over in the house. I think it was two or three boyfriends back, but it had only been one night and he'd not stayed long. More of a stay over after getting pissed kind of thing. Certainly no sex or sleeping wrapped in each other's arms.

I stopped abruptly, and Jason walked into me.

"Shit, I'm sorry," he apologized.

"No. Me," I said. Coherence was not my friend. But the sudden images of me taking Jason to my bed were as clear as watching a very tasteful porno—as if the pictures of us together were being pushed at me with no way to avoid them. "This way," I finally managed to say before gesturing Jason through into the small second bedroom, which was actually more of an office tucked into the eaves.

He sidled past, but the doors were narrow, and sue me if I didn't enjoy the feel of another man against me after all this time. He grinned at me, although he yawned again, which kind of ruined the effect.

"I'm gonna crash," he said in his soft drawling voice all husky from exhaustion.

"There's bedding in the box at the end of the bed, although it's not been used in a while."

"I don't need that, I just need to lay down," Jason insisted. "I'll be fine."

"Okay the, uhmm, bathroom is that way." I pointed behind me. "Although you know that." *Fucking genius.* "Help yourself to anything in the kitchen when you wake up, whatever time that is. The post office part of this house is separate and locked up, and for security you can't access the space outside opening hours."

"What if I need a stamp?" Jason deadpanned.

"I have those if...." I realized he was trying to be funny, and my serious-host-persona subsided as quickly as it had arrived. "Arsehole," I muttered and pushed against his arm with the flat of my hand.

"Night, Robbie," he said softly before closing the door.

Chapter Six

I stood for a moment rooted to the spot. For the first time since I'd left uni, I had a man living under the same roof. Okay, so it might only be for a couple of nights, and it was only as a favor, but hell, he was a gorgeous, sexy man, and I could've done with some of that in my life at that moment.

I made coffee and pulled out the old cookery book Maggie had given me. This thing, this object with all its flaws and additions and the stains and folded pages, fascinated me. I'd already picked up an awesome tip of adding mustard powder to beef stew that I resolved to try next time Mum and Dad visited, which wasn't for another couple of weeks. That reminded me that I really ought to phone and tell them that I finally owned something other than my car and clothes.

They were supportive of me to the point they pretty much left me alone with my sex life, or lack of it. They never worried I was gay, but my dad frequently lectured me on safety in sex and safety in alleyways. I think my dad believes all the sex I will ever have will be in alleyways without condoms; that's how much he worries about that part of my life. My mum is different. She wants me to find my forever guy, to see me settled and happy. She never mentions sex or alleyways. When I think of my forever guy, though, I never picture him as American. There again, I don't know how I picture him, really. I know I am drawn to brunets with interesting eyes and wide smiles, which means Jason fits very nicely in the category I have for future husband, but that is all.

I laughed out loud and scared myself at the sound of it in the quiet kitchen. I was no longer tired, and I pulled out my sketchpad and pencils and doodled for the longest time until my neck muscles burned and my eyes ached. When I focused in on the random patterns, I realized I had drawn water rushing down some old stairs and Jason standing in the middle of it all with a surprised O forming on his kissable lips. Tracing the outline of him in pencil, I stared down at the picture, and when I woke up, it was to complete darkness and a pencil stuck to my cheek.

The dreams that had chased me out of the kitchen and up to my bed were the weirdest I'd had in weeks—a garden with a tree and a very naked Jason imploring me to eat an apple. Not being the religious sort, I wondered why the hell I was dreaming the Genesis story with Jason featuring as Eve. Too tired to care, I stripped to my boxers, made sure my alarm was set, and fell into bed.

I really hoped the dreams followed me again.

Chapter Seven

I opened the post office and shop, and a quarter of my working day had passed before Jason appeared at the door separating the living and work areas. He was dazed, like he'd woken in a strange place and was confused as to why he was there. Luckily the shop was empty and no one sat on the sofas with books and coffee, so no one but me could see his adorable sticky-up bed hair and his sleepy expression.

"Jet lag," he explained with another yawn. He peered at his watch. "It's 5:00 a.m. at home."

"Have a seat." I gestured to the sofas, and he near fell into the closest one. I made him coffee, which I took over to him immediately, and bacon rolls, which followed a little later.

"Thank you for last night," he said after a while. Probably after enough caffeine had hit his system.

"You're welcome." I'm sure I'd already used that term with him, but I couldn't think of something else to say.

"And you're fine to stay as long as you need to. I have the room."

"I'll pay—"

"You don't need to. Just cover groceries every so often."

"Can I use your kitchen table?"

For what? I thought immediately. Images of me bent over the table were instantly vanquished as Jason continued talking.

"I wouldn't use much of your bandwidth, but I have some writing groups I join in with, and once I set up the laptop, you won't hear from me." Now that would be a shame. I quite liked listening to him.

"What is it you write?" I took my mug of tea and sat on the sofa opposite him, praying no one needed anything in the shop before I finished it.

"Drama, mystery, romance."

"Gay romance?" I blurted out. I'd read a bit of that and was partial to a happy ever after.

"Just because I'm gay doesn't mean I have to write gay stories," Jason offered. Well, that answered the question of Jason's inclination. He was indeed a living, breathing, tall, slim, sexy-arsed gay man, and he was in my house. All I could hope then was that he had a fondness for redheads with freckles.

"I didn't mean that...." I was flailing a bit, and I knew I was probably scarlet. One of the curses of my coloring was being unable to hide any form of embarrassment.

"I'm teasing you," Jason smiled and finished off the rest of his coffee. "As it happens, my books always have strong gay characters, either at the front of the story or in supporting roles."

"Are you published?"

"I have four books with a publisher, but the one I am working on now is something different, and I'm not sure who will want it."

Intrigued was an understatement. I was also kind of in awe that I had an author sitting opposite me. One who was probably successful when I partnered it with the money-is-no-object thing. I was an artist as well, although selling my work wasn't something I took lightly. What if people hated my quirky pictures, my watercolor takes on the irrationality of life?

Nope, I'm not taking that chance. I don't need to now that I own a house and the business inside it.

"Are you allowed to say? What you're writing about, I mean?"

Jason tilted his head a little and looked thoughtful, all narrowed eyes and cute. "Can I trust you?" he asked very seriously. Then before I could launch into my speech about keeping secrets, he continued. "It's my first historical, set in the Second World War, with the GIs over here and a mystery revolving around a baby."

"You're in the right place, then. RAF Chelveston is just up the road, I could take you there if you like." I was eager to show I could help Jason, be useful, and I loved Chelveston, or what was left of it.

"Station 105," Jason said. "That was what it was called in the war. My great-grandfather flew B-17Fs with the 352 Bomb Squadron."

I sat back in the chair. The coincidence was too much

to skip over. Jason's great-grandfather was stationed up the road, an American over here, just like Maggie's dead love. What were the chances that Jason's great-grandfather and Maggie's lover were one and the same? But then, Jason said his great-granddad was married to Maggie's sister. This was all too confusing to follow, and I should just listen instead of adding two and two to make five.

Jason blew my theory out of the water anyway. "He died last year. He was in his nineties. Three children, eight grandchildren, and at current count, there are twenty-one great-grandchildren and even three great-great-grandbabies. A good life, but he spent a lot of time last year back in the past. Alzheimer's."

"I'm sorry." And I *was* sorry for the loss that put a bleak sadness into Jason's eyes.

"I was closest to him, but I rationalize he had lived a long time and seen things that meant his life was full. He told me about his last bombing run, when he took a hit over Germany, and he managed to get the plane back to England and won a medal of honor for it. Said he wanted to get home for my great-grandmother, Annabelle. She was from Chelveston, worked in a pub there."

"The Red Lion?"

"I don't know. He couldn't recall, but all I do know is he loved her so much, but she died young in the early sixties. He didn't remarry. This book I thought could be based around their story."

I leaned forward in my chair again. "That's amazing. I love old stories like that."

"Me too."

"God, your family must be pissed," I blurted out, then

wished to hell I could call the words back. "I mean, losing this place." I waved around at the house I called home and the post office and the shop and the cozy seating area we were using. "I'm not even related."

Abruptly I imagined standing in court and fighting for the right to keep my home and wondered if perhaps I should even be talking to Jason.

Jason shook his head. "No one wanted this place or the cottage, you know, no one except me. I don't know how she knew it should come to me, although I think my uncle may have been in correspondence with her. She said in her letter to me that she knew I had a writer's soul." He closed his eyes, briefly recalling the words in his letter, I assumed. "And that I would find a story in Apple Tree Cottage, and probably love as well." He opened his eyes, and I was lost in the depths of the gray-green again as quick as a flash.

"That's weirdly worded," I pointed out.

"I know. You don't find love, it finds you."

I ignored the poet in his soul that made him create pretty words and continued with my own worries. "But the money from this place. Will I have your family contesting the will?" I wanted honesty from Jason, some kind of heads-up, and hoped he would recall I helped him on two occasions and that I was a nice guy who loved his home. Seemed like Jason knew where I was coming from.

"You never have to worry about that. Money is not something that worries my family. We have enough to last a thousand lifetimes. No one will come to England or want your home, I promise. It's yours. Maggie left it to you for reasons only she knew, the same as how she specifically left me the cottage. So it's okay to set up in the kitchen?"

The abrupt turn in conversation had me struggling to follow, but then I got what he meant. "Yeah, yeah, of course. The Internet isn't really hot here, but it's enough. The password is 'postoffice', all one word, but switch the o's to zeroes."

He stood and smoothed the front of his jeans, which looked perfectly unwrinkled to me. I doubted there was even a chance of wrinkling them given how snuggly they fitted him. I realized I was still sitting there staring at where he'd been for the longest time after he'd gone when I was actually roused out of my thoughts by the door opening and the small bell tinkling to warn me of a customer.

Going back to work with a lot of thoughts vying for attention in my brain was hard on the concentration, but somehow I muddled through the rest of the day. Maggie had a sister, who moved to the US with her American bomber crew boyfriend. I wondered why she'd never spoken of a sister to me. We'd grown quite close over the last ten years, enough that I was the only person to have been given the recipe for the applesauce cake. Not even Doris had that recipe, much to her dismay.

I guessed maybe if her sister died in the early sixties, then she'd been a distant memory. But what about her family? Clearly she had a whole group of people in the States who were related to her. I grabbed toast for lunch, and apart from a quick smile from Jason, he didn't stop typing at the keyboard, totally engrossed in whatever story was in his head that was somehow making its way to paper. Or laptop.

Between customers, I worked on a sketch of him on the laptop, the artist capturing the writer, and when I finished it, I made sure the sketchpad was turned to a blank page. I'd known this man less than a few days, and I wasn't ready for him to see my schoolboy crush in the lines on a page.

Locking up was delayed when Mrs. Wilkes absolutely had to, as priority, get stamps at one minute past five. I didn't point out that even if she put something in the post now, it wouldn't be picked up until eleven the next morning. That wasn't the purpose of this place. The shop-café-library was there as a comfort to the people around who knew that we would be there if needed. The station house was a hub that villagers and beyond relied on, and I liked that I was playing an important part in the landscape of Burton Hartshorn. It felt permanent and wanted.

"I need a drink," Jason announced when I went into the kitchen. He'd shut the laptop and sat back in the chair, rolling his shoulders and wincing. I gave a good massage, but there was no way I was volunteering. The day's soul-searching had me concluding I was coming off as a creepy stalker the way I'd been staring at Jason.

I spoke before thinking. "We could go up to the Red Lion and get dinner and a beer." Too late, I wished I could reword that whole sentence, but the words had left my mouth. I waited with bated breath that he would see right through my calm casual façade to the lusting guy beneath. The one who would kind of like to kiss Jason. *Now.*

"Sounds like a plan," he said. He stood and patted his

pockets in that age-old check for wallet and phone. Well, checking for the phone *is* a new phenomenon, I guess, but still it was kind of reassuring to see that he was more concerned about that than worrying that I had invited myself along for not only a beer, but dinner as well.

Chapter Eight

The Red Lion is one of those beautiful English pubs that was once a coaching inn. Built in the sixteenth century, it was older than Apple Tree Cottage. The inside was tiny, more a bar with lots of small rooms down dark, narrow passages. I loved it here. There weren't a lot of people inside, and we ordered food and carried beers through the pub and out into the back garden. Because this side of the village was on the hill, the views were stunning, add in the balmy late September evening and suddenly this was a place for romance.

Jason stood for a moment, simply staring out at the expanse of country before him, the greens meeting the sky in an undulating patchwork lined by hedges and dotted with distant houses.

"This is England," he muttered profoundly before striding around the tables and grabbing me by the hand to drag me toward the gate that led to the field behind the house. "What do you *see*?" he asked quickly.

My hand in his had shorted a few circuits, and the

intense, preacher-like focus of his gaze was doing a number on my head.

"What?"

"In your words. You live here, tell me what you see."

"Marchant's farm," I replied, pointing at the nearest farmhouse four fields away. "They own everything you can see up to that red building, which is a private school. The school own everything to the west of here. Uhmmm." I wracked my brains for something profound to say because he looked like he expected me to say something poetic and utterly perfect. I was doomed. I saw everything in color, so if he wanted history, then I was really fucked. "I can see the train line, or what's left of it. See the rows of bushes? That is the abandoned line that used to run through Burton Hartshorn."

"I get that," Jason said. "But what do you see?" He glanced across at me and squeezed my hand. "What would Maggie have seen?"

"Green. A lot of green, umber mixed with white, cadmium green in the firs, and the sky, it meets the land on the horizon and there is a haze of mauve, and the sky itself is a beautiful azure today." The words just tumbled out of me, and I felt impassioned by the end of it.

"There. That's it. I wanted to know through an artist's eyes."

I did my usual self-deprecating thing in which I belittled myself and let my lack of self-esteem trickle through. "I'm not an artist."

"You are so wrong. When I write England, I don't have your vision. I can write the characters, but the place itself, it's so different from where I live."

He released my hand, and together we wandered back to the wooden bench where our beers were. It took until I got back there to get over the disappointment that he had stopped with the holding hands part. How shallow was that, he was getting serious and having an epiphany over his writing and all I could think was that he had a very nice firm grip and a soft hand?

We made small talk that was a whole lot less unsettling than the artistic highs I'd just experienced, and that was just as nice. I listened a lot because his voice was gorgeous, and suddenly I realized I didn't actually know where he lived. I'd seen that envelope with a New York address on it, but that didn't mean it was his address.

"Where in the US do you live?"

He shook his head and gave a rueful smile. "Twenty-three floors up with a view of Central Park in New York. Go on, say it...."

"Say what?"

"That I am a typical cliché American from New York."

I recalled facts about New York, how it was always the first city to get destroyed by aliens or monsters or nuclear weapons in all the films I'd seen. Hell, even asteroids focused in on the small strip of land. I also somehow knew that the New York accent wasn't slow and drawled, wasn't it fast and clipped? Or was that Boston?

"You don't talk...." Yep, I went there. And I had no idea how to finish that particular sentence. "Your voice... isn't all posh and city, it's all low and stuff." And yes, I added that on, as if my embarrassment needed deepening. He took my idiocy in stride and laughed loudly. The laugh was sexy and deep, and it shook his whole body. Then he caught himself and looked at me seriously.

"What in tarnation did you expect? Y'all don't reckon I'm an American?" he said all deep and sexy with even more drawl. I was hard in a millisecond, and if I could've seen myself, I would've bet I had my mouth open in a parody of shock. Christ. I wanted him to say that again, and I would have asked him if our dinner hadn't arrived at that moment. *Thank fuck for steak and potatoes.*

Conversation turned to Maggie as really that was the only thing we had in common that was guaranteed I would have something to say. Not that I was particularly shy, but Jason had this air about him that screamed unobtainable, and I always went to bits when I gave in to that "fancying a boy" mode.

"My uncle e-mailed me today. I should show you what he said. The upshot was that there's more to this story than we will ever know. My great-grandfather had a twin brother who came over here in the same bomb squadron, his name was Evan. He dated Maggie, while it would seem that my great-grandfather dated Maggie's sister. Two brothers, two sisters. Turns out the brother died during my great-grandfather's last bombing run."

"Maggie's lover died," I said softly. "This Evan, he died in the war."

"And Maggie's sister went to the US with her husband, the twin who survived."

"That's a sad story," I offered in encouragement when Jason seemed lost in introspection.

"It's the story I am going to write. I didn't realize it, but after I read the e-mail, I knew there was a story there.

Two sisters falling in love with young dashing Americans, one leaving with her husband for a new life overseas, the mother of three children, who dies young. The other losing her lover to death and it changing her life forever."

I listened carefully. It sounded like the perfect story, but a kernel of worry balled in my chest. If this was going to be some great love story, then I didn't want Maggie consigned to the sidelines. I wanted her to be the focus of the story. I know it was selfish, but he didn't know Maggie. She wasn't some old woman who had given up, she'd been strong and had experienced the world and had friends and a life and a garden she loved to sit in. I had to know he would treat her right.

"Don't write Maggie wrong," I blurted out.

Jason looked up in surprise, a fork full of steak nearing his mouth. He evidently saw something in my expression that I couldn't hide and placed the cutlery on his plate.

"I won't," he promised me with sincerity in his eyes. "She's a major part of my story. I want to know why she and my great-grandmother didn't keep in touch, and why my great-grandfather didn't mention her to me."

Trust was something no person should give easily; especially not to a man I hadn't known that long, but there was something about Jason that called to me. And I didn't just mean to my libido, but to something way down inside me.

THE DAYS after that, four of them if I was counting —*which I was*—went fast, and somehow Jason and I had fallen into a routine of sorts. He would write and I would work, then we would go to the pub for dinner. We'd made it down most of the main meals list and took to sharing bits and pieces off each other's plates when we had different mains. He discovered he had a fondness for great big thick chunky chips, and I teased him when he asked for fries. That was how it went, soft and slow and all kinds of wonderful. He hadn't held my hand, but he gave out all the right signals. We would bump arms when we walked. He would smile at me like I brightened his day, and I knew damn well he brightened mine.

I made the cake again when the coffee group met next time. It just disintegrated into a huge glutinous mess, and that was even with Jason helping me out with the whole cup thing that formed part of the American ingredients list. He found me cursing in the kitchen and explained using a huge mug as my "cup" was not a good thing. No wonder the mixture was ballooning up and exploding over the sides of the tin. Still, nothing was quite right, and yet again I ended up giving the coffee group some of the other handmade cakes that Priscilla from the next village over baked for me to sell.

I could've copped out entirely and got her to see what she could've done with the recipe, but a large part of me felt that getting this cake right was my last connection to Maggie.

I poked at this failure like I did the last one, trying to learn why the damn thing hadn't worked. And I opened the notebook Maggie left me and attempted to make sense of what was in there. Apple trees and love and all that kind of stuff were scribbled in the margin, and even though some of it was smudged, I liked to think there was something I was missing that meant my cake-making skills weren't crap.

I scraped it in the bin and half listened as Jason talked to Andy about Apple Tree Cottage. Something about six weeks and scaffolding and boilers. Poor Jason sounded disappointed, but I knew damn well I wasn't. I liked having him there in my home.

I spotted a recipe for beef stew with dumplings and decided there and then that tonight we would be eating in, with wine. At least two glasses. Then I could make it way more obvious that I found Jason attractive and that I wanted to take a step in the direction of kissing.

"Did you hear?" Jason asked from next to me. "Andy said it could be six weeks or more until I get into the cottage."

I nodded. "I'm sorry."

"It's me that should be sorry," he said with a sigh. "I think I need to consider getting a place to rent or a hotel or something."

"You don't have to." *Please don't go. I like you being here.*

"It's wrong to impose on you like this."

I pressed a hand to his chest and gently gripped at the material of his shirt. The move smacked of desperation, but I didn't care. "You don't need to go anywhere." Then I did it. Like it wasn't me at all, I leaned in and pressed a kiss to his lips. The move was quick, and I was back and away in seconds. He said nothing, simply touched his lips with the fingers of his right hand. Slowly I released my hold on his shirt and stepped back. This was where he told me that he didn't want that kind of thing, that he wasn't looking for this at the moment, that it wasn't me, it was him. I'd heard it all before, as had every one of my single gay friends.

"I can't do this," he said softly.

Disappointment flooded me. In the space of a single second, I had fucked everything up to the point that no doubt Jason would be packing and leaving tonight.

"It's okay," I found myself reassuring him. That is what I do. I open myself up, get turned down, then find myself apologizing and trying to make the other guy feel better.

I took another step back and nudged the kitchen table.

Jason frowned. In one stride he was there, right up in my space. "I want to kiss you," he said carefully. The words were measured and calm, which contradicted the intent in his eyes. "But I want more, and I'm not the person you need for fucking and moving on." He cradled my face and stared right at me. "I love your eyes," he whispered. "The brown of them is so beautiful, and your skin, all those tiny freckles, I want to taste them all, and hell, this could be more than just fucking. Tell me."

He had me at the first time he used the word "fucking," which led to me getting so damn hard; add in him cradling my face, one of my favorite things, then talking about my eyes, and I was lost.

"I want more than that," I agreed, then swallowed to clear the huskiness in my voice. The words were sparse, but they were really all I could manage.

"There's something about you and this place," Jason murmured. "This could be everything to me." I didn't question or wonder at his words. He was the writer, and he evidently knew exactly what to say. I'm not sure if I leaned in then or he did, but somehow we were chastely kissing, his lips pressed to mine, and when he pulled back, he smiled that soft smile of his. "Okay?" he asked.

I rested my hands on his hips and tugged him a little closer. "Uh-huh." This time the kiss was more: he pressed the tip of his tongue to my lower lip, and I opened my mouth and welcomed the taste of him. The kisses were lazy and long, and I didn't move to grab at him or to grind up against him. This kiss wasn't about that, it was about knowing and discovery and all kinds of writery-type things that I'd read in books over the years. I wished I could've painted this emotion, capture the newness of it and the utter simplicity that was so powerful. Just a kiss and I was a puddle on the floor melting into him and craving more.

He shifted a little when we parted for air, not to get away from me but to move me so I was pressed against the counter, and abruptly the kiss was more. The embrace was quickly passion and need and want, and I shifted my grip on him to link my hands at the small of his back. The movement pressed us closer, and even in thick jeans I could feel him against me, hard and ready. I unlinked my fingers and freed the shirt from his jeans before trailing a path up to his shoulders and down again to rest on the belt loops of his jeans. They were too tight for me to get my hands where I really wanted them, but that was okay, this wasn't about sex or groping. It was heated, but it was only kissing.

When we finally pulled apart after god knows how long, Jason rested his forehead on mine. "I want to say let's go slow, I want to say the words that mean we make this part last forever." I knew there was a "but" somewhere, and I held my breath. "I've only... I don't know...." Somehow the wordsmith had lost his words.

"What?" I prompted gently.

"You want to take this upstairs?" He full-on dipped his eyes as if he was embarrassed.

Yes, yes, yes. God, yes. "I'd like that."

Chapter Nine

*a*t first we just kissed in the doorway to my small bedroom. The actual space was dwarfed by the large oak bed and sturdy chest of drawers; there wasn't much room for anything else. So when I stumbled back, it was fortuitous that the bed was right there. Because Jason tumbled with me, and we fell in a flailing heap onto the mattress. There was nothing awkward about the twist of arms and legs, and we slid up the bed as best we could until we lay side by side facing each other. I was lost in those gray eyes, and I wanted more of the kissing. Instead, Jason ran his fingers through my hair, then gripped the length of it, not to hurt, but to hold me still as he leaned up and looked down at me.

"I'll always picture you standing next to that car of yours that very first time I saw you," he whispered. "Your ass in those jeans and that shirt, which was like a second skin. I think I wanted this from that moment."

"You did?"

"It's not happened before," Jason admitted. "Something in my head was telling me you were special."

I couldn't help but kiss him after making a statement like that, and I reached up and locked my hands around his neck and pulled him down. He didn't fight the tug and instead sprawled over me and settled very nicely between my legs. We kissed and talked, and this was far removed from any kind of sexual contact I had ever had before. I wanted to climb inside him, be with him, just him.

We shed clothes in a graceless laughing race to see who could get naked first, and I won only because I wasn't wearing a belt. Finally naked, I arranged him how I wanted him, lying half on me with our cocks hard and heavy against each other. Paradise was just around the corner, and I wanted it badly.

The scent of apples wafted in from the open window along with the bonfire smokiness of the September evening, and I gave myself up to Jason as if we had been together forever.

He kissed a trail from my lips to my throat and across to one shoulder, then the next, followed by some crazy path that went from one nipple to the other.

"It's impossible," he muttered against my skin. "I can't kiss every freckle. I'd be here forever."

"They're not going anywhere."

"Next time I'll get these ones." He nudged my left nipple with his lips, then reached up and stole another heated kiss from me.

Next time? I wasn't sure I was going to survive *this* time. We rolled so I was on top, and I spent the time exploring my new lover. His skin didn't have freckles, but he did have an interesting birthmark on his left shoulder and a tattoo on the right. I spent the longest time kissing the acres of toned honeyed skin and realized this was as close to perfect as it could get. A light furring of chest hair led to a darkening treasure trail that I followed with my tongue. His erection bumped my cheek, and I had my first up-close and personal look. He was cut, and that seemed exotic and just this side of fucking sexy.

Jason's cock was dry and warm with just a pearl of precum on the tip, and I tasted every inch of it until Jason was writhing under me and warning me to stop. Bringing someone so close to the edge was intoxicating, and I backed off only to start again as soon as his breathing evened out. He whimpered—I swear that was the noise I heard—and he yanked at my arm until I pulled off and slid up his body. He flipped us so he was back in control and wrapped a hand as best he could around us both. I wanted in on it and lamely attempted to find a hook, but all I got was the chance to hold him and lose myself in what he was doing.

We were done so quickly from that point out, with everything that had been building for days being let loose in an instant. When he came he kept his eyes open, stared right down at me, and hell if that wasn't the sexiest thing I had ever seen. So sexy it had me losing it hot and wet right then. Only when Jason closed his eyes and slumped to the side of me did I realize the truth.

I was falling in love.

WE ACTUALLY made it downstairs to have dinner, but

when dinner ended up being cheese and fruit and crackers from the shop, we took it back to bed. How long we sat cross-legged opposite each other I don't know, but after a while, we lay down side by side. We talked about everything and anything, from Maggie to Jason's brothers, to the apartment in New York, to being a trust-fund baby, to me and how I came to run the station house.

"So why do you think she chose you to run the place?" Jason asked. He was threading and unthreading our joined hands, and the action was more than a little distracting.

"Something about being an artist and being rootless, maybe she just saw that I needed somewhere to make a life."

"And what about your art?"

"What about it?" I was good at playing dumb when I wanted time to consider an answer. I rolled up and rested my chin on his chest, our joined hands trapped between us.

"Can I see some of it?"

I knew he would ask that. I just knew it. The standard answers, including "one day" and "tomorrow" and "I don't have anything good enough," all failed to match what I wanted to say. Instead I leaned over him and opened the second drawer of my bedside cabinet and pulled out one of my many sketchpads. I could recall with clarity every single image inside, and I turned to my favorite, a simple watercolor of Apple Tree Cottage viewed through the orchard. Still supported by him, I held up the painting.

"There you go," I said in my most dismissive tone. I was giving him permission to hate it if he wanted.

He blinked at the image as if he couldn't properly focus, then he took the sketchbook off me and awkwardly turned the pages with one hand. Finally with a sigh of annoyance, he loosened his hold of my hand and wriggled out from under me before sitting cross-legged opposite me. I copied the pose and waited expectantly for what he was going to say about my art.

"Beautiful," he murmured. The blush started deep inside me. He was staring at my candid sketch of Maggie and her friends at coffee, and he'd called it beautiful. He flipped to another and then back to the painting of the cottage. "There's something quirky in every painting, isn't there?" he said cautiously.

I wanted desperately to reach over and take the book from him, but I didn't. I was much more naked sitting there than just as a result of not wearing clothes, and I waited for the axe to fall.

"I don't know which one is my favorite," he finally offered, "this one or the one of the old ladies and their cups and saucers and cake."

"You like them?" I hated myself that I even put the question mark at the end of that short statement. But even a first in art doesn't guarantee people would like my stuff.

"Not only is the artist cute, sexy, and in bed with me, he's also talented. You'll have to do the cover for my book. You have to. The one of the old ladies—"

"Maggie. That's Maggie with her friends. They meet up every week for coffee here, like a book club, and they exchange books."

"The expressions on their faces... it's wonderful. You should sell some of this art."

"I do. Well, I have some in a gallery in Buckingham,

some landscapes, some of Stowe Gardens, the usual. And they sell. I make a couple hundred a month off them."

"You could be bigger than that," Jason insisted, and my heart fell as he talked up this big plan for getting me in City galleries. That wasn't me. I wasn't about money; all I wanted was my village and what he wanted for me was the bright lights of success. Of course he would. He'd said money was no object for him, and I imagined he would want that in a partner.

He wants what I can't be. What I don't want to be.

I agreed with whatever he was saying, and then we curled up against each other and he fell asleep a long time before I did. Someone in this bed with me was a whole new experience, and I wished my headspace allowed me to relax. As it was, my sleep was fitful and I woke early. I realized I didn't know what to say to the man next to me, and I did the only thing I could think of.

I ran away. Showered and dressed, and with Jason sleeping through all of it, I was downstairs by seven. I rearranged displays, organized the counter, sorted the papers left outside the door, and checked the time. Seven twenty-five.

Only another hour and thirty-five minutes until we opened.

Chapter Ten

*J*ason appeared just before nine, and he had that look of confusion I'd seen on many a boyfriend's face when I couldn't face them for one reason or another.

"You okay?" he asked as he pulled me close for a morning kiss. He tasted of toothpaste and sunshine and smelled of shower gel and god knows what that had me hard again. "I'm sorry if I came on too strong about the art thing," he said firmly. "I know how hard it was for people to tell me I should try to get published. I hated them for it."

And there it was. He knew what he'd said, and he knew how I'd reacted. He understood. And just at that moment when the first person knocked on the door to be let in, I knew for sure.

I was in love. In the space of a week. Love.

Go figure.

"It's okay," I responded as carefully as I could so as not to let any of the love escape into words. "I'm sorry I freaked out." The knock came again, and I reluctantly pulled away. "Duty calls." I smiled at Jason, and he kissed me quickly before wandering off into the kitchen to write. I could've started every working day like that.

Since it was Saturday, the post office was only open until midday and the shop closed at four. Finally faced with Saturday evening and all of Sunday off, I stretched tall and walked my fingers on the low ceilings. I needed a beer and a kiss. Probably a kiss more than a beer, but I wasn't ready to admit that to myself out loud. I stole the kiss, pulled a beer from the fridge, and sorted through the pile of mail that had been redirected down from Apple Tree Cottage. I had that job because, as Jason said, I was the expert at it.

Jason saved whatever he was doing and closed the laptop. "Andy phoned, said he's managed to empty out the attic at the cottage. He's dropping stuff to us later, some toys and things."

"Cool." I discarded the junk mail and put two utility bills to one side. "I really ought to call the solicitor to talk me through the bills and things," I said absently. The last letter was a plain white envelope addressed to Maggie, and I tore it open and pulled out the contents: a check for £633.20 and a letter from a company whose name I recognized. I couldn't for the life of me recall where I had seen the name before. Then a couple of words jumped out at me. *Publishers. Books. Monroe Kitchener.* And a summary statement. The attached check was for second-quarter income, or so it said. Legal name, author name, breakdown of income. What the hell?

Abruptly I knew where I had seen the name. I left the kitchen and dived into the small front room with the view of the old railway siding and picked up the closest book I had been rereading. One of those from Maggie's box. Holding it aloft, I was back in the kitchen and placing the book next to the check.

"Maggie was a writer, just like you," I announced. Because that was the only thing that made sense. "She wrote under the pseudonym of Monroe Kitchener." Then it all made sense. The way she would share her love for these books, the way she obviously had income no one knew about. Hell, were Jason and I going to be getting checks like this every month? What would we do with the money? I sat down heavily, and fondness mixed with regret. If only I'd known, we could have talked about it. I could ask her what made her stop writing. Then I had another wave of inspiration.

"Are you okay?" Jason asked. He was wearing a shocked expression similar to the one I knew had to be on my own face.

"Can I use your laptop?"

He didn't hesitate, just opened it and switched it on. Then he turned it to face me, and I immediately went to Google and typed in the title of the last book in the series of ten books she'd written. There were a lot of matches, and I flicked through a couple until I came across what I needed to know. With my chest tight, I leaned back in the chair.

"When did your great-gran die?"

Jason frowned in thought. "The year my grandparents met, I think." He closed his eyes, then opened them as he answered, "1964."

I turned the screen back to Jason, and he glanced at it, although he didn't need to as I explained what I found.

"*Autumn Rains*, Maggie's last book, was published in 1964. Then nothing. Coincidence?"

"You think she stopped writing when her sister died?" Jason leaned on his elbows. "That's really sad. I wonder why?"

"Not sure we'll ever know."

Andy arrived at just after four with a cardboard box full of knickknacks—nothing of great value or worth to anyone other than those who might have had a sentimental attachment. There was a tiny china doll dressed in a faded pink sleep suit, a few tobacco tins full of beads, and a moth-eaten blanket. Seeing the box made me sad, and I couldn't help the emotion choking my throat. Maybe Maggie had sent the rest of her stuff away, given it to charity, but somehow the box was a final underscore that she was gone from there. When Jason hugged me, I leaned on him for every second of understanding he could give me.

"Grief isn't for the dead," he began in a soft tone. "It's for the ones left behind."

He was right.

September moved into October, and even though Andy had made the cottage habitable to the point that Jason could've moved back in, he stayed exactly where he was. Somehow his clothes were in my drawers, his shaving stuff in my bathroom, and suddenly nothing was "I" anymore but "we." I hadn't said the L-word, but neither had Jason. I just knew it was a matter of time. We ran together in the mornings, I worked, he wrote, I created art in my spare time, and we frequently had dinner at the Red Lion.

"My uncle e-mailed me," Jason announced on a lazy Sunday morning in bed. "I forgot to say. He's visiting my great-uncle to talk about what he recalls of my great-gran and Maggie."

"I ought to talk to people, you know. There has to be someone around here who knew Maggie when she was younger." I curled into Jason's side and kissed each line of muscle I could reach. I loved this man so much that it hurt. I wanted to be with him all the time, to love him and have him for as long as I could.

"We could research," Jason agreed. "After." He didn't say anything else, just rolled me so he was nestled between my spread legs and had both my hands captured with one of his. The sensation of being held was intoxicating, and I wriggled against him just a little. We kissed and rubbed against each other, but that small niggling need for more insisted on being heard. We had lube and condoms in the drawer then, but even though the lube had been used for many an interesting evening, the condoms had stayed put. I'd bought them maybe a week back and placed them very deliberately next to the old lube and the new unopened one. Jason would have had to have seen them, but he hadn't commented.

With slick fingers he pressed against my hole as he sucked my cock down. It was more than I could actually bear, and I was so damn close it hurt, but then suddenly he wasn't there. He was up over me and looking me directly in the eye. He didn't have to say anything, I knew what he wanted, the same thing as me.

"Please" was all I said, and I punctuated it with a slow roll of my hips, my cock pressing against his. *Please let him know what I mean....*

He stretched me with his mouth on my cock, and he edged and backed off and pressed and pulled, and my whole world, my entire universe, centered on this one man and what he was doing to me. He rolled on a condom and pushed against me a little at a time, kissing away the murmurs when it burned, swallowing the gasps I made as he went farther and farther, and then... I felt the pressure inside me, against my prostate, and that was it, I was lost.

Time didn't make any sense from there on in. There was only the battle to climb higher and higher and to enjoy the sensation of the orgasm curling from spine and muscle —until I shouted my completion and came between us without being touched. Jason pushed more, again and again, and with a curse he stiffened and arched into me. I grabbed at any part of him I could, my nails raking his sweat-slicked skin and gripping at his arms until he collapsed against me.

"Too heavy for you," he muttered.

All I did was wrap my legs around him as he softened and pulled out, and held on tight. "Never," I whispered. And I meant it.

Chapter Eleven

I was actually in the dream. Only watching, but I saw things that made me sad and angry and wanted to make sense of what it all was. I saw a much younger Maggie crying at a marker in the grass. A name and tears and a date and the strong arms of a man around her, me? I was Maggie, and the intensity of loss was utterly overwhelming. The dream was vividly real.

The loss I felt when I woke up was absolute, and I only woke up because Jason was shaking me and calling my name.

"Robbie." He kissed each of the freckles on the back of my right hand and whispered my name over and over as I finally lost the tenuous grip on the dream. Stunned and emotional, I curled into his embrace and held on tight. I'd never felt this needy before, as if all it would take was his touch and the emotions from the dream would disappear altogether.

"What was it?" Jason asked me, and I wished I could've said. All that remained was the sadness, and it lingered all through our first coffee and breakfast. Every so often I would catch Jason's concerned gaze, but I just laughed it all off and opened up the station house as normal for the usual run of customers. Individually, each person in Maggie's coffee group arrived: Doris with her long raven hair and tattoos, Audrey with her pearls and slim-fitted jacket, and Jemima with her knitting always by her side. Each of them had a story about Maggie, the time she pickled beetroot and it exploded, the different charities she donated money to, that one time she confronted a thief in the post office and threatened him with her umbrella. All about how good a person she had been. I knew these stories, I'd heard them before, but this morning, after last night's dream, I felt fragmented and thoughtful.

The door finally shut at ten minutes past five, late this time because Doris had popped back with cookies, telling me it was because I was sad. As soon as I had pulled the sign to Closed, I went into the kitchen to find Jason. I didn't even give him time to notice I was there.

"Can we check in on the cottage?"

He glanced up at me with that dazed expression he sometimes had when he was in the middle of writing a scene and blinked at me a couple of times. "Wha'?" he asked.

I felt such a surge of affection for this man who had fallen into my life. He was obviously tired, and I wondered if my dreams had affected his sleep as well. Still, he was smiling at me, and he reached up to grasp my hand and tug me close for a hug, with his face against my stomach and his hands around my lower back.

"I want to go and see the cottage."

"Mmm," Jason murmured and nuzzled at my shirt until he revealed the soft skin over my hipbone. He pressed a kiss there and squeezed his hug tighter for an instant. In a lazy move, he used me to stand up, then cradled my face to kiss me deeply. He tasted of cinnamon, and I laughed inwardly. Despite my latest attempt at the applesauce cake, a pile of crumbs with squidgy apple causing it to collapse, he had pulled it closer to his laptop and had actually eaten some of it.

We parted with matching smiles; then by unspoken agreement, we left the station house by the back door and walked up the hill to Apple Tree Cottage. There was evidence in the front garden of the work being done inside: a tumble of bricks and wood peeking out from under tarpaulin and several pallets of bags. The work was extensive, but they were only a week away from making everything right again. We bypassed the tools and stuff, and driven by something in my dream, I led Jason down the side path and round to the orchard behind the house. Apples lay scattered under some of the low-hanging trees, some of them rotting, some as bright green and fresh as if they still hung, ready to pick. I stopped at the closest tree, then closed my eyes. I recalled the things I had seen in my dream and had to focus past the overwhelming grief I remembered to the other parts of it.

"What are you looking for?" Jason asked after we had explored most of the orchard. Being under the trees meant the grass wasn't tall, but the weeds were slowly making progress in their attempt to find space to grow.

"Not exactly sure," was all I could really say. Thankfully he played along with whatever I was doing, and he dodged nettles and burgeoning blackberry bushes to follow me. Finally there was something familiar—a water butt collecting rainwater from the drainpipe on the cottage. I stood with my back to the icy water and faced out toward the orchard. The foliage in this garden was rich and green, and I squinted then... there... the tree. I stumbled as I twisted my foot on an abandoned hosepipe, but Jason caught me and I walked on. The tree had a distinctive shape. It was out of place, the trunk straight, not twisted in the way the other apple trees were. I crouched down in the long weeds and grass. Jason saw it before me. A glint of metal in the green, and we pushed everything back until we could see what was on the small plaque. I imagined it was a memorial to lost love or something dramatic like a clue to the reason behind why Maggie never fell in love again. Instead there was a date, and the plaque was nothing more than a flattened piece of metal with something scratched and scraped into it.

3 Sep 1942

I pulled my phone out and took some photos of the plaque.

"You think this was the date it was planted?"

"Or the date that Maggie's lover died?" I pointed out. Typical that I would immediately latch on to the more angst-ridden explanation. Still, after this, I felt more at peace, and for a little while, we stood holding hands and chatting about Maggie.

"Mr. Young!" a voice called from the house, and Andy crossed to meet us just at the gate to the pathway.

"Call me Jason," Jason reminded him as he shook hands with Andy.

"Kitchen's a couple of days short of being done, and I just wanted the say-so that we upgrade the plumbing to the utility room as well."

"That would be great."

"And that we found another of those boxes... hang on, I was going to bring it down to you." Andy disappeared back in the house, then reappeared almost immediately clutching a metal box that was a muted sage green and had stenciled numbers on the side. It was the kind of thing I'd seen in army surplus stores, and I was immediately intrigued. Jason took the box and tucked it under his arm. I wanted to open it then, but it wasn't mine to open. Instead we walked to the Red Lion for dinner and talked as we passed through the village.

"So your great-uncle says Maggie and her sister fell out?"

"All he could say is that there was resentment, something about decisions my great-grandfather made that affected how his brother may well have died. Rumors his brother wasn't ready for the gunnery position but that my great-granddad took his brother anyway. I'll let you read the whole e-mail on my phone when we sit down."

"Would make sense," I mused out loud. Something had caused the sisters to fall out, and made Maggie stop writing at the same time her sister died in the sixties.

The weather was warm enough for us to sit outside, and while we waited for the food to arrive, Jason levered open the box with his keys. The box opened, and this time the contents were a lot more interesting—papers, some photos, alongside a copy of Monroe Kitchener's, aka

Maggie, last-ever novel. The box had kept the book tidy and neat, and I placed it reverently on the tabletop.

"Recipes," Jason said as he flicked through the loose-leaf pages. An envelope fell from the bundle of them, and he picked it up. The fact that the envelope was new wasn't the weirdest thing—that would be the fact it was addressed to Jason and me jointly.

"Shall we read it?" Jason looked uncertain, and he passed it to me as if he thought I was going to be any better at dealing with a possible letter from a woman who had played such a big part in my life. I took the envelope and opened it carefully. There was a letter and an aged loose-leaf page. The words in the letter were short. This wasn't a flowery missive explaining the story of Maggie's life, this was succinct. I read it out loud in the empty garden of the pub.

"Dear Robbie and Jason. I understand you are probably confused as to why you have only just found this letter and that you have lots of questions. Long story short, I knew you would be good together, and this is my first matchmaking since I introduced my sister to her husband."

Matchmaking? I guess she meant me and Jason. I managed a smile across to him, and he nodded to encourage me. I cleared my throat and continued.

"Under the tree near the water butt is a plaque. The date on it is the date we planted the tree, and I had to move the plaque each year when the tree grew. The date is important because that tree was planted with love. Evan helped me dig the hole, we dug such a long way down, and we watered it and I remember we sat there on the grass and just stared at it. That was the first time Evan told me

that he loved me and I said it back. Then he asked me to marry him and I said yes. I was so deeply in love, and my heart broke when he died the very next day. I tried to be strong, but in my grief I was so stupid. I blamed my sister for having the brother who lived, I blamed Evan's brother for being alive, I blamed Evan for wanting to be a hero and for dying. I never spoke to my sister again. She left for America with her love still alive. All I had left was a box, this box, filled with the things the brothers left behind. The cookery book, papers, nothing that I thought had real meaning. When my sister died, I stopped writing. I didn't have the heart for it. But I found the cookery book and made so many people happy that finally I can say I regret everything and nothing. Maggie."

Jason sat back in his chair. "Wow."

Thinking on which part got to me the most made my head spin. I decided that the one detail I was focusing on was the matchmaking part. She had made it so we would meet. At the end of the day, we were co-beneficiaries. But she could not have known that Jason and I were going to end up in bed together. Abruptly I felt uncomfortable and instead focused on the cryptic end to her letter.

"She regrets everything and nothing," I murmured. "That's kind of profound."

"She regrets blaming everyone and losing touch with her sister, maybe she doesn't regret the path her life has taken."

I looked at the man who was so cleanly fitting into my own life, and I fell just that little bit more in love. He thought the same as me, that she was happy at the end. I put everything back in the envelope, and we ate dinner in a comfortable and peaceful silence and walked back to the station house hand in hand. When we clambered into bed that night, we kissed, but we were too caught up in making love to talk about the day.

But that was okay. I was kind of done with talking. I had thinking to do instead.

Chapter Twelve

A few days passed before I picked up the small
envelope again and checked out the loose-leaf
sheet that fit nicely into the book of Granny B's recipes. I
don't know why I didn't immediately go to find the book
that had helped Maggie find her peace. Perhaps part of me
wanted to keep the idea of a solution to everything out of
my reach. After all, who wanted everything easy?

I'd woken way too early for Jason to have emerged
from his side of the bed. He remained all wrapped up in
the quilt, only his tousled dark hair and the lump his body
made evidence that he was in there at all. Deciding I
needed tea or coffee, I took the recipe book and sat in one
of the comfy sofas in the corner by the coffee machine.
This time instead of flicking through the book, I carefully
examined each page.

Someone else's hand, not Maggie's, had taken each
recipe and added notes like Maggie had done, and not for
the first time, I wondered how old this book was—years
older than Maggie by the looks of it. Even though I knew

that it was American in origin, it still made me smile to see the odd way of measuring things with cups of this and cups of that. Not only that but every missing *u* and added *z* jumped out at me.

Some of the titles made me smile, and I checked a few more out. Under Chocolate Slab, the combination of chocolate, peppermint, and some kind of crumbly oaty mix, simply labeled "for sad times," Maggie had added one word, "worked," and some asterisks. I realized the asterisks meant that the ingredients were ones being rationed. Chocolate was definitely my go-to for when I was in the doldrums, and I heartily approved of the recipe even though I imagined the weight on my body if I ate too much. Others, like Beet Porridge, had comments like "for clarity," which didn't make much sense. I must admit I wasn't blown away by the idea of beet anything, but maybe I should try it at some point. The idea of the violently purple things I knew as beetroot being served up as anything other than pickled in a jar was alien to me.

I stopped at the recipe for Applesauce Cake again. The ingredients listed were the same as the ones I used from the recipe Maggie had written out for me. Exactly the same. Except for the words scribbled next to the apples. Something about referring to the applesauce recipe. I looked for that, but it was missing, and judging from a few torn remains, a couple of other recipes were also not there. I turned to the page I had just inserted—a recipe for chicken soup— and turned it over. There on the back, faint and spidery, was the recipe for applesauce. I gently eased the applesauce page from its loose binding and placed it flat on white paper. At least I could make out some of the writing now. Use *lone* apples, *sove* apples? The words said something like that in Maggie's loopy scrawl.

Sipping coffee gave me time to consider what that meant. Lone or Sove apples? What the hell was a Lone or a Sove apple? Crossing to the kitchen, I rummaged for the applesauce jar I'd bought from the supermarket and scrutinized the back. Lots of e-numbers and of course the single word "apple." Not lone or sove apple. Was that a type? Like Pippin or Granny Smith? Then it hit me like a block of wood to the back of the head, sudden realization of what Maggie maybe could have meant.

I let myself out of the station house and jogged up the hill in the light mist of early autumn rain, waving at the postman but not stopping to talk. I reached Apple Tree Cottage and jumped the low gate before locating the tree with the plaque. Without considering what the hell I was really doing, I picked a handful of apples and shoved them in my jacket pockets, the rest of them cradled in my T-shirt. How many apples was enough? *What the hell am I doing?*

When I returned home, I immediately dumped the apples in the sink and turned on the tap, seeing them bob to the surface and roll in the current caused by the running water. Excitement filled me, and I followed the short recipe, which had no other amendments scrawled in it, until I finally had a container of pale green applesauce that had the sweetness of added sugar and the tartness of the autumn-picked apples. Outside the window the light rain had turned heavier, and the sound of it against the windows was soothing as I mixed cups of flour and sugar and portioned out butter into the large mixing bowl. I hummed as I worked. Some part of me knew this was going to be the first applesauce cake that actually worked.

Halfway through cooking, Jason came downstairs, adorably rumpled and appearing concerned. "Everything okay?" he asked with a yawn. Then he pulled me into a tight hug. He smelled delicious, of fabric conditioner and citrus, and I returned the hug.

"Yes, I'm fine. I can't believe the rain, bloody typical of an English autumn day." I was talking for the sake of it, and he knew it. He settled me back and frowned at my expression.

"Sure you're okay?"

"Promise."

He kissed me gently; then by silent agreement, he settled in to write and I finished the cake and placed it in the oven before setting the timer. I dealt with person after person, all starting out with the usual comment on the weather and finally there was a break, when the alarm sounded to say the cake would be done. Maggie's coffee friends sat with tea, and I proudly pulled out the applesauce cake that looked nearly the same as Maggie's. Gently browned on the surface, it was raised a little and didn't collapse when I poked it. I cut slices and gave them to each woman there. For a second they all stared at the cake, then at each other with knowing smiles.

"What?" I asked, bemused. None of them tried the cake. They all just smiled up at me in that way people did when they had a secret. Damned infuriating it was as well.

"Did I ever tell you how I met my Sidney?" Doris asked. She tucked her long hair behind her ear, and I caught a glimpse of her tattoos. Doris and Sidney were as unlikely a couple as you'd ever see: him an accountant in the City, her a free-spirit craft maker who taught lessons at the local school hall in the evenings.

"No." I was unfailingly polite to Maggie's friends, and enjoyed their stories normally. Just, I couldn't be today. I wanted them to taste the damn cake and tell me what it was like.

"We'd been doing that whole thing where Sidney was telling me that he was too gray for me and that I was too bright to fit into his world. Maggie and I made this cake and I gave him a slice and that was it."

"It? How?" I asked. I couldn't help my own inquisitive nature pushing aside my need for them to eat the cake. So sue me.

"That was the day he said he couldn't keep the love inside anymore, and to Hell with his parents in their drab little house."

"Sidney said that?"

"And more." Doris laughed and placed the cake on the table. "You should give your young man a slice and see what he thinks." All three women looked at me expectantly, and I found myself nodding and leaving them to their tea and cake.

Back in the kitchen, Jason was writing up a storm, and I saw from the word count in the bottom left-hand corner of the screen that he'd already passed fifty-thousand words, and there didn't seem to be a letup in the ease with which he was placing words on the screen. I made us our own coffee and cut slices of cake, then sat on a chair at the corner of the kitchen with a clear view of the shop door—just in case we had a customer, even though the coffee group were as capable of watching the shop as I was.

The scent of coffee clearly broke through his concentration, and finally he stopped typing and gifted me with a wide and grateful smile. He rolled his shoulders, then leaned back in his chair. He sipped coffee and, abruptly, in among all this normality and perfection, I had questions for him.

"When do you have to go home?" I blurted out. I wanted him to say never, but that was impossible.

He spent an inordinate time staring into his coffee. "I don't have to," he finally said. "My mother was British, and I was born here. Although I've never visited, I have dual passports. It's a long complicated story."

And one I didn't want to hear just yet. There would be time for stories later. But what if I said what was on my mind? Would he just pack up and move into the cottage? He could then, it was safe and there was working plumbing. Fear gripped me that he'd laugh in my face if I actually said the three little words, and I swallowed them.

Pushing cake toward him, I tapped the plate. "Try some, see what you think."

He looked momentarily confused at the switch in conversation, and could I hope that was a little disappointment on his face? He broke off a piece of the cake and scooped the small chunks of tart apple onto the sponge. He placed it into his mouth, and I waited for the conclusion. He smiled, that disappointment disappearing from his expression, replaced by appreciation. Something inside me unfroze.

"I love you," I said simply. No frills, no explanations,

and certainly no expectation that he would return the words. To cover my sudden worry, I broke off my own piece of cake, and against the symphony of rain on the windows, I tasted heaven. The apple was tart, the sponge crumbly, the cinnamon soft and marked with heat. I opened my eyes.

I didn't even realize I had closed them.

Jason leaned over and grasped my hands with his. "And I love you," he said without hesitation.

Then we were kissing, the taste of apple and cinnamon and our new love sharp on our tongues. He scooted his chair around next to mine, and we hugged and kissed and told each other about all those moments that made us fall in love.

Warm and needed and oh so loved, I leaned into his hold and listened to the soft cadence of his words and the rain outside.

And in my thoughts, all I could focus on was that I was in love and I was loved back.

Thank you, Maggie. For everything.

THE END

Spirit Bear

Aiden Novak hides who he is. Losing his dad five years ago in the most horrific way has left him scarred and wary. He's supposed to inherit everything his dad worked so hard to build, but he feels nothing, and after a failed abusive relationship he is desperately combatting grief and isolation.

Mitchell's entire life changes when he hears a lecture on conservationism from Dominic Novak, and like the rest of the world, he's stunned when he hears Dominic has died. Five years later, he has worked hard to prove that he deserves a permanent position at Novak Park, he needs to show the new owner what an asset he would be.

Aiden wants to be seen as his own person, Mitchell wants a career, neither of them expected to fall in love. Could working together at a grizzly bear sanctuary in British Columbia be the answer for them both?

Chapter One

"No. Just no," Edward Brandon said in a horrified voice.

Anthony Novak sat back in the chair, shocked by the vehemence in his guardian's voice.

"But I don't see why not," he said softly. Edward was his dad's oldest friend and, more often than not, indulged Anthony in most everything he had wanted after his dad had died ten years ago. Since Edward had been the closest thing he had to family for so long, it was hard for Anthony to hear the 'no'.

Edward sighed heavily and scrubbed a hand over his face. He looked tired and Anthony knew he'd been up all night with the lemurs. "Because it's the most stupid idea in the long list of all the really stupid ideas that you have ever had," he said.

Anthony exhaled noisily and wished he didn't feel like a ten-year-old at the moment. He was twenty-four and he knew exactly what he wanted to do. His friend and mentor would come round to his way of thinking eventually.

"No one actually knows my real name at the moment," Anthony began. "It's been five years since I last hit the papers. I just want to stay under the pseudonym for a few weeks more. I don't understand why that is so difficult for you to understand."

"Because now you're coming here to the Park full time. You should be coming on as full partner as a Novak, not as Aiden Samuels. You have a responsibility to your father's name."

Something twisted in Aiden's chest at the mention of that huge weight pressing him down.

"I promise you," he said. "Whether I join the Park as partner or ranger, I'll be Anthony Novak. But just for three more weeks, let me be anonymous. I've lived five years as Aiden Samuels, twenty-one more days isn't going to hurt."

Edward contemplated him over steepled fingers. "So let me get this straight. You want to be part of the annual bear census at the Khutzeymateen reserve but you want to go under your assumed name. All in the hope that the bear census organizers won't realize who you are."

The Spirit Bear Park, an animal reserve just outside of Seattle, was named for the elusive pale-furred black bears that could sometimes be seen in the Great Bear Rainforest in British Columbia. Dominic Novak had spent a year studying them as a young man and he'd always said they were part of his soul.

"Dad was such a big part of the bear studies. If they knew I was there, his son, then yes, I wouldn't be just another ranger on his first educational placement, but someone they would expect more from."

"More?" Edward appeared puzzled and Anthony knew

he hadn't explained all this enough to make it clear to his dad's closest friend. He opened his mouth to explain but Edward got there first. "I know how difficult it is to live in the shadow of your dad." Edward was sincere in what he said. "He was a larger-than-life character, but you are his son and one day everyone will know that."

"But why does it need to be today? Can I not just have another three weeks of being anonymous?"

Edward was quiet. "I don't know what to say."

"I'm not my dad. I don't have his instinct with animals. All the books I've read don't mean I can share what I learned with others and show the level of passion he had."

"Your dad was a showman. You don't have to be just like him," Edward protested.

"But if I could have half of the success that Dad had in furthering conservation—or even a quarter—I would be happy. I know it's time for me to use my expensive education and work here at Spirit Bear." Anthony pushed away the edge of impatience in his voice. He wanted to work at the reserve, but he knew as soon as people knew who he was they would look at him with pity or stare with dollar signs in their eyes. Working on the annual bear census would be one way of getting into the thick of things without everyone's expectations hanging around his neck.

"Work here as the joint owner, with me." Edward said.

"I can't just walk into that. I want to learn from the ground up. I want to see it all, and just for a while longer I want to be Aiden Samuels, not Anthony Novak."

Anthony crossed his arms over his chest and eyed Edward, looking for a chink in his impenetrable armor, but he could see nothing. Okay, so working and living under his assumed name for a little longer was probably a bad idea, but hell, he just wanted to enjoy his time with the bears. If just for that short time longer he could be Aiden Samuels, new guy, then maybe he could find what that passion inside him without all the extra crap he would have to deal with otherwise.

Edward nodded slowly. "You were such a tiny baby when your mom died, and then losing your dad… I know it's hard. But to hide who you are now, I don't get that. Whatever the newspapers throw at you, we can handle it."

"I'm not sure *I* can. Just the three weeks where I can think about what I do and get a handle on it all. Please?"

"What about the ranger you would be going to Canada with? What will you tell him?"

"Nothing at first. I'll be Aiden for three weeks, then on the flight back I'll tell him who I really am." That much was clear in his head.

"That there is a recipe for disaster and could go all kinds of wrong. He'll feel like you lied to him."

"That's a chance I'll have to take. You're looking for a new ranger—look at the application I filled in."

Edward rifled papers, his lips tight, his eyes dark with indecision and questions, before finally sighing and moving the pen down the application form. "Aiden Samuels, twenty-four, degree in Zoology and college work placements, on paper the perfect candidate for a position here."

"But no real-life field experience, apart from the month in the Sudan. That is what I feel is missing, what I need to be comfortable in my new role," Anthony insisted. "How can I manage rangers who have more instinct with their animals than I do?"

Anthony knew he was right. He may well have had field experience as a child because he'd been a constant companion to his dad for the years leading up to Dominic Novak's death. But at the end of it all, he needed adult experience.

"Okay," Edward said thoughtfully. "Go to the placement with the bears, do the three weeks." He held up a hand to forestall what Anthony wanted to say. "Let me finish. Complete the three more weeks as Aiden Samuels and think about what you want to do when you come back. What I really want, and what you deserve, is for you to take your place as equal partner. Not as another ranger."

"Okay." That wasn't such a hardship. "Should I consider myself added to the bear count team?" Anthony asked softly. He could see the battle in Edward's eyes, knowing how hard it must be to see his friend's son, half-owner of the Park, sitting so hopefully for a decision on a placement that he could just add himself to anyway. But he needed to do this to get the missing passion and instinct in himself that he so desperately wanted to find.

Edward sighed. "Consider yourself hired."

The Spirit Bear Park Education Center wasn't new and it certainly lacked the sparkle of a new paint job. But it was lived-in and it was home for Mitchell in ways his own had never been. This collection of buildings with rooms to teach was a legacy from Professor Novak, and Mitchell was the assistant manager and lead teacher. Every day a new slew of students from schools tagged alongside students from universities on placements, and the mismatch and jumble of resources and knowledge was passed on to spread the word.

Spirit Bear Park had been established some time ago and large open spaces made it an award-winning attraction, but it wasn't just a place for people to visit on their downtime. The Park made a valuable contribution to conservation. It was a place where families could see animals roaming freely and learn more about the various endangered species that Dominic Novak had begun to re-home twenty years before.

It was Mitchell's first job and he was convinced it would be his only one, alternating with the rangers to experience the animals firsthand and then creating vibrant programs for learning at all levels. It excited him, it moved him, and it was his life. And he had friends here, including Scot, who had slumped into the chair in Mitchell's small office with disappointment carved into his face.

"I can't go to Khutzeymateen," Scot said softly, disappointment in his gravelly voice. "The wedding of the century is slap bang in the middle."

"How is that going by the way?" Mitchell smirked, knowing exactly how to get the rise out of his friend. Scot muttered a few choice words, which included the word lilac if Mitchell heard right. Scot's sister had met Alan, fallen in love with the guy, and then planned a wedding in the space of two months. Scot had been planning his rotation on the bear audit for two years. Mitchell knew family came first but it didn't seem entirely fair. "Couldn't you attend the wedding and then go on to the placement?"

Scot frowned. "Thought of that, but you know the whole grizzly thing is like a full-immersion experience; I can't exactly turn up halfway through for a week."

Mitchell nodded, that was the point of these occasional placements in areas of specialty—full immersion to experience and learn. He was gutted for his friend; Scot had been so hyped to get the placement at Khutzeymateen. His sister booking the middle week for her wedding was just really bad timing.

"So I was thinking… you should go instead," Scot suggested.

Mitchell hated snap decisions, hated amending his educational programs around forced change, grumped and groaned for weeks at any kind of disruption.

"They didn't offer the place to me," Mitchell said. Problem solved.

"They did, it was an open offer, two places for qualified rangers, and there is no reason why you shouldn't go."

"Do we know who else is going with you—sorry, was going with you—oh, you know what I mean."

"Some new guy, Aiden something. I heard he just finished at some foreign college, doing the placement before he starts at the Park. I don't know much about him, but he was the only other one qualified enough and who had expressed an interest other than you."

"I never expressed an interest," Mitchell defended quickly. "All I said was that it sounded cool to work with the conservation guys and the bears." Mitchell knew he was losing this discussion.

"Your last course finishes a few days before you would need to leave, I checked. Take the sabbatical, take the time off to do the practical stuff, Mitch. Get out of the classroom, it would do you good."

Chapter Two

*M*itchell had been sitting in the small plane for a good ten minutes before the guy who was going to be his teammate slid into the seat next to him, pulling the belt across himself and fumbling to close it, all the while muttering under his breath. Mitchell waited until five-ten of dark-haired guy stopped with the muttering and then he extended his hand in welcome.

"Mitchell Steward," he introduced himself. Blue eyes focused on him, and then his companion held out a hand to shake.

"I know," he said. "I'm Aiden." A Southerner by the sound of his drawl, Mitchell thought. He filed that away for future discussion; after all, he didn't want to use up all his conversation starters at once.

"So three weeks then," Mitchell pointed out quickly, aware he probably needed to say something. All Aiden did was send a confused look his way and slide iPod buds in his ears.

"Sorry," he said, turning the dial and closing his eyes, the tinny thump of music echoing in Mitchell's ears.

"Great start to a four-hour trip," Mitchell grumbled to himself, opening his collected research at the last page he was on and trying to get back into the detail. So much for getting to know this Aiden guy.

He was alternatively amused and annoyed seeing the white-knuckled fear as his companion's nails dug into cloth-covered armrests and then having to listen to off-tune humming that grew louder every time the plane hit any kind of turbulence. He felt like poking the sprawled guy in the shoulder at least a hundred times, especially as his companion had a decidedly loose definition of personal space. Mitchell spent some time pushing him back and the rest of the time staring at the guy's hands, his large hands, curled and strong, wishing he could concentrate on his freaking information sheets.

In the end he gave up on reading. He closed the sheets and pushed them into his carry-on. Leaning back in his seat and closing his own eyes, he leaned away from the heat from his fellow passenger's arm and the intriguing scent of his aftershave or deodorant or whatever he was wearing. Catching himself sniffing the air, he mentally chastised himself. His companion waking up and spotting what he was doing wouldn't bode well for them spending the next three weeks together. He briefly wondered what Aiden would do if the iPod charge ran out and was amused to be treated to the spectacle, halfway through the flight, of a panicking Aiden switching his purple iPod for a blue one before screwing his eyes tight and leaning back in his seat.

The captain made an announcement about descending

into Vancouver Airport, where they had their first stopover and a connecting flight. The plane came to a complete halt before Aiden pulled out his ear buds and finally looked Mitchell straight in the eye.

"Hey," Aiden said.

"Hello," Mitchell said quietly. Blue eyes regarded him intently.

"Sorry," Aiden added. He indicated the iPod, now laying quietly in his lap, and then waved his hand in front of his face in a *whatever* kind of gesture. "I'm not a good flyer."

Mitchell nodded his understanding and unbuckled. He was way beyond tired and probably wasn't in the right frame of mind to be commenting on how Aiden had been on the flight. He just wanted off the Air Canada flight and out into the fresh air. Pointedly he waited as Aiden untwisted his legs from the small space and stood, his head connecting with the overhead lighting and a muttered curse on his lips.

He appeared to be disoriented if the way he tripped and clambered with his carry-on was any indication. Finally he managed to make it to the exit, looking back at Mitchell with a very definite *well are you coming then?* kind of look. He backed it up with a grin, his ashen face getting more color into it even as he waited for Mitchell.

They had just over an hour and a half to connect to the next flight, and once they left the plane Aiden wanted to get coffee.

"Are you excited about this?" Mitchell asked when Aiden didn't seem to want to start a conversation. If anything, he appeared to find more interest in the sheafs of notes he had in front of him. They were brightly notated in purple and green. Evidently Aiden was more prepared than he was.

"I so am," Aiden said excitedly. He wiped a foamy moustache from his top lip with a napkin and looked back down at his paperwork. At this point Mitchell expected him to ask the same question back to Mitchell. Instead he tapped the papers on the table and launched into conversation.

"I think it is the grizzly bear's survival that will be the greatest testimony to our environmental commitment in the end," he said firmly. He was looking at Mitchell directly and his unwavering blue stare was curiously hot. Great, now he was crushing on the guy he was going to be in close quarters with for three weeks. Not good Mitchell. Not good at all.

"I agree," Mitchell said somewhat lamely.

"If we can get this right then maybe we can solve some of the other ecological and environmental messes we have made."

Mitchell remembered reading something along those lines in his online research. He considered if Aiden had read the same thing and was just adopting known comments or whether he'd actually came up with it himself. The British Columbia Grizzly Bear Conservation Strategy had been developed by the government of BC with the tenet *It will leave a permanent legacy for our children.* Just those few words had made Mitchell think almost as much as they apparently made Aiden talk.

"So, yeah, I'm excited. Recovery planning for grizzly bear populations that are at risk is kind of a critical element, y'know, in the whole conservation strategy," Aiden said.

"Critical," Mitchell parroted. *Those eyes are really blue and does his hair have red streaks in it and how long does he spend making it look so effortlessly tousled and cute?*

"So being involved in the rolling program to quantify population and habitat is kind of cool. Don't you think?" *He's talking. Listen to his soft, drawled words and for God's sake, say something clever.*

"Statistical analysis with multiple regression models and practical visual analysis is always cool," Mitchell finally said.

Aiden's eyes widened and then he grinned broadly. "Totally."

Spirit Bear Park sent two people each year to work here. He and Aiden would be looking at habitat, population, and any other factors that could affect the work that was being undertaken with the grizzly population they were to study. Canada and the US were encouraging international cooperation for management of the bear populations, some of which were in danger of extirpation, or as Mitchell's old species lecturer explained, as close to extinct as virginity at a frat party.

It wasn't only people like them, with their degrees and their experience, who saw how species were dying one by one. Extinction of species was at the top of most nations' to-do lists. Khutzeymateen was one of the most well-managed conservation areas, an ideal that other parks where grizzly populations were threatened aspired to.

"Extirpation of a species is a tragedy and if this work

revitalizes the indigenous bear population in BC and across the border then it's a win-win." Aiden caught himself as he chattered and looked down at the papers in front of him. Mitchell saw the flush of embarrassment on Aiden's face as he tucked his hair behind his ear. *Hella cute and—oh hell, I didn't just think that.* "Sorry. I can go on and on if you let me," Aiden added. Mitchell instantly wanted to reassure the other man and chuckled. He jumped in to save Aiden with a conversation extension.

"I know the population of grizzlies at Khutzeymateen is considered viable and that it's a stable population that needs assessing. I just wish I'd had more time to read up on all this." Aiden looked up and Mitchell indicated the paperwork spread out in front of him. "I only got everything last night. I was a last minute change replacing a friend."

Aiden frowned. "You wanted to come though?"

"Yes, but the last project I was on was Kenya, it's been a while." He didn't have to try hard to put enthusiasm into his speech. "I work in the Education Center at the Park," he offered, because Aiden hadn't actually asked. "So I know all the facts, I just didn't have a chance to analyze the charts and statistical data we have so far from previous teams."

Aiden tapped a finger against his temple. "We'll be okay; I have it all in here. We can work on that when we get to the first night's stop."

Aiden pushed his hair behind his ears again. The reddish brown mess of flicks and layers fell around his face and he was evidently irritable with it. When Aiden mumbled something while looking back down at the table,

Mitchell realized he had just found Aiden's tell. It appeared he was nervous and when he got like that he touched his hair and lowered his gaze.

He didn't mean to make Aiden anxious. Maybe he was staring a bit too much. Deliberately he concentrated on the caramel macchiato he had in his paper cup. A lot of time in the rainforest would pass before he got more coffee like this and he needed to remember it.

The second flight was as quiet at the first. Another color iPod and yet more tinny music meant Mitchell had time to think about Aiden. The younger man appeared wary of Mitchell, even though Mitchell had generally been on his best behavior. He could hear Scot's voice in his head, *Angsting much, gay boy*? Just… there was a vulnerability about Aiden that intrigued Mitchell. A combination of clumsiness, shyness, enthusiasm, and the finest ass on either side of the border had Mitchell wondering if there was any chance Aiden was gay, or even just a little bit bi. That would make the three weeks fly by when, instead of cold nights in individual sleeping bags, there could be hot sex in bags zipped together. He chastised himself and willed his sudden erection to fuck off. Not only was Aiden a new member of staff at the Spirit Bear Park, but he was too young for Mitchell. Hell, he couldn't be much more than twenty-three or -four. Aiden was at least seven years younger than him, and Mitchell was really feeling that difference.

As the plane banked and dipped through the clouds, Mitchell got his first look at this beautiful part of Canada and its distant snow-tipped mountains. Finally, after a long couple of hours they descended from high wispy clouds and landed at Prince Rupert Airport. The plane continued taxiing, rolling to a stop at the end of the middle-of-nowhere runway. Mitchell moved to look out the window at the flat space beyond. Excitement curled in his stomach like a kid before Christmas, the unknown beckoning to him beyond the thick glass, and he shifted in his seat, a now-blinking Aiden looking out the same window.

They climbed down steep metal steps, standing uncertainly at the base, both looking for the contact that was supposed to be meeting them. There were people around them—passengers and flight crew—each seemingly moving with purpose towards a shelter to one side. Exchanging inquisitive expressions, both men followed the herd, so to speak, to come in behind a guy with a note board and pen.

"Fowler and Samuels?" he asked officiously. "Do we have a Scot Fowler and an Aiden Samuels?" Aiden spun on his heel, his eyes widening, and he shouted a quick 'here'. Mitchell added the fact that it was he, Mitchell Steward, and not Scot Fowler that was on the flight. The officious man tutted, but then he crossed the two names off his list.

They followed him to the baggage claim, a wooden table with chairs around it that appeared as if someone had cleared away dinner to use the top for cases. Both men grabbed their bags. Digby Island, where the runway was located, was a bus and ferry ride away from the mainland, and Mitchell hoped like hell that Aiden wasn't afraid of boats or being driven. He wasn't sure he could handle another minute of muted tinny Lady Gaga. Instead Aiden chose to inundate Mitchell with a non-stop dialog ranging from his fear of flying, his apologies for appearing rude, his love of animals, and the fact that the grizzly bear was perhaps the greatest symbol of the wilderness.

It fell to Mitchell to facilitate Aiden's talking with the insertion of a few nods and *uhms*. To be fair, he did agree with most of what Aiden was saying, sensing a fellow soul in his quest for species survival and conservation. If only he could concentrate on that instead of feeling like a kid with his first crush then all would be fine.

"It's gorgeous, isn't it?" Aiden said. He was taking photos with a tiny digital camera and moved from one end of the ferry to the other like a kid hyperactive on cola.

"Beautiful." The water was a sapphire blue and the mist rising amongst the trees was amazing. He couldn't think of any more words to describe the stunning vista. He leaned against the rail of the boat and breathed in the cold Alaskan air that filtered along the BC coast and then inland to where they were.

The ferry nudged the dock, and Aiden was first off, jumping the space between boat and dock with an agility that seemed to belie his clumsiness on the plane until he caught his leg on the rope and almost fell flat on his face. Mitchell climbed off as the boat was tied, feeling much older than his thirty-one years as Aiden started to babble on in unashamed excitement. It unnerved him to have Aiden near bouncing on his toes. In his mind the movement didn't come over as particularly professional when their contact from Khutzeymateen crossed to them, looking faintly shocked when Aiden grabbed his hand and shook it with both of his own.

"How long will it be now?" Aiden asked quickly as Mitchell shook the guy's hand a lot more sedately. They followed the man, who had introduced himself as William Helin, to a black 4x4.

"It'll be a good four hours," he answered. He encouraged both Aiden and Mitchell into the back. "Easier to nap."

"I'm too hyped to sleep," Aiden replied instantly, at the same time knocking his head on the roof of the 4x4 as he tried to fold himself into the small space.

"Jeez, man, are you trying to kill yourself?" Mitchell commented softly, helping Aiden with the belt and pulling the door shut. Aiden turned to face Mitchell with a flush of scarlet coloring his cheeks.

"Sorry," he apologized and subsided to look out the side window. Mitchell frowned and was concerned at Aiden's response. He hadn't meant anything by his comment. The other guy looked uncomfortable and way past embarrassed. And now he was quiet and that was just plain wrong.

"I didn't mean anything," Mitchell started, and Aiden turned to him, an earnest expression on his mobile face.

"It's okay, I know I can sometimes be a bit—" He shrugged. "—y'know, clumsy, hyperactive, and shit. You just need to say if it gets too much. I always thought I might have ADHD or something 'cause I don't sit still, when I'm nervous I can't shut up, and I fall over things all the time."

"No," Mitchell was quick to apologize, "really, it's

cool." Mitchell wasn't sure if that was the right thing to say, but it had the desired effect. Aiden went back to looking out the window, but at least Mitchell saw a small smile on his face before he turned. What Mitchell needed to think about is why that smile and that happiness made him feel so damn pleased. Scot was right when he said that Mitchell's gay side was getting him all emotional. He leaned back on the headrest, watching as small-town living gave way to Canadian wilderness, an excitement building inside him that not even being tired could stop. They climbed into the snow line, high into the peaks some 6500 feet above a valley of wetlands, old-growth temperate rainforests, and the large estuary. Mitchell imagined the air outside the window was cold and crisp and clean, like this land was new and untouched.

The last part of their journey was off-road; because of the area's high sensitivity and strict conservation orientation no one was allowed into the conservation area outside those who worked there. No campers, no families, no hunters, just acres of unspoiled wilderness and the bears.

William was talking about the park as they bumped and slid along trails that Mitchell wasn't even sure actually existed outside of William's head. "This area is just off the watershed of the Khutzeymateen River."

"I read that it's an important hunting and fishing site for First Nations people," Aiden said. Then he subsided with a murmured *sorry*.

William nodded. "The Gits'iis, one of the nine tribes making up the Allied Tsimshian Tribes. The park was created in partnership with the Gits'iis people." Aiden was nodding along, agreeing as William commented; he had obviously done his homework. Although Mitchell knew about the First Nations people, he hadn't researched that side given the short notice for attendance. "The park is managed jointly with BC Parks and the Tsimshian Tribal Council."

"What does the name Kitsimdeen mean?" Mitchell asked. He was sure he was butchering the pronunciation of the word.

"You say it K'tsim-a-deen," Aiden interrupted. "It means 'valley at the head of the inlet'." Mitchell wasn't surprised Aiden knew that. He seemed to know an awful lot about this placement.

"Will we get to have any interaction with the tribes?" Mitchell queried, blinking as Aiden sent him a look of mild amusement.

"I think you'll find you already have been interacting," he said softly, laughing along with William. "William's surname is Helin." The next part he directed at William. "I guess you are related to the tribe elders?" Aiden was throwing it out as a question, but William was still laughing, and Mitchell could do nothing other than smile along with them.

Mitchell knew a lot of information important to this placement. He knew bears were as fast as racehorses, whether on the flats, going uphill, or going downhill. They're strong swimmers with good eyesight, good hearing, and an acute sense of smell. He knew that all black bears and young grizzlies were agile tree climbers; mature grizzlies were poor climbers, but they had a reach up to four meters. He had made it a point to know that if a bear is standing up it is usually trying to identify you and that it wasn't looking to hurt you. He had worked the bear rotation at Spirit Bear; he knew enough, and really, wasn't that why he was here? To learn? But so he didn't know William was related to the elders, sue him. Aiden looked over at Mitchell ruefully and Mitchell realized his inner annoyance must be showing on his face.

"Sorry again," Aiden said, too low for William to hear. "I didn't mean to laugh." Mitchell shrugged it off, suddenly feeling very stupid; he didn't know why Aiden's laughter got to him like that. He couldn't get a handle on this clumsy man who worried about what other people thought of him, who spent his whole time apologizing for what he was or what he knew. The whole package fascinated Mitchell and he thought that maybe he'd like it if he and Aiden could end this three weeks as friends, if only so he could stare at him some more.

"My grandfather," William said, answering Aiden's original question. "At least fifty percent of the people tending to the area are locally sourced from the Tsimshian. The rest are people like you: researchers, graduates, and the like. We are a closed community." Aiden nodded, and Mitchell frowned to himself, he bet Aiden had known that too.

"I know they are more prevalent on the islands, but do you think we'll see any Spirit Bears?" Aiden asked. By this time he was leaning forward to listen to William and Mitchell realized he could probably stare at the high cheekbones and long dark eyelashes framing those stunning azure eyes all day.

"Moksgm'ol. They are known to the Tsimshian people

as Moksgm'ol. And I expect you will," William answered. He turned the wheel to avoid an obstacle in the road and Aiden slid sideways against the belt until his thigh rested against Mitchell's. *I'm going to hell*, Mitchell thought immediately.

Chapter Three

*A*iden yawned widely. Early evening had painted the sky a muted mauve by the time they reached the hostel, a small one-story building that slept six. Tonight it would just be Aiden and Mitchell. William was going home and would be back the next day, bringing with him the team leader who was assigning Mitchell and Aiden their area for assessment. The cabin was primitive, rustic, but—thank God—windproof and even kind of warm.

After stamping snow off his boots, Aiden slid onto the bed nearest the door, lying back on the thin cot, twisting his lips ruefully as he realized even his five-ten was not going to fit onto a five-six cot. Still it wasn't anything new; Aiden never really felt comfortable anywhere, too clumsy and uncoordinated, too *Aiden*. Mitchell chose a bed a few down, sitting and sighing as William waved from the door and shut it behind him.

Aiden bounced back up off his cot, opening a cupboard

and finding cans of stew. He considered the stew, gas burner, and other supplies that they had been left with. Within ten minutes, while Mitchell sat writing in some kind of journal, Aiden had stew simmering in a pot and fragrant coffee in tin cups.

"This is good," Mitchell said as he virtually inhaled both. "Thank you."

Afterwards, they sat on the beds, lying against thin pillows while nursing coffee, and Aiden wondered who was going to speak first. Inevitably it was he who broke the silence. He hated awkward silences.

"I'm looking forward to starting at Spirit Bear, y'know, after this," he offered into the silence.

"It's a cool place to be," Mitchell responded carefully. "I love the center, and the animals, but sometimes people don't want to hear about it as much as I want to talk about it."

"Well, I want to know." Aiden shifted to face Mitchell with a curious expression on his face.

Mitchell smiled. "I've been there coming up on seven years now, straight from college; I was so lucky to get the position."

Aiden already knew that, but saying so meant revealing who he really was. That wasn't happening anytime soon, at least, not until they got home to the US. It was inevitable Mitchell would find out but he would at least have had three weeks of anonymity where he could be treated as just another guy at the Park.

Maybe I should just tell him now and get it over with. Aiden immediately dismissed the thought. People looked at him differently when they found out who he was. Given that he was, for all intents and purposes, Mitchell's boss, all Aiden could foresee was problems if he revealed himself too soon. Knowing him, it would come back and bite him in the ass but for now he could convince himself everything would be okay. Denial was his friend.

They chatted for a few hours about everything and nothing—football, animals, college, religion even.

"So, I guess as we are spending the next three weeks in close proximity, now may be a good time to tell you I'm gay," Mitchell suddenly said in amongst the discussion of his momma's church bake sales.

Aiden just blinked owlishly, he was quite obviously losing it if his gaydar hadn't picked that one up. "Oh" was all his klutzy head could come up with. Anything more eloquent was lost in the eagerness to sit up and say *me too, me too*. What were the chances that he would have that in common with the guy?

"Me too." Okay, that had sounded a lot more clever in his head. "I mean. I'm gay. I have been ever since I was…" *Shit, stupid, stupid, stupid.* Aiden gave in to his rising embarrassment and ducked his head. Tangling his fingers in his hair, he smoothed the longer lengths behind his ears. He really needed to figure out the most reasonable and easiest way to look after it.

"Well okay then," Mitchell said, finishing his coffee and crossing to the door. "That might make the trip a little more exciting than just the fear of being eaten by a bear."

Mitchell was teasing, Aiden knew that, but it didn't stop him from turning scarlet.

Mitchell shivered. "Jeez, I don't want to but I really need to go outside to take a leak," he announced. He shrugged on his bulky parka and slipped outside, pulling the door closed behind him. Even after Mitchell left amidst a few swirling wisps of snow, Aiden remained sitting, still bright red.

There was nothing positive to be said for hiding. Hiding his name, his identity, never letting anyone in, sticking to casual, and having nothing in the way of meaningful sex, was bad. He had never really had a relationship, barring one loser, but there were just too many secrets, too many lies, too much being scared and open to public scrutiny.

Add in his hyperactive brain, his clumsiness, and realizing when he turned fourteen that he wasn't right in his own skin—unfortunately, the same time his dad died—and it was no wonder Anthony felt better behind the mask that was Aiden. He'd accepted himself but he didn't tell people. He wasn't sure why, although the therapist he'd seen at seventeen had had a field day with his issues. Aiden was shocked that he admitted even as much as he had to Mitchell. To hear Mitchell so clearly and confidently admit to his sexual preference… it just frightened Aiden spitless, all of it.

Mitchell returned, muttering something about it being colder than a witch's tit and stamping his feet dramatically. It was all Aiden could do to not ask Mitchell how he managed to sound so sure of himself. How he could be gay and so seemingly at peace with it, when all it was for Aiden was yet another reason to hide.

Instead Aiden watched Mitchell pull off his parka and

remove his boots before climbing under blankets and saying goodnight. Aiden shrugged on his own coat, then opened and closed the door and stood outside, his face to the cold, swirling snow, his gaze fixed on a point in the far distance. The panic inside him started to grow and emotion choked him as one of the attacks he was so used to started to pull him under until his breath wheezed and his head grew black with unaccountable fear. Every single confident thing he had done today simply slipped away under the weight of grief and fear that constantly dragged him down.

How was it he had become this? From a child that had been so full of life, so independent, and so in tune with the world around him to this scared idiot? Tears of self-pity were scrubbed away by gloved hands, his spine stiffening as he talked himself down. A year of therapy and many more years of yoga and relaxation and he could do this, but sometimes he just had to let it out. Slowly. *Slowly.* Finally calmer, he pasted a smile on his face and went back inside. He needn't have bothered; Mitchell was still curled under his sleeping bag on the bed, his own height of maybe six foot causing him to look like a pretzel. Not a good look. Aiden dreaded getting comfortable on the small bed. Were all the other rangers and naturalists under five-six? Were they all children? He laughed to himself and puttered around tidying up until he had to give in and get some sleep.

As he slipped under his own blankets while listening to Mitchell's deep, even breathing, his head was filled with questions, the same questions that plagued him day and night, that caused him to fail in everything he did.

His dad never had stupid panic attacks or felt like he couldn't deal with people. His dad had been brave and strong and wouldn't have let negative emotions stop him from doing anything.

Aiden just wished he were more like his dad.

Chapter Four

*T*hey woke up with seemingly similar levels of discomfort, Aiden unfolding his frame from the tiny bed and hopping as bare feet dropped on the cold floor and Mitchell yawning and stretching and cursing quietly as he tried to loosen his feet from under the end bar of the cot. It hadn't been the best sleep, and Aiden was on edge, wondering what was going to be thrown at them today. He had woken up every so often in the night only to see Mitchell awake also. They had exchanged commiserating looks as they twisted and turned to get comfortable.

"I'm not sure I signed up for torture," Mitchell groused and lowered himself to the chair at the small, uneven table. Aiden pushed a mug of caffeine his way and Mitchell closed his eyes and groaned appreciatively as he swallowed the heat, running his tongue over his lip to chase the taste of the coffee.

Aiden just watched. Or rather he tried not to watch. Well actually he tried not to watch too obviously as his colleague pulled what could only be called a sex face over caffeine, complete with tongue peeking out. Aiden swallowed, damping down the immediate attraction to this hazel-eyed man that had sparked inside him. This is how it always happened. Aiden stared at the unobtainable, the partners he would never have, in this case, the gorgeous Mitchell who would run as fast as he could in the opposite direction. He'd felt it yesterday as soon as he slid into the seat next to the quietly composed man with the inquiring gaze and the smell of expensive aftershave. He had felt the man was unobtainable, diametrically opposed, the absolute pinnacle of a non-Aiden-type boyfriend.

Said other category, an Aiden-type boyfriend, was difficult to actually quantify in detail or with much thoroughness given the sparse, tumbleweed-strewn landscape of his love life. He had a severe lack of relationships that lasted past date one, since he inevitably came across as a mix of some kind of drunken idiot and a child in a man's body. No one had to tell him that one day he would eventually meet someone that saw through his clumsiness and his overly enthusiastic interest in the world about him. But, looking at the man opposite him and remembering his shocked reaction to some of the stupid crap Aiden pulled yesterday, it wasn't going to be this Mitchell guy. Aiden had experienced his share of unrequited crushes, but it didn't stop him from looking, did it? Which was when Mitchell chose to look up, his eyes widening, and Aiden knew what he saw. *A pathetic staring person.* For all Mitchell could have said or commented, all he actually did was frown quickly and then drop his eyes back to his coffee. With that single move Aiden had a reprieve, and he stumbled to stand, knocking the chair back against the wall and tripping over his own feet to stumble-curse out the door and into the snow, grabbing his parka as he left.

"Freaking stupid." He stamped around in circles, his breath puffing in the frigid air. "Stupid social skills." He was being hard on himself, he knew that. After all, it wasn't as if his life had ever been normal. He had been dragged from jungle to desert and back again until he was fourteen, then dumped into a spotlight he didn't want. Private school, a British University, and thrust back into the legacy his father left for him. How could he expect to know what the freaking hell to say to people, especially gorgeous, confident, gay—and out—people? He breathed deeply, the cold climbing into his lungs, the purity of it dizzying at this height, and he sighed, trying to pull together the growing embarrassment at the whole staring thing that was threatening to produce awkward-Aiden from the mix.

He heard the door open and Mitchell made his way to where Aiden stood, digging his hands into voluminous pockets and burying his face deep in quilted padding. Aiden didn't say anything, wasn't really sure what he could say, trawling his head for small talk. He dismissed every sentence that led to a discussion on either sports again, of which he wasn't really an expert, or the weather, which was fairly much in their face anyway. Instead he was relieved when he didn't have to. Mitchell did enough talking for both of them, explaining a bit more about the Park they were both going to be working together at after the census work was finished here. The older, more experienced ranger explained that it had been difficult the last two years, ranger numbers had been down, although the animals were still cared for and the Park had decent visitor numbers. Mitchell reassured Aiden about his job, because their bosses, Edward Brandon and the absent Novak Jr., were pumping more money into the animals, the staff, and, last but not least, Mitchell's baby, the education center.

"It's almost as if they have given the education center a blank check." Mitchell laughed, and then shivered. "Man, let's get more coffee before William arrives."

Aiden blinked steadily at Mitchell. He wanted to say, *It's my check, I am the one putting the money into the center. I want to spread the word, safeguard the jobs. Can you see me?* It was so wrong to be hiding like this. As soon as he sat down on the plane he should have said, *Hey, man, keep this to yourself but my real name is Anthony Aiden Novak, pleased to meet you.* They could have done the whole awkward uncomfortable thing, got it out of the way, then settled in to work. As it was now, Aiden had something else to worry about. He would have to listen to Mitchell bitch about funding, then praise the education schemes, comment on visitor numbers, laugh about colleagues, and the whole time pretend he wasn't Mitchell's boss. Edward had been so right. This was a bad idea. He even opened his mouth to explain who he was and then realized he couldn't say the words.

They sat for another ten minutes drinking coffee in silence, each deep in thought, until nine a.m. when William and the team leader arrived, stomping off snow and grinning widely. William dumped a box of supplies on the floor and began pulling out maps, spreading them out on the table as they exchanged good mornings. The bottom left of the map was highlighted in blue, an area roughly the size of a large town, and assigned the reference T87.

"This is your area. We already have data for the two bordering areas to the North, and here to the West." He added a satellite phone and a small netbook to the pile with the map. "This is a satellite phone in case of emergency but also a way to keep in contact. There are solar recharge stations in the cabins on your route, but I'm sure you won't need the phone. You will probably come across the odd Khutzeymateen ranger, or K-ranger as we are called, as I know there was a bit of a problem in that corner with hunting since it is so close to the river."

Aiden and Mitchell exchanged glances, Aiden deciding an emergency phone sounded good. Clearly Mitchell agreed. Whatever the communication coverage was in the denser parts of the forest, hunters, K-rangers, and bears all sounded in his head like a recipe for some kind of drama.

"So, you have your map, we just need to check your route and your stops and then your kits," William continued, efficient and to the point. So it went for a good hour, before the two men gathered their resources and took the first step on the trail that was more like a narrow path —a path that was only due to last some two miles before dumping them into the wild side of nature.

They set out on a good pace. Aiden concentrated on every footstep, determined not to let his body pull him over a branch or down a hole, the snow making each step difficult as it hid the ground below. It became easier as they moved downward, as the snow gradually gave way to frost and then to a ground mist when they passed the snow line. Then the trees drew in closer, the path suddenly disappeared before them, and parkas were unzipped away from faces.

The trees were tall and close together and several were covered in moss for as far as Aiden could see. The space was ancient with old roots spreading and clinging to the rock until there was a network of entwined wood that made the going a little more difficult. At this point the forest was muted greens and little sunlight made its way through the canopy above.

Mitchell had taken the first turn to orient their way down the mountain, the compass around his neck keeping them on course and Aiden following behind. Aiden tried really hard to listen to Mitchell's instructions, but Mitchell's deep voice distracted him enough that at some points Aiden had to stop to avoid falling over due to lack of concentration on the terrain.

"We stopping?" Mitchell asked, hefting off his pack and pulling at his parka, after the third time Aiden halted. The deeper they got the warmer it became, or rather, as warm as it could be with the icy wind in the air. Aiden was feeling the heat in his insulated coat, and by silent agreement they leaned against a tree and broke out what could be described as lunch—two energy bars, trail mix, and water. Eating in silence allowed Aiden to look around him at the ancient trees and tangled mossy roots.

Aiden considered himself fit. He ran and frequented a gym, but the ache and burn in his legs as they descended the shale cliffs that marked this side of the mountain reminded him that his idea of exercise and the actual training that a full-time K-ranger would undertake were actually very different.

"You realize," he started, a wry smile on his face as he passed trail mix over to Mitchell, "we need to walk back up the mountain when we are done."

Mitchell looked back the way they had come, up through the dense trees and the light-blocking canopy, and grimaced. "Goddamn," he offered softly, stretching out the muscles in his legs. "Still, it's actually harder on the legs to walk down than to walk up."

Aiden smiled in agreement. He just wondered if both his lungs and his klutzy nature were up to this, and hunching in on himself, he crouched down, drinking water and losing himself in imagining the journey back up to the snow-line ranger cabin. Mitchell was going to regret being partnered with him when Aiden fell over and broke an ankle or possibly got eaten by a bear. Aiden had imagined both scenarios and they had been figuring even more strongly in his head the deeper into the trees they travelled.

"Two and a half more miles before dinner," Mitchell offered, carefully looking at the compass and checking against the map. "We have a cabin again tonight with provisions and beds." The last he said with a smirk, offering a hand to Aiden to help him stand. Aiden hesitated to take the hand for a moment, as if gauging whether Mitchell may offer the hand and then drop Aiden at the last moment or something equally dire. As it was, something very different happened, and it was probably that singular moment in Aiden's life when everything changed.

Aiden stumbled as he stood—of course he did—and

Mitchell grabbed at the younger man's arm to steady him, a chuckle on his lips as he helped him stand free and clear.

"Sorry," Aiden offered by instinct and backed away into the tree behind him, putting space between them, looking warily at the unreadable expression in Mitchell's hazel-gold depths.

"It's okay," Mitchell replied softly, his hands not moving from Aiden nor from the support he was unconsciously giving Aiden by holding his arm. They stood for an indefinable moment until Mitchell dropped his hands and backed away, starting the walk away from the point they had stopped while muttering about maps and directions and bears. Aiden hesitated for a long minute, watching as Mitchell forged ahead missing tree roots and stones with a confident stride Aiden wished he had half of —alongside Mitchell's composure.

Sighing, he started to follow. He couldn't help but continue replaying that moment back against that tree with Mitchell only inches from him, his hands anchoring Aiden, holding Aiden, with something in those fascinating eyes that made Aiden's heart ache.

Want? Lust? It definitely wasn't sympathy or pity.

That was new.

Chapter Five

After a billion years of geological activity, from the fury of volcanoes and clashing tectonic plates to the ice that carved valleys, the Canadian landscape had twisted, turned, and morphed into various forms. From jagged mountain peaks to sea cliffs and sand dunes, and from marshes filled with rich green sedge to the start of the ice of Alaska, Aiden knew the geology of the area like the back of his hand. He could touch the stones, the grass, and the trees and almost feel a connection to the history. It wasn't just animals that Aiden had learned inside and out.

In his classes for conservation biology he had excelled in ecosystems planning and the conservation area design, knew the science, with a clear certainty, of the requirements for the protection of species and ecosystems. He outclassed the lecturer and even went as far as submitting academic papers for publishing, all under his pseudonym, Aiden Samuels, and all with great success. He studied advanced geology and conservation, pushed past anything that conventional degree-level education could teach him, eager to learn, eager to know.

He had studied the plans to protect the key areas in British Columbia and plans to keep people away from the old growth watersheds along its West Coast, a land of fjords and mountains and islands. When Edward had mentioned the opportunity for a full-immersion experience in the study of the area he had jumped at it, much to Edward's amusement. Apparently someone named Fowler was going to partner with him, the Park's lion and tiger expert, and Aiden remembered being wary when he saw the papers Edward had pushed his way. Scot had looked kind of big and rough and ready, just the kind of person that turned barely-coherent-Aiden into completely-spazzy-Aiden in the space of minutes.

Still, what twisted him up inside the most was that the replacement, Mitchell—tall, broad, gorgeous, in-his-thirties Mitchell—was having the same effect but for very different reasons. As Aiden dragged his fingers over the trunk of the nearest tree, he focused on the fact that he felt like a five-year-old whenever Mitchell even looked at him, let alone talked to him. So far he had managed to avoid major conversation, but he sighed inwardly as he heard Mitchell clear his throat and knew without a doubt that Mitchell was going to start talking to him. His heart started pounding in his chest. *Jeez, what now?*

"You touch everything," Mitchell observed from behind him. "It's very tactile the way you trace fingers over lines in the rocks or touch the bark of the trees." Aiden looked back, startled, immediately dropping his hand from the tree he had been examining.

"Sorry," Aiden immediately replied. It was his standard answer.

"No. I'm sorry." Mitchell took the two steps to reach Aiden and placed his own hand on the bark, tilting his head in consideration. "Don't stop. I didn't mean it to sound like a criticism. I want to touch history all the time; I kind of get why you do it." Aiden half smiled, shifting from one foot to the other and replacing his hand on the bark of the old tree.

"This area lost a lot of trees to logging," Aiden explained softly, curling his fingers against the rough texture underneath them. "And these old trees, they're rare. I mean, there are hundreds of them, but in the grand scheme of things, they are rare."

"So when you touch what do you see?"

Aiden shrugged. He focused on what he knew. "More than ten feet of rain falls on this part of the coast each year, y'know," he started.

Mitchell nodded. "Hence the waterproofs and the tent."

"Yeah. Well this forest has an almost primeval feel to it. The bark is damp and deeply cut, and I guess—" He paused, dropping his gaze and swallowing. "—I imagine in my head the bears that have passed here, the First Nations people who have lived here, the things these trees have seen."

"Is it the same with the rocks you touch? I see you touch the rocks too."

Aiden caught his lower lip between his teeth, still with his eyes downcast, and mumbled something that he knew Mitchell wouldn't quite hear.

"Say again?" Mitchell prompted, reaching out a finger

to gently lift Aiden's chin, the stubble of two-day-old beard catching on the tip. Aiden looked everywhere but directly at Mitchell, discomfort was surely obvious in the way he stood and the fact he wasn't talking. "Aiden?"

"The rocks?" Aiden swallowed what he wanted to say, the sudden passion inside him banking as he tried to explain what he felt in words that wouldn't freak Mitchell out. "Well I guess if you think about it, they are older than the trees, ancient, billions of years old, carved by ice, and well, they fascinate me."

"Do you know anything about geology?" Mitchell asked curiously. "I mean beyond the obvious stuff related to our degrees."

Aiden swallowed his immediate reply that he knew a whole lot about geology. *Way to come off as a nerd.* "I just imagine the valley choked with a bulldozer of ice, grinding the walls into sheer cliffs, creating ledges, thousands of feet high, with all the waterfalls." Aiden backed away from Mitchell, stumbling over a loose root and grabbing at the tree to steady himself.

"You okay there?" Mitchell asked. "I'm sorry if I made you uncomfortable. My brain is sometimes way behind my mouth."

"You didn't, I just am really a huge dork about these things."

"Thing is," Mitchell began, "this touching thing, man…"

Aiden looked back over his shoulder, waiting for Mitchell to tease him. "Yeah?" he asked nervously. He stopped walking and waited to see what Mitchell was going to say.

"Well, when we get to the estuary," Mitchell started in his most serious voice, "will you be touching the bears?"

Silence. All Aiden could do was stare. Then suddenly, he processed the whole thing and realized that Mitchell was indeed teasing, but in a nice way. He grinned broadly. "Wait and see," he replied, his voice low and husky with laughter. He turned to follow the compass down the barely there ancient pathways, leaving a chuckling Mitchell to walk two steps behind him.

An hour of stumbling over roots later and they reached the first camera station. The cameras were dotted all around the paths down the mountain and Mitchell was grateful when Aiden volunteered to play monkey and climb to them. The wooden structure was built high in the trees, and they had already been scrambling through the dense vegetation of the forested areas for a good five hours. Mitchell was fully aware that species protection depended on the conservation areas being the right size, the right shape, and in the right place. The bigger and more *middle* less *edge,* the better. Having the habitat encompass the whole lifecycle of a species was better, but just now, when his shoulders ached from the pack and his feet hurt in his boots, he wondered why this particular sanctuary had to be so freaking big and so freaking middle and so freaking *natural*.

His stomach was protesting a lack of food even as Aiden climbed the last few roughhewn wooden steps to check the first of the remote cameras on their list, at what was cited as station forty-six.

Aiden did his checks, listing them over and over out loud so he didn't miss anything, and then jumped the last few steps to the mossy ground, righting himself against the tree itself as he slipped on the damp earth, and then sighed. "'M so hungry," he said quietly into the closing evening.

"Zero point three miles to the cabin," Mitchell offered helpfully and marked off the camera position on the map, his only role in the whole climbing-trees business, and very happy he was with that role too. In his opinion only monkeys—and seemingly Aiden—climbed trees, and he was more than pleased just to be watching Aiden, with his tight ass, scramble up and over thick branches and dense foliage. That freaking ass, wriggling in Mitchell's face as Mitchell gave Aiden a leg up to the first branch, reminded Mitchell that he should keep away from thoughts of any Brokeback-Mountain-type scenarios. Scenarios that may or may not, at this moment, be prominent in his mind. Aiden struck him as fragile, almost sad, and Mitchell imagined there was a big no in the column next to 'easy fuck 'em and leave 'em sex' on Aiden's to-do list. He was lost in his thoughts, really trying very hard to ignore his rampant imagination, until the guy stood there, right in front of him, dimples and all.

Aiden rubbed his stomach. "I can feel myself fading away," he joked, looking up under hooded eyes, seemingly for Mitchell's reaction. Mitchell couldn't help himself and he smiled at the humor, watching as Aiden visibly relaxed. Aiden was a good guy, not one to bitch and moan.

"I can't believe I am feeling freaking excited about beans or stew," Mitchell grumped, lamenting the supplies he guessed they would find at the first stop.

"And coffee?" Aiden suggested, to which Mitchell visibly brightened.

"Jeez, coffee."

They made it to their overnight stop a while before it was time to sleep, and if Mitchell had thought last night's accommodation had been primitive, then this was surely much worse. The cabin, for want of a better label, was fairly ramshackle and had almost been absorbed into the forest, roots and leaves twisting and climbing on seemingly ancient wooden walls. It looked rain-tight and sturdy enough to keep them safe from curious wildlife, or at least it did at first glance, but Mitchell imagined that it was going to be damned cold in the dead of night. There was a stove, some limited canned supplies, and three barrels of collected rainwater that stood outside the cabin. Mitchell felt grungy and tired, and used to showering each day, he ran a hand over stubble and had a momentary pang for a hot shower and a razor.

"We can wash," Aiden said enthusiastically, bringing in a container of rainwater and dumping it into a pan on the stove to boil. Mitchell looked dubiously at the heating water, wondering if that was really Aiden's idea of a bath.

"Or not," Mitchell offered dryly, concluding that Aiden did in fact mean to use the small pan of water as some sort of wash-down container.

"Not that," Aiden said, laughter in his voice. "The water tank on the right is marked as wash water."

Mitchell looked momentarily horrified. "But it's cold and it's outside." He wasn't actually sure which was worse.

"Your loss," Aiden smirked, shrugging off his overshirt and leaving his arms bare in a thin T-shirt before leaving the small cabin and pulling the door shut behind him. By the time he returned, Mitchell had coffee and was wondering whether he should go and check to see if a wandering bear had eaten his colleague. He looked up as Aiden entered, the teasing words on the tip of his tongue swallowed immediately in an inhalation of *oh my god.*

Aiden's hair was pushed back from his face, damp and close to his head. His face was flushed with the cold air, his eyes wide and awake, and he looked freaking gorgeous, relaxed, free, edible, and available. Mitchell stood abruptly, cursing himself as he startled the relaxation from Aiden's eyes. Mitchell pushed past Aiden to move out the door, pulling it shut behind him, breathing the cooling air deeply, and willing down the attraction that curled in his belly. Jeez, what he wanted to do to the quiet man inside the cabin would probably scare the living shit out of him.

Outside, Mitchell hovered for a good few minutes, his hands just above the icy water, willing the courage to plunge them deep into the black depths. He had slipped off his shirt and T-shirt, his skin bare to the evening air, pulling his jeans low on his thighs and dropping his boxers. If he was going to do this then he was going to be *damn* clean. The ice took his breath as his fingers broke the surface, and he had the quickest clean in the history of quick cleans, shivering and cursing at the cold. Every muscle in his body was shaking as he shook his short hair free of droplets and toweled himself down with his T-shirt. It was only minutes before he realized his skin stung with heat as he moved the material across himself, invigorated and clean, and he finished the wash with a smile on his face. He had even managed to clear his head of his instant Aiden fantasies, which was no mean feat in itself, and feeling more awake than before, he clambered back into the cabin, a stupid grin on his face and words he shouldn't be speaking on his lips. Aiden looked up, startled, as Mitchell stumbled into the cabin, closing the door and slumping on his own bed, grabbing at the coffee Aiden had left on the table next to him.

"Awesome," Mitchell spluttered, looking over at a bemused but smiling Aiden. Smiling. Aiden. Dimples. Aiden. Blue eyes. Aiden. "Can I ask you a question?" he added, and Aiden shrugged.

"Sure."

"Do you have a partner? A boyfriend? Someone at home?"

Aiden blinked, evidently he wasn't really expecting a question like that. "Erm no, I don't."

Mitchell relaxed back onto the bed, sipping at hot, fragrant coffee and nodding to himself. "Me neither, that's good," he pointed out quietly. For several minutes he just stared at Aiden, dropping his gaze every time Aiden looked up at him. There was confusion on the other man's face and Mitchell thought long and hard before he finally decided to hell with it all.

Mitchell moved quicker than he thought possible, and

in seconds he was sitting on the side of Aiden's bed, his hands twisted in his lap.

"Is it okay if I kiss you?" Mitchell asked softly, leaning closer until mere inches were between their lips.

Chapter Six

*A*iden was struck dumb, couldn't form words if he had tried as Mitchell leaned impossibly close, a spark of something in his eyes that scared Aiden. He moved closer and closer until only breath separated them, then Mitchell paused, waiting for affirmation, waiting for the okay. It never came, not in words anyhow. Aiden reached up to meet the kiss and they simply brushed a warm touch, mouths closed and eyes open. Aiden slanted his head, getting a better position, and opened his mouth on a breath. He tasted Mitchell's lower lip, his tongue insistently asking for entrance, until on a low groan Mitchell returned the touch.

It was a match to fuel, ignition instant and all-consuming as Mitchell curled his hands into Aiden's still-damp hair, pulling him closer and closer, Aiden's hands on his shoulders sliding down to grip in soft cotton and settling in to kiss. Long minutes passed, how long Aiden couldn't tell, until only a desperate need to breathe forced them apart. They paused momentarily, staring at each other, then Mitchell crawled up to curl around Aiden, pulling him in for more drugging kisses. Aiden had never been kissed like this. It stunned him and shook him.

He was also very confused even as he kissed, even as Mitchell was hard against him, he couldn't see how Mitchell was this aroused, how Mitchell could want him this much. It built and built inside him until finally he had to push Mitchell away.

"Wha—?" Mitchell said, looking confused, his eyes half closed, his lips bruised and swollen and his breathing hard.

"What are you doing?" Aiden asked as Mitchell pressed forward, trying to capture Aiden's lips again, but Aiden pulled back. "No." He leaned back, way back, his hands still curled into Mitchell's shirt, and Mitchell opened his eyes fully. "What are you doing?" Aiden asked again.

"What am I doing? What are we doing, you mean."

Pushing down the need to just let Mitchell carry on, Aiden knew he needed answers. He wanted to get on with the humping and the kissing, but he wasn't sure he wanted Mitchell just because of proximity. He couldn't afford to expose himself—or Anthony Novak—to an inappropriate, but probably wholly satisfying, hot, sweaty sex session. Mitchell leaned back also and gently curled Aiden's hair around his fingers. Aiden could see the confusion in Mitchell's eyes. There was disbelief there and Aiden forced himself to continue meeting Mitchell's gaze.

"Why do you want to kiss me?" he asked.

"Why wouldn't I? You, me, a cabin, alone." Mitchell waggled his eyebrows suggestively. His teasing stopped when Aiden couldn't summon a smile to give him back.

"I've not really done a lot of…" Aiden gestured with a hand and hoped Mitchell understood what he was trying to say.

"You really don't see why I want to kiss you?"

Aiden couldn't imagine where to start with that loaded question, capturing his lower lip between his teeth and worrying at the kiss-bruised flesh. No, he really couldn't see why Mitchell of all people would want to kiss him, not after what happened at college. He hesitated to answer, knowing that whatever he said, however he tried to explain it, he would just come across as the idiot he always did. Why would Mitchell want to kiss *him*? What was special about him. Apart from his dad and his money? Still, Mitchell didn't know about any of that, not the fact that he was the son of Dominic Novak or that the Novak estate was worth a shed-load of dollars. So if Mitchell didn't know these things and he still wanted to kiss Aiden, then he must see something that Aiden, nor any of his friends or partners, ever had. But just what that was Aiden didn't know.

So he said the only thing he could in answer to Mitchell's probably rhetorical question. "No, I can't see why." He cringed at his own words, someday he hoped his honesty was going to work for him, but he didn't expect that day to be today, not here in this cabin with the promise of more kisses on the plate. He saw the full-body sigh that trickled through Mitchell, the careful half closing of eyelids, and the cautious tightening of the grip in Aiden's hair. He knew what was going to happen now, the same things that normally happened. Any man who showed an interest in him just wasn't ready for baggage; none of them wanted to carry out actual meaningful conversation with him. He knew he carried enough shit for seven men: childhood issues, sex-connected issues, the experience in college. Ben.

And there it was. Ben. Ben Warner and his gray eyes and his dark hair and his I-want-to-be-your-friend hugs. God did Aiden fall for that one, the only person outside of his family whom he trusted with his secrets and the one who let him down so spectacularly.

"Okay," Mitchell finally said, leaning in for one last kiss, a lingering touch just of lips and breath, his eyes open and questions in the hazel. Then he pulled back, untwisting his fingers from Aiden's hair, and sat cross-legged at one end of the small cot. Aiden scooted to mirror the position against the head of the mattress, defensively crossing his arms across his chest. They sat quietly for a long while, Mitchell tapping his fingers on his knee to some internal rhythm, his head tilted to one side in thought. Aiden began to squirm under the scrutiny.

"You are just the right height," Mitchell finally said with a nod.

"Too short," Aiden countered quickly.

"I like my men a couple inches shorter than me," Mitchell argued. "Makes kissing nice and easy. And you're built just right for my hands."

Aiden dropped his gaze, suddenly more embarrassed than he had ever been.

Mitchell considered more. "Your hair is so soft," he pointed out. "It's the most gorgeous color, all browns and reds."

"It's too short," Aiden said with a hand curling into his

bangs and brushing them back. "If I don't cut it short though it just curls, but longer means it kinda hangs there." Aiden moved his hands from his hair back to his lap and was suddenly conscious of the layers that were drying in disarray after the wash.

"Short is sexy, but jeez, the thought of you with long hair—to be able to wrap that hair round my hand—" Mitchell paused. "—to hold on to your hair, while I'm kissing you... Your eyes are beautiful."

"Blue," Aiden dismissed out of hand, "sometimes gray, never deciding which color they want to be."

"Startling blue with flecks of silver—so intelligent and clear, you carry every one of your emotions in your eyes."

"Hmmm," Aiden said softly, no one had ever looked that closely at his face before. Did he really have eyes as beautiful as the ones Mitchell described?

Mitchell jumped straight back in. "So let me tick this off: eyes to your soul, height and a slim build that just freaking turns me on, hair that is so soft, kisses that shoot straight to my cock, and to top it all, you know all the shit there is to know about the bears. What more could I want?"

Someone whole. Aiden didn't answer out loud, instead he started to roll off the bed. He intended to move and pour more coffee, to kill time, to delay answering, but Mitchell pulled at his sleeve, encouraging him to stay sitting down.

"I don't know who hurt you, what made you so nervous here." Mitchell paused, curling his fingers into the soft cotton of Aiden's sleeve. "But we have three weeks to come to an understanding whereby you see yourself as hot and I help you to see it." He released his grasp and half crawled onto his own cot, and with a quiet, "Night, Aiden," he curled into his thermal bag and relaxed into sleep.

Aiden watched Mitchell give in to sleep, feeling the same fatigue he knew Mitchell suffered from. He lay down, the half dark enough to mean he could focus on the black when he shut his eyes. He was still half-hard from the kissing—*from the freaking kissing*—that was a first.

He pulled his sleeping bag around him and concentrated on trying to sleep. He wished away the confusion in his head, but dreams came to him quicker than he wanted, hard and fast and too clear not to remember. It was same dream as always. His dad, the blood, the death, and then his dad again, dying, it was almost as if he could guide himself through these dreams without trying.

And then there it was—college. It had been a long time since he had consciously or unconsciously thought of his time in college and Ben but the thought had crystalized today from nowhere. It hadn't been long, just six weeks of college, of being Anthony Novak. He'd left his private school and was utterly determined to be a normal guy at college. The help he'd been getting with his social difficulties, with coming to terms with who he was, with losing his dad, had all worked to make him halfway confident. In hindsight, he realized he had been a young man still in one or more stages of grief, still struggling to come to terms with what had happened to his dad. Ben had been a friend, and in the space of a week they were boyfriends, a first for Anthony, his first boyfriend, his first 'I'm gay' statement to the world, and it was good. Well most of it was good. The hugging, the talking, the kissing, that was good, but the sex, that was difficult. Ben was experienced and Anthony couldn't go as fast as Ben. Ben wanted it rough and hard, and he didn't always stop to see what Anthony wanted. But it was okay, Anthony was okay with that; it was the way the sex had to be. Ben told Anthony he understood why Anthony sometimes didn't enjoy the sex and was mostly supportive about it.

The only dark cloud that Anthony could see was that *they* knew, the journalists, the ones that seemed inordinately interested in him. They knew Anthony was gay, it was never hidden, and jeez did that give them *more* grist for the mill. Ben was fine with that, protected Anthony from the cameras and the questions, and placed himself between them and Anthony at every opportunity.

Unfortunately, Ben was also getting his rocks off with a distinctly female student a block over in his spare time, something the paparazzi made a quick connection to, cornering a bemused Anthony in a coffee shop and thrusting photos under his nose. *Was Anthony aware that Ben was fucking around behind his back?* Anthony denied what he saw, denied that *his* Ben was doing that to him. But finding Ben, following Ben to ask him, what Anthony heard from Ben and the tiny blonde on Ben's lap was the end of it all.

Ben trying damage control with his girlfriend? He heard the excuses and the reasons why she should ignore what was in the photos left on her desk. He heard Ben admitting to her he was only with Anthony because, well, his dad was famous, had been famous, so he must have money, and student loans weren't enough to see him through four years. So Anthony listened, as Ben, his lover, his friend, the one person he spoke to, revealed what kind of person he *really* was. That was when Anthony's heart broke into its final small pieces, and Aiden Samuels became real. Aiden Samuels with his late start at Cambridge University in England, with his new identity, his new backstory, with no money, a new beginning. The betrayal was heavy in his heart, enough to isolate this new Aiden, enough to have Aiden burying himself in studies, becoming the best at what he wanted to be.

His father.

When Aiden woke from his nightmare, he was damp with sweat and shivering with the cold, his sleeping bag pushed down off his chest and his hands shaking. He focused on his breathing, trying to will away the panic attack that was building. He pushed at the material that restricted his breathing, but his fingers were at his neck and his brain was telling him *no oxygen no oxygen*.

Chapter Seven

*M*itchell woke with a start, noises in the room alarming him and sending him upright instantly while looking into the semi-darkness for the source of the noise. Had bears somehow got in? Wolves? What the hell?

Aiden.

In seconds Mitchell was next to the shaking man, listening as Aiden gasped for air, hand hovering uselessly as he wondered what to do. Okay. Panic attack, fright. Aiden wasn't asleep, he was staring helplessly up at Mitchell, this wasn't a dream Aiden was in the middle of. With a soft touch Mitchell smoothed warm hands on clammy skin and began to talk nonsense, gently and calmly. "Shhh, it's okay... I'm here... it's okay... breathe... 1 2 3... it's fine."

Over and over he used the gentle tones, his touch becoming more insistent as Aiden's breathing settled, and he watched as Aiden's hands dropped from his throat and fell curled into his lap. Mitchell didn't want to know why this had happened, scared it had been his own fault, that maybe his insistence on getting physical with Aiden and teasing him had created this midnight terror. Finally Aiden was quiet, his breath hitching, his head bowed, and the hands in his lap now twisting together so hard his knuckles were white. He didn't look up, didn't talk, just lay back down and curled into a ball, seeming so small for a grown man, and Mitchell tucked the sleeping bag around him, ensuring that there was no gaps to let in the frigid air. He returned to his own bed, a million questions in his head and finding it hard to sleep again.

Morning happened far too quickly from Mitchell's point of view. A quick glance at his watch showed it was only six a.m., and with a groan of protest, he rolled to face Aiden's bed, thinking maybe it was Aiden that had woken him. Aiden sat on the side of his bed, his face pink from what Mitchell assumed was another wash in the cold water, and his expression a combination of sad and bemused.

Aiden half smiled. "Hey," he said softly. He twisted his fingers together as he spoke. "Sorry," he added.

Mitchell blinked the morning into his sleep-deprived head and forced himself upright, sitting cross-legged with his toasty warm sleeping bag around his shoulders. "No worries," he started. "You okay?"

Aiden sighed. "Thanks. For last night. For the panic attack, I mean."

Mitchell dipped his head and shrugged. "It was nothing."

"They happen," Aiden started, then stopped. Mitchell

didn't interrupt or encourage, simply observed as Aiden stood abruptly. The water was hot and Aiden concentrated on making and handing Mitchell a metal mug with the coffee that would kick-start his day.

Mitchell whispered his thanks and gratefully inhaled the rich smell of the instant coffee. "Go on," he prompted gently.

"They're... uhmm... well they... the damn panic attacks... are labeled as a manifestation of depression," Aiden began, dipping his head, again unable to meet Mitchell's concerned gaze. "I lost my dad when I was young, kind of had a rough time coming out as gay, and then had a pretty shit start to college, all that and my own self-esteem issues and I am one ball of neuroses."

"I'm sorry," Mitchell said. He thought about his mom and dad, alive and well in Ohio, and his sister and brother who lived with the sole purpose of annoying the middle brother. Losing a family member and coming to terms with his sexuality all at the same time? That couldn't be good. "Tell me about college." That seemed like a safe topic.

Aiden started at the direction Mitchell had chosen. "Ben was college."

"Your first guy?" Mitchell asked.

"Yeah, really, there wasn't a lot of opportunity before —private school and no real chance of healthy experimentation before college." Mitchell didn't say anything but he thought the words Aiden was using sounded like the kind of things a psychiatrist would say. Aiden continued. "He was my first *anything*. Only it wasn't an exclusive relationship as I found out; he was sleeping with Alice Esterson from PoliSci at the same time."

"Shit."

"Exactly. I switched schools, used some of my dad's contacts, went overseas to study. Well away from everything and everyone." Mitchell listened as Aiden spoke, an unreasonable urge to kill this Ben rising inside him. "So, I guess I buried myself in academia, and now I know an awful lot of details about a whole lot of things. I'm twenty-four and I still haven't had what I would call useful relationship experience of any kind. So you see, last night, what I was trying to say…"

"Go on."

Aiden tucked his hair behind his ear and then placed a hand flat on his own chest. "This is me, hopelessly inept and prone to panic attacks. Not such a good prospect, eh?" Aiden smiled. He didn't appear to pity himself, and there was nothing in his voice other than a simple and sad resignation. "I'm also not so good with people. So I guess this is my first real experiment at being a real grownup." He huffed a laugh but Mitchell didn't see much amusement on Aiden's features.

"So why this placement? Why the bears?" Mitchell was curious; a man buried in academia didn't do field trips into the wild as far as Mitchell was concerned. They taught in dusty universities and had letters after their names.

"Instinct. I want to touch and to learn."

"Like you do with the trees," Mitchell said, injecting a smile in his voice. Aiden nodded, and Mitchell stood, sliding socked feet into his boots and shivering as he pulled on layers of flannel. It was still way too early to be up.

Aiden pulled his lower lip between his teeth, a sudden look of nervousness on his face, and Mitchell waited. Evidently Aiden had something else to say.

"I guess I have something to ask you—and I can totally understand if you say no."

"Okay?"

"You said last night... I mean, the whole kissing thing... I could get behind that... if you felt you could put up with the shit... kissing and maybe other stuff... just fooling around. Not taking away from the job we need to do, but at night. It wouldn't have to continue after we get back, but just to—I've been awake the last two hours trying to find a way to ask this."

This beautiful, sexy, complicated man was asking Mitchell to show him what sex could be like and coming up empty every which way he tried to express the need? Mitchell was kind of bemused, kind of turned on, and kind of happy. He crossed to Aiden's bed and leaned down to capture soft lips in a gentle kiss. He pushed back thoughts of how awkward this could be when the three weeks was up and only had two words to whisper against cold-water skin.

"God yes."

⸻

Despite Aiden cringing inwardly about baring his soul to Mitchell, nothing changed between them as they got ready for the day and the journey they needed to make farther down the mountain. The second day turned out to be much like the first, pushing through tangled undergrowth and chasing down camera locations forty-seven and fifty-one. There was more climbing of trees, only this time Mitchell didn't hold back, giving Aiden the required push up with hands firmly on his tight ass, offering appreciative noises that sounded to Aiden like lewd suggestions that he was totally getting behind.

When Aiden had jumped down at camera fifty-one, falling to a crouch, Mitchell held out a hand and pulled him to stand, pushing him gently back against the aged bark of the gnarled tree and stealing heated kisses.

They talked, Aiden telling Mitchell as much as he could about Ben that didn't involve revealing his actual identity or the whole paparazzi thing. He still wasn't ready to reveal who he was and he didn't question why. He liked being safe in the anonymity of Aiden Samuels. Mitchell was interested in Aiden without knowing about the money or the fact Aiden was actually his boss out there in the real world beyond the Great Bear Rainforest. And that was it. The real world was hundreds of miles away in another country, so far away that Aiden was forgetting.

Mitchell listened and talked about his college experience, how he had met and shared a room in the dorms and then a house with Scot, the same Scot who was scheduled to be here with Aiden but had to attend his sister's wedding. The same Scot who got Mitchell drunk, got Mitchell high, got Mitchell into bar fights, in fact seemed to get Mitchell in trouble at every turn. The same Scot who made Mitchell's college years a time of enjoyable experiences and memories. Aiden was envious that Mitchell had a friend that went that far back, a friend that accepted him for who he was and who he worked with. The official side of him, well that side was a little concerned that this firebrand that was Scot Fowler was working with *Aiden's* animals, but still, Mitchell said Scot loved his work and that he had settled down a lot since college.

They had their first evidence of the bears as they neared the stop for the next evening, evidence of last fall's denning in a thick pile of brush forced up into the hollow of a tree. Aiden noted it down and managed to get the coordinates from the mapping and the GIS system. For a few minutes they explored the surrounding area and added to the notes, and Aiden was surprised when Mitchell moved up behind him and pulled him around for a kiss. When they parted Mitchell was grinning ear to ear. The smile was infectious and had a promise of more kisses.

They made it to the next cabin shelter around four. This was an even smaller affair than the one the night before and had two small cots pushed close. At least they were longer beds, so they wouldn't have to assume a pretzel position. They broke out dry rations and water, and then by silent agreement they climbed into bed. Aiden concentrated on the insistent rain that had started earlier. They didn't get inside sleeping bags, simply laid out blanket rolls and then slid under the unzipped bags together, only inches apart. It was dark inside, neither wasting batteries on light, and they lay side by side, just talking softly.

"Tell me what it was like with Ben?" Mitchell asked. It was a question Aiden wouldn't normally answer, couldn't normally answer but for the dark that surrounded them giving him a feeling of security.

"It was okay," he began. "Normal I guess, kind of rough, but y'know, it's two men, it's gonna be harder. I wanted to like it, but I didn't really enjoy it as much as he did."

"Did you tell him?" Mitchell asked curiously.

"Tell him what? Oh, you mean did I tell him I wasn't enjoying what we were doing? Yes, on several occasions. But I didn't know any different, I still don't know any different. All I know is that I felt out of control and not really wanted. I was forced, pushed into things, and I felt trapped. Like there was no control for me to have."

"I'm listening to you and you use words like forced, pushed, trapped, control. That's not right." With a tug he pulled Aiden onto his bed and maneuvered him so he lay half over Mitchell. "Let me show you." He shifted slightly until the only comfortable position Aiden could find was with his leg lying across Mitchell's thigh. Mitchell was hard against him. They were in boxers and T-shirts and Aiden could feel every inch of Mitchell.

"Take my hands," Mitchell said softly and Aiden did as he was asked, his face inches from Mitchell's, his eyes widening as Mitchell pulled his own hands, with Aiden's fingers interlaced, above their heads to lay flat on the cot, exposing Mitchell's neck. The move put Aiden off balance slightly and he shuffled a little to get settled properly again. The new position put Aiden firmly in control, and in seconds Aiden was harder that he had ever been, pushing insistently against Mitchell and waiting for what he was supposed to do next. In the dim light provided by the moon outside, his gaze wandered down the stubble-rough skin and to the graceful stretched neck laid out under him.

"Aiden?" Mitchell prompted, pressing up into the man above him. Aiden groaned and dropped his head into the hollow next to Mitchell's neck.

"I want to…" Aiden whimpered into Mitchell's skin.

"It's good. You can let yourself go," Mitchell said. Aiden finally snapped, dragging lips and teeth over neck and pulse and ending up kissing Mitchell deeply. The kiss was explosive, clashing, needy, hard. Aiden unconsciously tightened his grip on Mitchell's hands, pressing him harder, a rhythm as old as time between them, but Mitchell didn't stop him. The cabin filled with the sounds they made, sounds of need and want, expletives cut off by deep kisses and promises as they rutted like teenagers.

"Aiden. Please."

Aiden kissed away the words, tasting Mitchell, cutting off his breathy moans with sounds of his own, gasping his release, followed shortly after by Mitchell, and collapsing sweaty and tired against Mitchell.

"I've never—never felt—" Aiden stuttered and then said nothing else. He released Mitchell's hands and fell against his own bed, wet and breathless, questions on his lips. He didn't ever remember a time when just rutting and kissing could make him come so freaking hard. *Oh my god, rutting.* With a small mewl of embarrassment he covered his eyes with his arm, waiting for the inevitable fall out. Jeez, he couldn't even get kissing right.

He felt Mitchell pull at his arm, but a childish need to hide kept him from making it easy.

"Aiden? Aiden—don't freak out on me here. Aiden?

Aiden…" Slowly Mitchell's voice filtered through Aiden's shame and he peeked from under his arm at Mitchell's face. Seeing Mitchell's smiling face, Aiden slid his arm up again over his eyes, a groan in his throat.

"Sorry," he mumbled almost under his breath, feeling and hearing Mitchell move and imagining the slide of come on his fingers as he wiped it away. Should he clean himself up? Should he wait for Mitchell to sleep before he moved? Would he be forced to sleep all night in damp boxers after wiping himself off?

Aiden moved his arm, watching as Mitchell concentrated on removing the damp underclothes, used a T-shirt to wipe him off, and then settled the sleeping bag over Aiden's legs, pushing his own legs under as well. In a flurry of sudden movement and with an undignified squeak, Aiden was laying half over Mitchell again touching skin to skin. He opened his eyes, having shut them in the general being-manhandled thing, to look down at a softly smiling Mitchell.

Mitchell reached up a hand to twist in Aiden's hair, guiding lips to lips. They exchanged soft kisses, Aiden at first very slow to react and every so often leaning up to check that Mitchell was okay with this. He was getting hard against Mitchell again and he could feel Mitchell hard against him as well. It was as if he was a teenager again, every ten minutes he could get a hard-on just by freaking looking at a guy. Mitchell ground his hips up at the same time he kissed a red mark into Aiden's neck. It was sensory overload. Aiden wasn't holding Mitchell's hands this time. Aiden was free to feel, to run his fingers across warm skin, stare into the autumn colors of Mitchell's eyes, watching each hitch in his breath as Mitchell bared his neck and lost himself to sensation.

Aiden was doing this, was causing Mitchell to writhe under him, and a strange feeling of sudden strength began to coil under his skin, bubbling and hissing and demanding to be let out. Emboldened by the noises Mitchell was making, Aiden took it a stage on from kissing, circling Mitchell's cock with his broad-palmed hand, twisting from base to tip and back again. He stopped the motion, looking uncertain, pausing, hesitating. Mitchell started to move under him, started to push his cock through the circle of Aiden's hands. This wasn't hard to do; Aiden knew how to handle his own cock, someone else's should be the same.

"There. Harder." Mitchell's breathing became even more ragged under Aiden's hands as they kissed, more exchanging breaths really than kissing, just needing to touch.

Mitchell was the first to lose it, hot and wet between them; Aiden's hands slid through the slick, his own hard cock slotted into the space against Mitchell's hipbone.

"He said…" Aiden started to speak and groaned, his head full of so many conflicted feelings, everything Ben had said pushing its way to daylight, every hurtful word, every put-down, every tiny point Ben made. "He said I was bad at this—said I was useless." The last word was a groan even as orgasm began to curl and twist in his spine, his vision blurring as emotion choked him. "He said I was useless," he repeated, arching his back, the rhythm against Mitchell's hip enough for Aiden to come hard onto Mitchell's skin.

He leaned his head down against Mitchell's sweat-damp neck, feeling his lover's heart beating, seeing the evidence of life in the flickering pulse at his throat.

"I'm not useless," he finally whispered against the skin he found there, reassured as Mitchell wedged a shirt between them to soak up the mess, pulled the sleeping bags tight around them, and then dug fingers deep into Aiden's hair, massaging and gentling.

"No, Aiden. You're not."

itchell didn't think he'd ever been more relaxed. They collected more data as they moved closer to the marshes at the base of the mountain. The air was warmer, the grass thicker, and the canopy of trees a lighter green, not the verdant lushness of the rainforest they had been passing through. He said so to Aiden. He was saying a lot to Aiden; they were talking all the time.

More spilled out from Aiden about the bastard that was Ben, a man Mitchell was going to kill if they ever crossed paths for his put-downs, his comments, his general crap that he laid on Aiden. If Mitchell thought there was more to the story he didn't say, he wasn't going to push Aiden. This Aiden he was starting to know was a man but he also had a fragility about him, and Mitchell knew better than to rake him over dying coals. He tried to change the subject a few times, but there seemed to be a few things Aiden was reluctant to talk about—like his family, for one. They agreed on football teams, agreed to disagree on basketball teams, and agreed on good Mexican food, made more poignant as they were eating trail mix at the time.

"What made you want to work with animals?" Mitchell prodded after they had exhausted a play-by-play discussion of the Duke/Ohio State Final Four game and the astonishingly bad showing of Mitchell's team, which Aiden crowed about.

Aiden was walking ahead and Mitchell swore he saw Aiden's back stiffen, but that could have just been his imagination.

"Family business," Aiden offered carefully, "my dad." He paused. "He worked with animals."

"Like you are now?"

"Kind of," Aiden finally offered. "What about you? When did you decide you wanted to work with animals?"

"That one is easy," Mitchell began. "It started with Oscar."

"Oscar?"

"Yep, Oscar, my boyfriend in college: tall, dark, gorgeous, love-of-my-life, etcetera, ad nauseam. Bastard fucked me over." Aiden stopped walking at this and cast a look over his shoulder. Mitchell took one step to bring himself level with Aiden, offering him a protein bar and stopping to lean back against the nearest tree. Now was as good a time as any to stop for a break and they passed a water bottle back and forth as Mitchell continued. "So, I am all set for a career in IT, you know, declaring my major, all the usual stuff, then Oscar…" His face twisted in a sneer at the name. "Well, he didn't get the grades in the prerequisites, so Daddy, millionaire Daddy, bought his son a place in the college. The Johnsonn IT wing was a great success. Of course, it came with provisos. For Oscar's dad, Senator Johnsonn,"—Mitchell emphasized the word Senator—"it didn't sit well to have a gay son. So one night Oscar is declaring undying love while buried balls-deep, the next day he is telling me we can carry on, but hey, he needs a girlfriend, 'cause he can't let Daddy down."

"Oh." Mitchell looked at Aiden, who was staring at him wide-eyed. Maybe it would help Aiden to know he wasn't the only guy who had been used and thrown out like garbage.

"I won't hide who I am, Aiden. That is what he wanted me to do. I can't be hiding and lying. If there is one thing in this world we should be, it's honest, otherwise, you know, everything goes to fuck. So anyway, there I am in the main office, and I can't bring myself to declare IT, but it is so late there is only space in Zoology. I slink into the first lecture, deciding which college I should be transferring to, and then it happened." He stopped, waving his free hand in front of him with a smile on his face; he loved telling this story.

"Go on." Aiden smiled back. "I'm sensing this is a cool story."

Mitchell laughed. "So this professor was visiting, giving some speech on, I don't know, conservation was my guess at the time. Similar to here, the setting up of areas of wilderness. He kinda grabbed my attention, and I couldn't just let it go. I was hooked. He had a passion in him, a love for conservation, for the animals he worked with, and that

passion just spilled out from him like I don't know what."
Mitchell screwed the cap back on the water bottle, pushing
it back in his backpack and sliding down the trunk to sit a
while. "So, to finish the story… you gotta promise not to
laugh though, man."

Aiden raised an eyebrow. "This is going to be a funny
story?" he joked and then he held up his hands and added,
"I promise."

"This guy who stood there, well, people were
muttering like his opinion wasn't valid. There were
whispers that he was some pretend wildlife guy, that he
hadn't lived the life, or walked the walk." Aiden nodded,
and Mitchell frowned as he remembered back to those first
hours in Zoology. "Well, it was this guy who used to do
this mainstream animal show and his name was Dominic
Novak."

Aiden coughed and spluttered coffee on his jeans, and
Mitchell stopped talking long enough to pat him on the
back.

"You said you wouldn't laugh."

"Went down the wrong way," Aiden finally offered. He
looked a little pale and Mitchell filed that away in case
Aiden was coming down with something.

"Anyway," he continued. "You know what, by the end
of that lecture he had people eating out of his hands. It was
awesome and the rest, as they say, is history. I wrote to
him, you know, we exchanged a few letters, then of course
he died, tragic, that was bad, really bad."

"He died," Aiden repeated.

"Anyway, that is how I ended up at the Park. I wanted
to be part of his education program, so here I am, working

for his ex-partner and the elusive Novak Junior and loving every minute of it."

Aiden nodded, lifting his pack and moving to settle it on his shoulders. "Half a mile to the next camera," he said simply, and Mitchell shouldered his own pack.

"Great, more tree climbing," Mitchell muttered and exchanged wry looks with Aiden, "more freaking tree climbing."

———

They journeyed a little longer and Aiden knew he was being quiet. The shock of hearing his dad's name, of finding out his dad was responsible for Mitchell even being here was almost enough to have him blurting out his real identity. What would Mitchell actually do if Aiden told him? Would he freak out? Hate him? Not want to kiss him anymore? The thought of the last thing happening was enough for Aiden to keep his secrets to himself.

His dad had been an amazing and inspiring man. A teacher and a TV presenter, he'd worked with the Spirit Bears here for a whole year when he was the same age Aiden was now.

Aiden looked down at his feet, at the indentations in moss that they left as he walked. His dad could have walked this way, looked at the same distant waterfalls and mountains. Had he been as overwhelmed as Aiden felt now?

"We'll need to be careful over the next channel of water," Mitchell interrupted Aiden's thoughts. "There's a note here about fallen logs and trees." Aiden stopped walking and Mitchell stood next him. Together they considered the waterfalls that fell from a great height and converged into this river tracing down to the main inlet. There was a bridge of sorts twisted in with fallen branches and a large tree. The water underneath wasn't fast flowing but it looked deep.

"Can you swim?" Mitchell joked.

"I bet that water is freezing," Aiden pointed out. "Melted snow and rain." The bottom of the river was visible, and where it shallowed out there was the unmistakable splashing of the salmon that made their way here every spawning season. The air was fresh and clear, the rush and noise of the water exhilarating, and nature was slap bang in your face. Aiden couldn't be happier. Pushing aside all thoughts of secrets, he hunkered down at the edge of the bridge and pushed one of the supports with his hand. Casting his eye across the entire twelve feet to the other side, he assessed what he was seeing.

"Solid, stuck here," he summarized.

"Agreed," Mitchell added.

"One at a time."

"Short straws?" Mitchell laughed and adjusted the straps of his rucksack so that the bag sat squarely on his back.

"No need. I'll go first," Aiden said with a smile. Neither man was really concerned. Well, Aiden wasn't, and Mitchell's smile indicated he wasn't either.

"Wait. Look. Jeez. Bear." Mitchell grabbed his arm and said the words really low in his throat. Aiden turned in the direction Mitchell was indicating and he had his first look at one of the huge black bears that made the rainforest their home. Lumbering in the water, it was every so often spearing at a salmon, and if the bear hadn't been only thirty feet away and within running distance, Aiden would have joked that the bear didn't look that good at fishing. He hoped the bear caught a salmon soon considering how close they were. He didn't want the bear catching their scent and thinking human may be more tasty than fish. When it caught a fish Aiden breathed a sigh of relief. The bear held it aloft, the sun glinting off the scales of the wriggling salmon, and Aiden wished he had gotten his camera out of the bag and had it ready for a shot.

"Oh my god, look," Mitchell whispered. Aiden peered closer and there, just to the rear of the bear, the leaves were rustling and he could make out two tiny forms. When the leaves parted and two bears tumbled out into the water Aiden couldn't help the gasp of excitement. One of the tiny cubs was the black of its mother, but the other was a Spirit Bear, born to a black bear but with the rare genetic trait that turned its fur creamy white.

The fur stood out in stark relief to the greens of the bushes and the two men watched, mesmerized, at the sight before them. Momma bear ate the fish and regarded her cubs with the patience only a momma could have. They played in the shallows, tumbling and growling and falling all over each other. It had once been believed that black bears were carnivores, but closer studies showed that they were actually omnivores. Their diet included nuts, berries, fruits, acorns, roots, deer, moose, carrion, and the spawning salmon that the momma bear had caught. If salmon were plentiful in the waters of the top of the river, it probably meant a healthy population of bears. It was now Aiden and Mitchell's job to back that assumption up with expert observation.

"Four, maybe five months, just babies. My camera," he said softly. Taking a step in front of Mitchell, he waited for the other man to pull out his camera, and then in rapid succession took a whole series of shots. The bears were either used to the presence of humans or hadn't scented them enough to worry. For a good thirty minutes they stayed in the bright sunlight and then suddenly Momma bear picked up the dead fish and wandered back through the bushes, her noisy, rambunctious babies following with happy jumps over stones.

That wasn't the last of it either. After the bridge and almost to the basecamp, the evidence of denning and the bears that had inhabited the area grew more and more. By the time they finally hit the marshes at the base of the mountain, they had both seen enough to point to maybe six or seven bear trails, all duly logged and notated in the journal.

The basecamp cabin was two stories high and bear-proof. There were also hides made from canvas and wood layered high in various trees, much to Mitchell's disgust.

"I'm not climbing any trees," he groused. "I'm too old for that."

"You're never too old to climb trees," Aiden said back.

"Wait until you get to be thirty-one and tell me that then."

The cabin was set back from the waterline and not dissimilar to the one with the water barrels. The thin ladder from the ground to first level was near flat to the wall, and at first Aiden thought he was going to fall backwards and squash Mitchell. The wood of the cabin was old but solid and names carved into the wood all around indicated the names of the people who had been here before. Aiden wondered if his dad's name would be there. The bottom level contained a small boat and two barrels that Aiden assumed were for water. The upper level had four beds, a stove, and even a small refrigeration unit.

The inside looked undisturbed, and it had a thick heavy wooden door that caught on crumbling clay steps and probably woke up the entire bear population of the area every time it opened. There was fuel and limited provisions, but enough of both to make the first night there much more comfortable than the other nights on the journey down.

Solving the problem of the two men in small cots was easy. Aiden slid two beds together and declared they would sleep diagonally, to which Mitchell replied they wouldn't be sleeping much. Aiden just blushed.

Aiden made coffee and he and Mitchell stood on the small overhanging excuse for a balcony with the whole of the estuary set out before them. Where marine and terrestrial entwined was an utterly beautiful place and it was hard to believe they were only three hundred miles north of the city of Vancouver.

The deep inlets and fjords from the Pacific touched the land here and formed a place of mist and mystery. In the distance they could hear the deep growls of foraging grizzlies.

"We were so lucky to spot a white bear on our first sighting," Aiden said.

"They're so rare," Mitchell added.

Rain cloaked the cabin in a veil and they were in each other's arms and kissing with the backdrop of natural paradise behind them. Aiden wanted skin. Wanted to touch. He guided Mitchell back and through the door and placed their coffee mugs on the table.

"It's late," Mitchell teased.

"It's only seven," Aiden said.

"We need to get to bed. Early night. Big day tomorrow. And look what I found in the medical kit." He held the small plastic jar aloft and Aiden's eyes widened. "We have Vaseline."

"No condoms though," Aiden said disappointedly.

"No. But you can do all kinds of things with the help of a little slick." He sat on the edge of the bed and toed off his boots, lifting them and placing them on the chair with a sweatshirt over them. Pulling and tugging at his jeans, he looked up at Aiden, who couldn't tear his eyes away from Mitchell's body as it was exposed an inch at a time.

"Like what?" Aiden asked. He coughed when his voice sounded scratchy.

Mitchell very deliberately picked up the small jar from where he'd placed it on the pillow and turned it over in his hands with a thoughtful expression.

"Well. I could slick my fingers, open you up, find your sweet spot, and then suck down until you explode."

The words sent blood rushing south and in a rapid movement Aiden began removing his clothes, copying Mitchell's action with his boots and making sure all his clothes were up off the ground. Whatever the impetus to strip, they both knew creepy-crawlies had a way of finding nooks and crannies and an insect in your boot was an unsettling experience.

"Or you could do that to me," Mitchell said thoughtfully.

"I don't know how," Aiden immediately said. "I'll hurt you."

"Trust me. You can't hurt me." Mitchell lay flat on his back with his knees up and bent. "Come here."

Stripped naked and shivering at the sudden cold air on his skin, Aiden climbed on the bed and shuffled closer to Mitchell. For a long while he just looked at Mitchell's hard length, at the base of it in curls of near black, at the weighty balls and the secrets that lay behind. He'd never done this before. How difficult could it be? Put Vaseline on your fingers, press them to the hole, move them a little, and push them in.

"Suck me first," Mitchell said gently.

Aiden felt like a fool. He'd given blow jobs before but mostly with the guys holding his head. He didn't like the feeling of not being able to breathe, but they seemed to get off on it. Mitchell had his hands on the pillow on either side of his head and didn't seem to want to be gripping Aiden. Crouching over Mitchell, he nuzzled against his erection and licked the tip gently. The soft moan that Mitchell made was enough to encourage Aiden to do more.

With fingers curled at the base, Aiden sucked Mitchell down to about halfway and then moved back up. He peered up at Mitchell to gauge his reaction but Mitchell had his eyes closed and was now gripping the wood of the wall behind them with both hands. Emboldened, Aiden swallowed deeper and then set a rhythm of lips on the down stroke meeting with fingers on the up until Mitchell's soft moans turned to pleas. When a hand nudged the Vaseline closer to Aiden he got the message.

"One finger first," Mitchell breathed. His voice was a groan and Aiden watched as his lover's body arched up instinctively. He obviously wanted Aiden's lips on his cock, which was an incredible feeling of power. Aiden coated his finger with gooey slick, and he pressed against Mitchell's hole, rubbing until it pushed in. Mitchell moaned again.

"Did I hurt you?" Aiden said curiously. It must have hurt, it used to burn when Ben…

"No you didn't… more…" Mitchell encouraged. "Your mouth. Please." The last 'please' was more of a whine and Aiden didn't argue. He swallowed Mitchell down and pressed another finger in. Stretching the muscle, he searched for the sweet spot he had read about and that Mitchell had mentioned. He clearly had found it when Mitchell arched up into his mouth and groaned.

"There," he said on a moan. "God."

Aiden concentrated on gently rubbing and sucking and loved every second of hearing Mitchell lose it just by his touch alone.

"Aiden… close…" Aiden sucked down one more time and kept pressing inside. Leaning back, he moved his hand up and down Mitchell's wet cock and watched as Mitchell reached orgasm and long ropes of come splattered up over Aiden's hand and onto Mitchell's belly.

The erotic sight of Mitchell writhing on his finger and the sound of him shouting his completion was too much. In a frantic scramble Aiden used his free hand and brought himself off in just three short strokes, his come mingling with Mitchell's. Finished and completely and utterly spent, he reached for the nearest material, his Muse T-shirt, and wiped them down. He even paid gentle attention to Mitchell's ass, and then pulling the sleeping bags over them, he cuddled into his now-dozing lover and wondered how life could get any better.

Chapter Nine

*B*etween them they named the cubs Vanilla and Cocoa. Mitchell loved watching them and was constantly thankful that the momma bear tolerated the human observation. They didn't know the sex of either but they'd taken to calling Vanilla a girl and Cocoa a boy. Aiden had asked him which was his favorite. But which of the little mites, with their bright eyes and inquisitive temperaments, could he pick? Vanilla was the shyer of the two, easily spooked when a salmon splashed or a bird called. Being the cautious one would probably serve him or her well. Cocoa, on the other hand, was an inquisitive little shit. He was forever jumping out at poor Vanilla and scaring the life out of her. Cubs were weaned at four months, but probably being January or February babies they were likely around the five-month mark. Tiny babies. Adorable tiny babies. With a grumpy three-hundred-pound Momma.

"What are they up to?" Aiden asked. He sat down next to Mitchell on the balcony of their cabin.

"Playing. Cocoa smacked Vanilla round the face and Momma slapped him down. He's in the bush sulking."

"Did you write it in the book?"

Mitchell tapped the notebook. "All done."

"I need to get up into the third hide. The camera feed is cutting out every so often."

"You want me to do it?" Mitchell asked. Despite hating climbing trees he felt like he should offer.

"Nah. I'll do it." Aiden leaned over and dropped a kiss on Mitchell's head before he climbed down the ladder. Warmth suffused Mitchell at the casual touch. Aiden wasn't anything like any of the men he'd been with before. There'd been no more panic attacks and Aiden was relaxing, but at the end of the day he was still a little on the shy side. Nervous in bed to start, he was now up for most things. Mitchell squirmed a little at the memory of Aiden this morning losing it when Mitchell was exploring him with lips and tongue. Aiden was sensual and in tune with his body, and having the man in bed with him was an experience that Mitchell wanted to remember every minute of.

Mitchell wanted more. This morning when he woke with Aiden's arms around him was the perfect moment, one of those singular moments in your life that you will remember forever. When they got home maybe they could carry this on. He didn't want it to end. They worked together, so yes, it may be a bit awkward, but Scot was dating Debbie in Administration so he knew it wouldn't be frowned upon. Edward was a good guy and the missing Novak son wasn't around to be interested.

Vanilla sat back on her haunches and Mitchell

observed as she watched Aiden climb the tree. His eyes went from Vanilla to Aiden and he couldn't help but admire the figure of his lover as Aiden lithely jumped the steps and onto the bottom branches. Even Aiden's clumsiness around the cabin had eased as he became more relaxed. He swiveled his gaze back to Vanilla but she had disappeared from sight. Narrowing his eyes, he scanned for her, and thank god she was a pale color and stood out because she was climbing the damn tree after Aiden.

Cocoa was out of the bushes, momentarily standing on the dark rock and then walking on the shale along the bank. He trailed his sister, stepping in water, causing ripples and splashes, and Momma bear watched with lazy interest from her perch on a large flat rock. The babies could climb trees like monkeys, much faster than a man. Concerned, Mitchell stood from his position on the ground and wondered what the hell to do next. They wouldn't hurt Aiden but Momma bear wasn't going to be as easy to push away if she thought her cubs were in danger. The radio on the floor next to him crackled and Mitchell instantly scooped it up.

"Mitchell. Did you see?"

Mitchell nodded and then realized that wouldn't be obvious to Aiden since he was hidden from Aiden in the shadows of the cabin. He stepped forward and waved at his lover, who was well above the steps and up into the hide.

"She's maybe six feet below you."

"What is she doing?"

"Probably wondering why the strange-looking bear thing is climbing one of her trees."

"Ha freaking ha."

"Just stay where you are. She'll get bored."

By this time Cocoa was sitting at the bottom of the huge tree and looking up at his sister. Great. They didn't need both bears up there.

"I can't be up here too long. I'm hungry," Aiden said.

"You're always hungry," Mitchell said. He wasn't far off in that statement; he wasn't entirely sure where Aiden put all the food he could eat—it certainly didn't show on his slim frame.

"Can you make a noise? Get them to move away."

"Zero interaction," Mitchell reminded him. They weren't supposed to mess with the bears in any way. Bears had a unique intelligence that combined with their exploratory skills made it very challenging to watch the bears without them becoming used to humans. Bears that don't fear people became vulnerable to hunters, and with the recent spate of hunter visits none of the trackers to this area became too close to the animals.

"What if I need the bathroom?"

Mitchell laughed at the joking in Aiden's tone. "You've heard the one about bears shitting in the woods right? Same goes for rangers."

Momma bear wandered over and pushed at Cocoa with a large paw. Cocoa immediately jumped on his mom, cuffing at her ears and scratching in play. A low growl from Momma bear and the inquisitive Vanilla was scrambling down from the tree and bouncing alongside her brother until all three bears disappeared into the forest.

The family usually foraged in the early morning and evening and rested during the day, and they weren't the only bears close by. The notebook was full of observations.

"You can come down now," Mitchell confirmed.

Aiden climbed down and jogged the small distance to the back of the cabin before climbing the ladder. He was laughing and when they sat next to each other on the balcony looking out over the water and the trees everything was perfect.

The census was going well; the two of them had identified and logged separately some twenty-five bears feeding from the fresh-flowing water and eating the lush vegetation around them. The bears tolerated Mitchell and Aiden but still eyed them with suspicion. Bears were solitary animals by nature, mothers stayed with their cubs only until the cubs are ready to leave the den. Vanilla and Cocoa were well looked after, and it was fascinating to watch as they learned the world around him. Mitchell was fully aware that both black and grizzly bears were dangerous creatures; however, he also knew that they would not attack unless they were startled or provoked and he and Mitchell both spent hours in either the hide or in trees detailing everything they saw and feeling safe.

Mitchell hadn't seen evidence of the hunters that William had mentioned, but he and Aiden kept their vigil, kept their silence, and kept their records. And hell if he wasn't falling a little more in lust-love each day with a confident, at-ease, kind-of-toppy Aiden.

It was the seventh night of being at the base camp, nearly two weeks into this whole experience, when Mitchell woke to a sharp crack that split the still night air.

He shoved Aiden awake and then stood at the plexi-glass window, trying to look out into the gloom.

"Come away from the window, Mitchell," Aiden said worriedly. "That sounded like a gun."

"You heard that, right? Hunters, maybe."

"So we stay in here, we don't go looking. You heard William when he said that."

"It could be one of the cubs hurt though, or the momma," Mitchell said. He huffed at the glass, trying to clear a space to see, thinking he saw the glint of light on metal outside. Pulling on his boots he moved to the door, Aiden at his side, sure as stupid that they were doing this thing. Neither was armed nor had any kind of protection, so they rounded the trees cautiously. The moon was weak in the cloud-filled sky and Mitchell strained to see through the dark. His eyes adjusted and he thought he saw movement ahead. Vanilla sat alone on the bank of the water, almost hidden by the green sedge, and Mitchell held Aiden's arm as he took a step closer.

"Where's Cocoa? And Momma bear?" he said softly. They skirted where Vanilla was and saw Cocoa halfway up a tree. The family had been split up.

"Is that blood?" Aiden asked. Mitchell saw what Aiden did: Momma bear, curled in on herself, her breathing labored.

"Did they shoot her?"

"Shit," Aiden said softly, "she's hurt." He stepped closer, the undergrowth beneath his feet cracking and snapping, and the bear lifted her beautiful head. Her muzzle was pulled back in a snarl and her eyes were wide with fear. Vanilla ambled over to sit by them and they began to back away. Getting between cub and Momma was not happening.

"We'll go back, use the satellite phone, and get a veterinarian in."

Vanilla's mewling was enough to have Momma bear pull herself to her full height, nearly as tall as either man and twice as wide. They stood frozen, a bear would attack if they felt their cubs were threatened, add a significant wound and blood loss and Mitchell knew they were in the wrong place at the wrong time.

Momma bear moved slowly, her lumbering gait looking so uncoordinated, but they knew she could run, knew how fast she would be normally, and with no words spoken, they turned and began to run back to the cabin and the phone. Mitchell was just behind him when Aiden tripped, both men tumbling to land in the watery sedge, the mud oozing to hinder them. Momma was close behind though, and they scrambled to their feet, only seconds ahead. Aiden pushed Mitchell in front of him; they were almost there, the ladder only inches away. Mitchell jumped and scrambled the height. Aiden jumped as well but his foot hooked a step on the ladder, delaying him from getting up and over the top.

Aiden shouted behind him and in a sudden yanking move, Mitchell had dragged Aiden up and over onto the balcony. The bear stopped below them. An unholy scream ripped the air around them and Mitchell shuddered.

"Fuck," he said. "That was close." He pulled the satellite phone from his pocket and began to dial the emergency number. He turned to face Aiden. Aiden who was strangely still, looking unfocused, his eyes glassy, and... blood? *What the hell?* Blood dripping from his neck, blood matting in dark hair and circling Aiden's neck in small rivers.

"Mitchell," he managed to say before he just fell in an unconscious heap on the floor where he had been standing. Mitchell made it to him just as his lover reached the cold wood. He touched the scarlet that was running freely from the wound, and he scrabbled desperately for the dropped satellite phone, dialing and screaming their position, calling for air evac, their needs, the urgency, the injured momma, the cub.

Help. Help the bear. Help Aiden.

Help us.

Chapter Ten

*I*t didn't matter that it had been Mitchell who came in with Aiden covered in Aiden's blood and holding Aiden's hand; they still wouldn't tell him a damn thing.

How badly hurt is he?

Is he going to be okay?

Can someone just tell me?

Instead he was left to pace, wondering if the person who he had connected with in such an open, honest way was even alive. He stopped at the door marked 'Staff only'. His hands hovered over the white surface, his gaze tracing each letter, only standing back when someone came through. He wanted to have the courage to just push through, to have the right to be at Aiden's side.

They had taken him in the helo; the medics weren't sure what had happened past a bear attack. They weren't helped by Aiden being unconscious and Mitchell being unable to form a coherent sentence. *Are you hurt?* they asked as they stretchered Aiden to the helo, the blood stopped with padding, stats and numbers determining Aiden's life, sparking and hissing in staccato form over the noise of the rotors. *Sir, are you hurt?* they repeated as the helo left the ground, pulling back only when Mitchell shook his head.

They landed at a community clinic in Port Simpson, and Aiden was wheeled through the door Mitchell now stood outside of. That had been more than two hours ago.

What was he going to do? How could he lose this man when it seemed he had only just found him? He'd seen so many changes in Aiden the last few days, from shy and quiet to a man that held himself tall and started to have confidence in how he could be with Mitchell. This just couldn't be happening. Why the fuck had he thought it was a good idea to go and chase down noises and bears, leading Aiden out into God knows what?

"Mitchell?" The single word cut through Mitchell's thoughts, and he turned quickly, his hand going to the wall to steady himself.

"William." Of course he would be here, the clinic must have his number as an emergency contact for the bear census program.

"How is he?" the older man asked softly. He laid a calming hand on Mitchell's arm. "Have they said?"

"Not to me," Mitchell answered, looking back at the door. "I'm not family. They won't tell me a damn thing." William caught the next person through the door, a nurse in scrubs. Mitchell didn't even want to think where the blood on the green material came from.

"I have consent forms to be given information on a patient and a medical consent form he signed."

"The bear attack?"

"Yes."

"Wait here," she said. She vanished back through the door and reappeared with a doctor in tow. The doctor came out with a frown on his face.

"Here for the bear attack?" he asked William, who nodded.

"How is he?" Mitchell asked abruptly.

"He presented with the normal pattern of orthopedic injuries, lacerations, and punctures to his neck and right shoulder. Surgery went well to repair the nick to the carotid artery, and he is currently in an artificial coma and under observation." It was simple and to the point, and William nodded, passing over a folder of paperwork to the doctor.

"Aiden... he's going to be okay?" Mitchell didn't even want to ask, to hope, but he had to know.

"Couple of days, assuming everything goes well and he comes out of the artificial coma okay, and we can probably discharge to your care," the doctor confirmed, copying details from William's papers to his own notes and nodding as he did so. William had no more questions and Mitchell was just relieved to know that Aiden was safe.

"Can I see him?" Mitchell asked softly. The doctor looked at William, who just nodded and took back the paperwork and insurance details.

"Wait here, I'll get the nurse to take you back."

It was twenty-four hours before Aiden started to pull out of his unconscious state. Mitchell hadn't moved from the chair the whole time apart from drink breaks and to use the bathroom that was attached to the room. A couple of times Aiden had muttered in his sleep, asking for Mitchell, asking for help, obviously lost in a dream, a nightmare, and all Mitchell could do was touch him and try to reassure him. When Aiden did finally manage to push through the morphine to speak in the otherwise quiet room, it startled Mitchell. He leaned in so Aiden could feel the reassurance of Mitchell being there.

"Mitchell?" Aiden spoke with a soft voice, husky with disuse, and blue eyes half opened to the stark white of the room. Mitchell blinked sleep from his eyes and leaned over the bed, close enough he could hear the soft voice. "Wha'th'fuck?" Aiden slurred.

"Bear" was all Mitchell said. Aiden blinked, moving subtly and graying when he moved.

"Shit," Aiden forced out, "can't do an'thin' right." His voice was all long and drawn sleepy vowels, exhaustion in every sound, but it made Mitchell almost instantly angry to hear the self-pity in his lover's words. Unconsciously he stiffened and pulled back from Aiden, ready to set him right. "Don' go," Aiden interrupted Mitchell's train of thought, so softly Mitchell had to strain to hear.

"Enough now," Mitchell responded firmly, pushing back the irritation that Aiden had immediately felt he couldn't do anything right; after all, it hadn't been Aiden insisting on diving outside the cabin to see what the noises were. "Shut your eyes and sleep, I'll be here when you wake up."

Aiden did as he was told and Mitchell watched as his lover's breathing evened out.

"Sir?" The same nurse from yesterday was at the door. "I'm wondering if you could help us with something. I would ask Mr Helin but I didn't want to call him back here. You're friends with Mr Samuels?"

"Yes. We work together."

"Could I ask a couple of questions?"

"I'll try and help." *Great.* She was probably going to ask if all his shots were up to date or something obscure that he wouldn't know the answer to.

"The names on the medical form are different than what I have on the admissions form. I wondered which one we should be using for medical information."

Mitchell frowned. He held out his hand for the two pieces of paper. One he remembered they filled in on day one, a medical form with insurance details, allergies, that kind of thing. He glanced at the signature part at the bottom and the neat capitals. Peering closer, he couldn't believe what he was reading. Not Aiden Samuels at all.

Anthony Aiden Novak.

Aiden didn't know how long he slept, he had no comprehension of time in his morphine haze, had completely lost track of everything. He didn't even know what day it was. He blinked and looked around the bright room, realizing it was a nurse checking his notes that had woken him.

"Good morning, sleeping beauty." The nurse smiled.

"About time you woke up, we were wondering if you were faking." Aiden forced a weak smile, disoriented and only half-awake.

Where is Mitchell? Is he here? He didn't realize he had said it aloud, only caught the nurse twisting her lips in confusion. "My friend," he managed to force past cracked lips. The nurse smiled then, moving to open the door, telling whoever was outside the door to come inside. Aiden felt his heart leap, Mitchell was here for him.

"Aiden? How you doing?"

William? Where was Mitchell?

Aiden sat up with the nurse's help, questions on his lips, his face pale and sweating, and William hovering, wincing as Aiden groaned in pain.

"He's got a room at a hotel close by," William offered softly. "I sent him back to get a shower and some sleep. He looked tired and he wasn't talking much. He'll be back this evening."

Aiden leaned back on the pillow, the stitches pulling, and tried to get his head around the whole Mitchell-not-being-here thing. He was being unfair to expect Mitchell to be sitting by the bed like someone in one of those cheesy Lifetime movies. But, he'd gotten used to seeing Mitchell every time he opened his eyes.

"How long have I been unconscious?"

"A couple of days now. They kept you under."

The door opened behind William, and Aiden looked past him to see Mitchell standing at the door. William was right. He did look tired. Gorgeous, rumpled, sexy, but tired.

"You were supposed to get sleep," William admonished. Mitchell shrugged.

"I had stuff to do," he said.

Elation filled Aiden. Mitchell was exhausted yet he was here for Aiden.

"I'll leave you to it then," William said. He said his goodbyes and left the room, pulling the door shut behind him until it was only Aiden in pain and Mitchell staring at him left.

"Why didn't you tell me?" Mitchell asked immediately.

"Tell you?"

"Who you really were?"

The question hung there between them and Aiden realized exactly why Mitchell was here. This was the confrontation. This was every single one of Aiden's self-serving lies coming back to bite him.

"I didn't mean to *not* tell you," Aiden offered finally.

"Two weeks as friends, lovers, and colleagues, and you never once thought to mention your real name or the fact that you are actually my boss?" There was no anger in Mitchell's voice. He simply sounded resigned.

"I'm sorry. I can 'splain." Aiden attempted to move again and winced as the site of the stitches pulled violently. Grey misted over his eyes but he blinked it away. This was important.

"They asked me about insurance and papers, some problem with mismatched surnames, and then it became obvious." Aiden put his hand to his chest and shut his eyes. The cannula in the back of his hand pulled tight but he welcomed the tug on his skin. Emotion choked him.

"Aiden? Do you need a nurse, are you in pain?" Mitchell asked gently.

"Tired," Aiden forced out. Then emotion washed over him, the pain and the self-pity and the sheer stupidity of what he had done balled in grief in his tight chest.

"I would have understood."

"You would have judged me."

"Would or could? You know me now. Do I seem like the kind of person who would judge you?"

Aiden focused on how he had lied to the only person in his life beyond Edward and his dad that had ever seen him as someone to love.

"I didn't. I do," Aiden attempted to explain. "God, I don't know. You said you hated liars, and that was me so I was really afraid to saying anything after that, and I know I should have just told you at the beginning. I just have this stuff in my head…" For a few seconds the two men simply looked at each other. What else could he say apart from *sorry I was stupid*? His head was so muddled, and exhaustion and pain combined to make him wooly and unable to actually explain to Mitchell how he felt.

"You look like shit," Mitchell finally said.

"Feel shit," Aiden managed.

Mitchell placed the palm of a hand on his forehead. The weight of it was perfect and Aiden hoped it was not the last time he would feel Mitchell's hands on him.

"Get some sleep. I'll be back in the morning."

"Thank you."

It was only when the door shut behind Mitchell that Aiden realized he had forgotten to ask about Momma bear and her cubs.

Chapter Eleven

*M*itchell's cell showed it was three in the morning and it took him five minutes to get Scot to answer the phone.

"Someone better be dyin'," Scot said grumpily. He was half-asleep and clearly frustrated.

"Sorry, man," Mitchell apologized immediately.

"Mitch? What the fuck you calling me at ass o'clock in the morning for?"

"He lied to me, Scot, and I feel like a child who found out there's no Santa. I'm trying to be grown up and understanding but this guy is my boss. I want to get on a plane and come home but then I don't and I wish I knew what to think."

Silence.

Mitchell swallowed, the emotion choking his throat.

"Okay," Scot said slowly, "I'm trying to process here." Mitchell could picture his friend lying on his bed and staring up at the ceiling, blinking away sleep.

"I met someone," Mitchell started. He pushed the fingers of his free hand into his jeans pocket.

"On the plane?" Scot sounded confused.

"No, at the—with the bears—dammit." Mitchell stood suddenly, like he needed to release some energy, and started to pace. "He lied to me, but the weight of his secrets must be so heavy. I met Anthony Novak."

"The missing son?" Scot asked. "You met Novak? There *is* a Novak Junior then? I need coffee. Is this a coffee talk?"

"Please," Mitchell said wearily. He needed for his friend to listen while he talked. Maybe placing all of his thoughts out in the open would help him make sense of things.

"Okay, I'm in the kitchen. Start from the beginning."

"The guy you were supposed to go with. Turns out he's Dominic Novak's son. We got close when we were working on the census."

"Close close, or *close* close?" Scot asked.

"We kinda had a relationship." *Relationship?* What kind of word was that? "He was this flighty, fidgety kid—"

"Kid? How old is he?"

"Twenty-four or something."

"So he's not a kid then."

"He seemed like it when I met him. He tripped over stuff and he wouldn't stop talking and he had panic attacks and it turns out he has issues," Mitchell finished lamely. Issues didn't cover it.

"He saw his dad die in front of him, mauled to death on TV. Of course he's got issues."

Mitchell hadn't expected to hear Scot siding with

Aiden. He wanted unqualified support from his friend, not statements of the obvious. The he kicked himself. Scot wasn't exactly siding with Aiden; he was only repeating what Mitchell knew anyway. Mitchell was more than aware of how Aiden's—*Anthony's*—dad had died. He recalled seeing the pale, wide-eyed teenager who stood stoically at the funeral and the hoard of journalists who crowded him afterward.

"He should have told me," Mitchell said. His own coffee, from the hospital waiting room, was cold. "Even when we slept together and we were so close, he still didn't tell me he was my boss."

"Okay, I finished my first coffee and I'm listening to every word. You met a young guy and you had a thing and he was lying to you about his name. Is that it in a nutshell?" Scot sounded very patient and Mitchell knew he had phoned the right person. Scot was seeing probably far more than Mitchell wanted him to. He said the right thing at the right time as if he knew Mitchell needed to get this off his chest

Mitchell scrubbed at his eyes with his hands and wished for more coffee. "I think I'm embarrassed. I stood there and told him about the day I met his dad and how what he talked about made me move all the way to Seattle to work at the Park. I feel like an idiot..." Mitchell couldn't actually pull the words together.

"You need to sleep, get some perspective. He's the owner—part-owner, whatever—you could probably sue his ass for sexual harassment or something. He can't fire you—"

"He won't fire me. He's not like that."

"Okay. But you told me he lied. What reason would he have?"

Mitchell could only guess. He wanted to think that knowing he was spending three weeks with the new boss of the Park wouldn't have changed how he had been, but he wasn't stupid. The guy had the kind of tragic history that you couldn't even make up. Mitchell attempted to convince himself he wouldn't have judged Aiden but he probably would have. Not in a bad way, but he would have been different in how he was with the man. Guarded. Careful, even. Was it possible that Aiden was just protecting himself from that? That he just wanted to be seen as another ranger, a normal guy, without the tragic loss of his dad and his whole life story available at the click of a button on the internet? His first real boyfriend had used him; why would he expect anything different from Mitchell after only knowing him a short while? Mitchell sighed. He'd seen the real Aiden. He was convinced of it. The confident, funny, sexy guy that was buried under expectation and panic was the man he'd started to imagine a relationship with.

"I asked him but he's drugged up to the eyeballs," he finally said.

"He's an addict?" Scot sounded horrified.

"No. He's... I'm calling from the hospital. He was hurt when a bear clipped him on the neck."

"When did this happen?"

"Two days ago."

"And you're still at the hospital?"

"Yeah."

"Then you need to ask yourself why you're still there."

"I want to make sure he's okay is all," Mitchell defended.

"Can I go back to bed yet?" Scot asked over a yawn.

"You haven't given me any advice, asshole."

"I did. Ask yourself why you didn't get on the first plane home."

Mitchell sat for a few moments and listened to his heart. Aiden had been this helpless young guy, and Mitchell had fallen for him in the worst way. But when he found out what Aiden had done, instead of running away he'd waited to talk to Aiden. Even then it wasn't to shout at the guy or accuse him of lying. Then it hit him what was worrying him the most in all of this.

"He's going to think that it matters to me who he is. I fucked this up big time," Mitchell said.

"How did you fuck it up?"

"I didn't immediately say we'd talk and get this sorted out. I should have said that."

"There you go then. So what else are you going to do? Are you coming home?"

"No. I'm waiting until morning and then getting the whole story from him."

"It sounds like you're serious about this guy, Mitch."

"I am. He's funny and clever and sexy, and the things he can do with his hands—"

"Enough with the description of your homo-love," Scot interrupted with a laugh. "It probably helps he's rich."

Shit. He'd not thought about the fact that Aiden inherited his dad's legacy plus a part-ownership in the Park. "His money isn't even something I'm thinking about," Mitchell said quickly.

"Mitch, man, I'm joking with you. I'm going back to bed. Can you manage on your own now?"

"Thanks, Scot. I owe you one."

"Not sure I did anything."

They exchanged goodbyes and Mitchell held his cell in his hand and watched as the digital display went from 3:08 to 3:09. Only when it reached 3:20 and his thoughts were calmer did he leave the hospital and walk to the Days Inn next door. He needed sleep.

But all he could do was think. He loved his work at the education center, loved knowing he worked in the place that was the legacy of Dominic Novak, for the man who had started him on his career path when he was younger. Leaving the Park would be a huge wrench. He wasn't going to leave; he would work this out. Aiden may not have told the truth but Mitchell was prepared to listen to the why and hoped Aiden hadn't been taking him for an idiot.

He remembered what Dominic Novak had written about the death he had seen in the wild, that fragile circle of life that was normally continued and synchronized, only disrupted by man. Mitchell had asked him about that in his first letter, the one telling Dominic how he had been inspired to study zoology because of him, the one asking how the older man could reconcile nature and the evolution and balance that was at its core with man and what evils man could do to that nature. Dominic had been so pragmatic. *Man was part of nature,* he had said. His opinion was that it was man's job to disrupt nature so that nature could become stronger, more resilient. It was an idea that freaked Mitchell out at the time and so they wrote a lot about that concept, about the hows and the whys. They became friends for the short time until he died, and they talked about so much, about animals and environments—and about Anthony.

Anthony. So very full of life and so interested in the world around him, he was a natural and a child after Dominic's own heart. He was a man now. No longer was he a fourteen-year-old boy who'd had a wild monkey as a pet or was homeschooled so he could travel the world with his father. Not a child who saw the same murders as his father and who pulled his father back from the grief he was lost in. No, this Anthony was a man—a confusing, complicated man with self-esteem issues. He was a man who had been used as a stepping stone by his first and only real boyfriend, one who had been—and was still being— hounded by the press, forced to relive his father's awful death over and over all in the name of entertainment. This was the man who had stolen Mitchell's heart, the man who now sat within reach and who probably should hear all of this from Mitchell.

What would happen now if Mitchell walked away? Aiden had his secrets, but Mitchell could see why, well no, actually Scot had *made* Mitchell see why.

Chapter Twelve

*a*iden woke to daylight and a nurse hovering by his side. Like it had just happened, Mitchell's visit last night was his first real thought. He should have told Mitchell everything, and now he may well have screwed up the most positive thing he'd ever had in his life.

Aiden was determined; he needed to see Mitchell face to face—he had to. If Mitchell pushed him away, railed at him, accused him of things that would never be as bad as what Aiden could imagine for himself, then Aiden would be okay with that, because at least if he could just get in two words—*I'm sorry*—then maybe that would be enough to let Mitchell go without a fuss.

He missed Mitchell, missed the warmth that was his lover, the softness of skin pulled taut over hard muscles. He wanted the sound of the rhythmic breathing and the heartbeat that would vibrate against Aiden's touch. He realized he hadn't understood just how much he had grown to rely on Mitchell being there.

He lay there silently, his thoughts a mass of confusion, the only clear thread in his head was that he could sell his half of the Park, move on.

God the drugs were messing with his head.

"Hey."

"Mitchell!" Aiden exclaimed. He couldn't help the sudden press of relief that spilled into that single word. They both waited until the nurse left. "Did you get any sleep?" Mitchell looked even more exhausted than the night before.

"Some. I heard from the K-rangers. Momma bear's wound was a through and through. They darted her and she's already back up and around."

"Vanilla and Cocoa?"

"With their mom. The conservancy is on top of it all."

Aiden quickly changed the subject, hoping to get at least part of his explanation out there before Mitchell could leave. "You know that if the K-rangers had known who I was then they would have treated me differently. The son of the man who spent a whole year living with their bears. A special man like my dad that they respected. I couldn't live up to that."

"Aiden, that's stupid."

"Well then, maybe I didn't want to feel like I had to live up to my dad's memory."

"You don't see how special you are, do you? It's you that I fell for. I talked to Scot to try to figure things out, and it's not your money, or your name, or… shit, look… I don't know where to start—"

"I'm sorry," Aiden interrupted desperately. "Please can we just forget it all? I promise you I had my reasons."

Mitchell looked down at him with a considered expression, and then finally he pulled up a chair and sat inches away from Aiden. Reaching out, he grasped Aiden's hand and held it firmly.

"We need to talk," Aiden said. "I want to explain everything to you. I have to explain to you." Mitchell shook his head and moved closer to Aiden, leaning against his good arm.

"I do want us to talk," Mitchell started, "but I'm not sure what we need to say. It's just, you didn't tell me who you really were."

"Mitchell—"

"No, Aiden, I'm okay with that," Mitchell reassured him. "I swear. At first I had this entirely juvenile reaction to being lied to. But I'm not in school; I'm a grownup. Talking to Scot helped me think things through, helped me realize why you did what you did. The paparazzi hounded you as a child, then when you finally find what you think is happiness Ben tried to use you. I'm not surprised you wanted to hide who you were." When Aiden nodded carefully and started to answer, Mitchell just placed a finger on Aiden's lips and smiled, leaning down and capturing his lips in a kiss. Aiden chased the kiss as Mitchell pulled back, despite the pain in his neck.

"Aiden?" Mitchell's voice was raw. "I'm sorry I walked away from you last night like that. It was wrong."

"Shhhh," Aiden whispered with his kisses, not wanting to hear apologies, not even needing them. "I fell in love with you, Mitchell. Can you ever feel the same way about me?" He waited for the disappointment of hearing excuses that he knew would be the result of laying his entire self out like that.

Mitchell appeared to be considering his reply and then gently kissed Aiden again.

"I'm falling in love with you too."

"Tha-that's good then," Aiden stuttered.

"I do have a question though," Mitchell said.

"Go on."

"Are you still Aiden, or should I call you Anthony now?"

"Anything you want," he answered immediately.

"I fell for Aiden," Mitchell said softly. Then he gripped Aiden's hand tightly and smiled.

"I like that." Aiden felt warmth building inside him.

Aiden was good.

Epilogue

"Aiden?" Mitchell's voice was low and right next to his ear. "Are you awake?"

Aiden murmured a 'yes', but buried beneath the quilt it was doubtful Mitchell would be able to hear. Squirming free of the material had him backing up into Mitchell's warm body, and he smiled to himself when he felt the hardness of his boyfriend's body behind him.

"What time is it?" he asked on a yawn.

"Just after six." Mitchell pressed his lips to Aiden's forehead and Aiden scented the mint of toothpaste. Evidently Mitchell had been awake a while. Pushing back the covers, Aiden stumbled to the bathroom for a piss and to brush his teeth. They weren't due up until seven, which meant an hour in bed with minty fresh breath and preferably naked. Back under the covers, he faced Mitchell and cuddled in close. Six months of waking up with Mitchell and every new day was filled with so many possibilities.

"Love you," he murmured. This time there was no way

Mitchell could avoid hearing the words and he answered with a soft smile.

"I love you too," Mitchell offered.

They kissed gently for a while until the kisses turned from slow and gentle to fast and hard. It was always this way for them. Simply being close to Mitchell had Aiden turned on faster than he had ever imagined was possible. Sexy, confident Mitchell was Aiden's anchor, his reason for getting up every day. He didn't think it was possible to love anyone as much as they loved each other. Sometimes when he was low—which wasn't often now—he would imagine a life without Mitchell. An empty life like he'd had before, filled with nothing but academia. Aiden wriggled closer and in a swift move had his lover on his back and under him. Mitchell huffed in disapproval but then grinned up at him.

"I'm sure it's my turn," he deadpanned.

"I'll fight you for it." Aiden smirked. They'd fallen into bed at around midnight after yet another problem in the lemur enclosure. Two escapees and a recurring viral infection had all available rangers either in a search pattern or attempting to separate three of the lemurs from the others for medical treatment. There had been no time for lovemaking when all they were capable of was a shower and tumbling into bed.

"I'm taller than you," Mitchell protested.

"Size isn't everything."

"I'm sure pushing me over the sofa the night before last counts as your turn."

"So not listening," Aiden said firmly. He loved that they could tease each other. Not just that this was such an intimate thing to do but that he was confident enough with Mitchell to be able to tease back. This man in his arms had shown him so much love and affection that it was almost impossible for Aiden to believe he was anything less than perfect in Mitchell's eyes. Every so often he would doubt that but Mitchell would work to bring him around. He was so patient.

"Can we at least talk about moving in together?" Mitchell asked. He cupped Aiden's face in his hands. Aiden looked down into serious hazel eyes.

"After," he replied. "I need to be inside you first."

Far from a situation with Vaseline and no condoms in the middle of a bear forest, the two men were tested, clean, and had lube stashed in every room of both his rental and Mitchell's sprawling apartment. Another thing Aiden loved was the fact that he and Mitchell were so in tune. Mitchell wasn't scared to show that he wanted Aiden just as much as Aiden wanted him.

Aiden kissed Mitchell deeply and moved higher so he could trap Mitchell under his weight. He reached beyond them to where the lube sat on the side table, and in smooth, experienced motions he was spreading Mitchell's legs and pressing inside. Mitchell arched up into the kiss and moaned low in his throat. This was Aiden's favorite part: when he had Mitchell writhing under him, when he could push him to the edge and watch him fly or decide to tease and hold off actually pressing inside. When two fingers began to stretch and a third had Mitchell begging for deeper, Aiden unerringly located his sweet spot and suddenly Mitchell was forcing himself back down onto Aiden's fingers.

"Now," Mitchell gasped into the kiss.

Slicking himself up, Aiden had to control the need to lose it from just the touch of his hand. He pressed against Mitchell's hole and pushed inside the barrier. For a second he stilled as Mitchell screwed his eyes shut and let out a noise that was half sigh and half groan.

"Mitchell?" Aiden waited. He wanted to see hazel eyes when he was inside, wanted to read Mitchell's expression. They had this routine where they told each other everything—how they felt, when to push, when to go deep, when to back off.

"Move," Mitchell demanded. "Just move. Please."

Aiden began to move but didn't for one minute stop looking into Mitchell's eyes and kissing his lover. When he was close, so close he could come just at the slightest push, he watched as Mitchell arched under him and orgasmed with a shout. That was enough to push Aiden over the edge and he came deep inside the man who was the other half of him.

"I love you so much," he whispered into damp skin. Mitchell pulled him in a close hug and whispered into his ear the same thing he had every day for the last four weeks.

"Move in with me."

The same as every other day, Aiden didn't answer. Mitchell wanted him to move out of his rental and into this apartment. Aiden was hardly ever at his own place and spent more time here anyway. But moving in seemed so permanent. Did Mitchell really know what he was taking on? Rolling off his lover, he smiled down at him and held out a hand.

"Come on, lazy ass, we have the unveiling to get to. Last one in the shower gets the he cheap shampoo."

Mitchell didn't ever pressure Aiden about moving in. But today for the first time, he looked a little sad. The emotion was fleeting in his eyes but Aiden knew he had put it there. Mitchell wanted commitment and Aiden was just plain scared. He still had the odd moment when the control he wanted over his life slipped, and he didn't want that to happen when he had nowhere to run to.

***

The sculpture of Momma bear and her cubs was unveiled at ten a.m., and the journalists were out in force. Seemed Dominic Novak's son had arrived to take over where his dad had left off and they loved that. There had been double-page spreads with the story of Dominic Novak's death, but they were balanced with what he had achieved in his life and for that Aiden was happy. Of course he was mentioned, and his sexuality was questioned; hell, they even pulled up the story on Ben. But in the end, none of it mattered when Mitchell was at his side.

Edward was giving a speech and Aiden looked over at him with a great amount of pride.

"Dominic came to me one day, not long after he'd made money from his first season of wildlife shows. He wanted to invest money into Spirit Bear Park and he had this big idea. He envisioned a center that could be used to educate students all over the state and beyond. I remember asking him how he'd got this idea. He said it wasn't even his idea." Edward paused and glanced over at Aiden.

Aiden wasn't sure where this was going but he nodded encouragingly and smiled.

"Anthony was probably no more than maybe ten or eleven, and apparently he'd come to his dad with an idea. Kids shouldn't have to go to school." He paused and the people grouped around him—journalists, staff, a camera crew—all laughed. "Anthony was of the opinion that all children should be able to learn like he did. He wanted them to have access to all kinds of animals and learn about them in their environment. He told his dad that they wouldn't learn this stuff in classrooms." He looked back at Aiden.

Aiden was shocked. He never realized the center had been inspired by one of his wild youthful wishes that every child could live on safaris with their dad.

Edward continued, "Dominic and I talked. He wanted to offer hands-on education for all ages, for all classes, all kinds of people, and we built the education center based on that. Today it gives me great pleasure in opening the new extension, the aptly named Vanilla and Cocoa wing." Edward cut the ribbon and Aiden was the first to clap for his honorary uncle as Edward entered the new building followed en masse by the rest of the group.

All except him.

Him and Mitchell.

"You okay?" Mitchell asked.

"I never knew that," Aiden replied. "I never knew it was me that inspired all this." He waved his free hand at the center. His other hand was very firmly being held by Mitchell, who smiled down at him and pulled him into a one-armed hug.

"Mitchell, you're wanted for the presentation," Edward said, back at their side.

"I'll be right back," Mitchell said. "Five minutes."

As soon as he was alone with Edward, Aiden began to talk. "I didn't know about the Center, you know."

"He listened to every word you said. You remember he would organize his trips around your home schooling. He was so damn proud of you, talked about you all the time, how you were so clever like your mom. He said you knew more than he ever would about animals, their habitat, the cultures of the continents around you. 'A walking encyclopedia', he called you."

"He did?" Aiden didn't disbelieve Edward. Clearly he had just forgotten everything in the wash of grief.

"He wanted you to grow up strong and unafraid. It is all he wanted for his boy, to have a life that you loved. You can have that with your young man."

"It's not been long with Mitchell," Aiden said. He needed to talk about this with someone he trusted and Edward was the only man for the job. "He wants me to move in with him. I'm not sure I'm ready for him to see me day in and day out. What if I fuck it up big time?"

Edward smiled. "And what if you don't? What is it that's stopping you?"

Aiden wished he knew. Six months had passed since that fateful trip to British Columbia and he and Mitchell had more or less spent every available moment outside of work together. Aiden was working his first rotation at the Park with the wolves and Mitchell was deep in controlling construction of the new wing. In that time they'd grown so close, there was no *falling* in love—they were in love, plain and simple. "I don't actually know," he finally admitted. "Maybe I'm just waiting for him to see the real me and run."

Edward sighed. "The real you is pretty special, Anthony Aiden Novak. I wish you could see that."

"I do. I mean I don't. I mean… jeez… Mitchell makes me feel like I could be special."

Edward chuckled. "Then go with your heart and start a whole new life that is all yours. I can see you love him. He loves you too, of course, it's obvious."

"I know," Aiden said softly. "I know he does." He saw Mitchell walking back to them and stopped talking.

Mitchell rejoined them. "They're happy watching the video presentation on their own, but I'm going to stay and answer questions if that's okay with you?" he asked Aiden.

Aiden smiled. "I'll meet you at home." He still wasn't entirely comfortable around journalists and relaxing on the sofa with coffee and a good book sounded like a good idea.

"Your rental or my apartment?" Mitchell asked gently. The question was loaded with so much meaning. Mitchell was asking for an answer from Aiden. What came next was possibly the most important thing Aiden had ever said. Mitchell owned his apartment, it was bigger, and it was there that Aiden would be able to start his new life with the man he loved.

He kissed Mitchell full on the mouth and then stepped back. "Our apartment."

THE END

Child of the Storm

Ben Hyland is excited to be showing Yorkshire to Cory Vasilyev. Cory scouts locations for film studios and needs the right inspiration for a new film version of Wuthering Heights.

Problem is, Ben wants to share his passion for the story and for the wild moors, but Cory just wants to go home.

Until abruptly he doesn't want to leave at all.

Chapter One

*B*en Hyland shifted in his seat as they passed signs for M1 North. They were about twenty miles into their journey and they had left London where tangled roads had given way to endless motorway. The guy in the driver's seat hadn't said much so far. Then again, the rental car, a brand spanking new Ford Focus, was right-hand drive and given his companion was American there had to be a lot of concentration going on behind his hazel eyes.

The very last thing Ben wanted to do was snag the driver's attention by talking needlessly. Still, they had a long way to go up the spine of the UK and to have silence for hundreds of miles would definitely grate on him. Ben Hyland liked his quiet times with his books and his academic study, but when in social situations he hated the dreaded dead parts. That was why he had a reputation as being the one who spoke before he thought. Just to fill the empty space. He searched his brain for the right thing to say to A, an American, and B, possibly the most gorgeous guy he had seen in years, perhaps ever.

"What film is it we are scouting locations for?" Ben finally asked. Breaking the silence felt good. "Am I allowed to know now that we are in the car?"

His companion, Cory mumbled-surname, the aforementioned American with the blond hair and the come-to-bed eyes, flicked a glance at him. He looked so damn serious and there was a definite frown line marring his otherwise smooth forehead.

Eyes back on the road he answered. "It's not a secret. Of course you're allowed to know. It was all in the briefing pack that my company emailed you." Unspoken was the added 'didn't you read it, you idiot?'.

"I didn't get an email," Ben defended himself.

The frown briefly reappeared on Cory's face.

"I'll follow that up," he said. "You should have received the full confidential file with all film details." Cory's company was scouting for more than the one film location and Ben was just one of four lecturers at South Bucks University that had applied to assist. He bet every one of the other three had received their briefing information. Bloody BT Mail. "The short straw we pulled is a costume drama set in Yorkshire."

"Yorkshire? I love Yorkshire." Ben was excited, certainly not feeling for he had drawn the short straw.

"You mean you didn't even know where we were going?"

Ben shrugged. "When you went M1 North I assumed we were going upwards." Ben laughed and emphasized the up by pointing his finger to the sky.

"Hmmm." Cory didn't seem impressed. "Anyway, the working title is *A Child of Storm*."

His summary wasn't exactly all forthcoming with a plentiful amount of detail and didn't really give anything away. For a second Ben stared at Cory waiting for more. Cory simply concentrated back on driving but Ben really was interested in knowing more details. He would stop asking questions as soon as Cory said Ben was getting on Cory's nerves.

"Is that a remake of *Wuthering Heights*?" Ben asked. "*For he, like her, is a child of storm; and this makes a bond between them, which interweaves itself with the very nature of their existence.*" Ben added the quote with a grin. It was one of many he could recall at the snap of his fingers. He refused to think it made him odd. He was just passionate—that was all. And the chances of him being lucky enough to assist in finding locations for Heathcliff and Cathy? That was not something that happened to Ben Hyland.

"Yes," Cory answered carefully. He was evidently uninspired by Ben's pretentious excerpt from the book. "That is what the script calls for reference too."

Ben felt a fluttering of excitement in the pit of his stomach. *Wuthering Heights* was his favorite book; from studying it at GCSE right through to writing his degree dissertation about the Brönte sisters—or more accurately, the demise of their brother Branwell. Hell, Hollywood would probably fuck it up, but the journey to get there, an excuse to spend three weeks in Yorkshire—Brönte country—was suddenly the best thing to happen to him all year. This all-expense-paid trip with a salary at the end of it for just three weeks work was exactly what he needed.

"Really? *Wuthering Heights*? Heathcliff, Cathy, and the whole moors thing?" Ben tried hard to tamp down his excitement but Cory was clearly thinking of something else as his response was a bit lackluster.

"Uh huh," Cory replied. Yep, clearly distracted.

"God, you are going to love what I can show you in Brönte country," Ben continued. He waved his arms animatedly as much as the inside of the car would let him, already envisioning where they could look for parts of the film. "Oh my God, I know the perfect Heights, and you know the part where Catherine is running in the rain to find Heathcliff—"

"I haven't seen the old films," Cory interrupted coolly.

"Oh, not the films, sorry, I was referencing the book—"

"I haven't read the book."

That stopped the conversation dead.

Ben bit his tongue for less than thirty seconds. "We're scouting for locations for a film based on a book you haven't read?" Ben said with shock in his voice. "Does Sony Pictures know this?"

Cory let out a long-suffering sigh. Evidently he was asked this question a lot. "Sony employed our company because we are the best at what we do. They don't question our methods. They don't need to be aware of whether the people they employ have read some old book. You don't need to read the book to be a locations manager; you just need to find the right scenery depending on the script." Cory was talking at Ben as if he were a kid. All calm and careful and perhaps a little condescending. Ben wished he wasn't so damn focused on how gorgeous the man's voice was when clearly Cory was a bit of an idiot. Cory continued, "I expect most of the film can be shot against green screen with the correct scenery placed in after. Possibly even using bigatures."

Ben had no idea what a bigature was, and even though he wanted to ask, he sensed that he was pushing it with the questions. His usual optimism pushed aside the fact that the good-looking guy was a complete prat with a stick up his arse. Three weeks of immersing himself in beautiful countryside was something Ben was not turning down. He had signed up to be the assistant, the one with knowledge of his country, not to make friends with a guy who was flying back to the States in three weeks.

Cory couldn't have been much older than Ben. He had a serious, focused expression sketched on his expressive features, tanned skin, and the most startling hazel-green eyes. Dark blond hair was cut in a style that looked effortless but probably took hours and a huge amount of product to keep tamed. Cory's voice was soft and there was a definite drawl to the vowels. Ben wondered where in the US his companion came from. The hot and sultry south, the serious east, or the laid-back west—if indeed any of those stereotypes actually existed outside of characters in films.

He was shorter than Ben's six foot. That much had been obvious at the first handshake at Heathrow Airport. He had given his name as Cory *something*, but Ben was too polite to ask for clarification of his surname.

Ben had taken his hand, holding it possibly longer than

perhaps he should, but jeez, the guy was really bloody pretty and serious with Hollywood-perfect teeth and —*God. I need to let go of his hand. Now.* Dropping his grip, Ben had seen the curious expression on Cory's face but strict British reserve had Ben taking a step back and inclining his head. That was enough of a hello. Any more touching of the solemn yet pretty could-be-an-actor man was likely to get his dick in trouble. Picking up the rental car and turning north around London and out the other side took up a lot of time, but once on the open road he had wanted to learn more about Cory. Films captivated him; the film industry with all its ups and downs fascinated him.

"I was lucky to get this gig," Ben said. He had managed to break the silence once. He could do it again. "Maria, from our drama and film department, answered this ad and said I should do it too. My boss, that's Oscar Huntingdon, wanted to get involved as well. He's not a bad boss, just a bit odd. I am not sure he likes the English department much, nor drama, come to think of it."

"Uh huh," Cory commented as he switched lanes and then pulled back in front of a bus full of school-aged kids who were making rude gestures at every car that passed them. Undeterred, Ben forged ahead in the 'breaking the uncomfortable silence' project.

"He was the one who handed out the matches for us. Maria got the gig in Wales, 'cause she's Welsh. Which helps, you know."

"Sure."

"So anyway, Oscar took your company rep who is scouting London for some steampunk thing. Oscar is all 'I teach physics, it should be me that handles the serious stuff.' I guess he hasn't seen Sherlock Holmes, because I watched that and I loved it. I mean who wouldn't—it's Robert Downey, Jr. and Jude Law in one film. Have you met them?" There was a pause and Cory seemed to be considering his answer.

"Not one-on-one. No," he answered.

Ben was gratified that Cory had actually been listening to his rambling.

"Anyway, I think Sherlock is very steampunk. So the boss could be disappointed if the sci-fi he is on is more Robert and Jude bromance and less *Contagion*. And then you'll never guess what he said to me."

"Surprise me," Cory said. There was no dry sarcasm in his tone, merely a fond amusement like a dad tolerating the ramblings of a small child. Ben ignored him. He was good at that.

"He then said to me that only Yorkshire and the costume drama were left. He announces that he chose Yorkshire for me because—then he just stopped and looked at me and I was so ready for him to say something about 'my people liking costume dramas or being a sausage jockey or wearing pink'—the usual bollocks he throws at me about what he says is my 'alternative lifestyle'. He wimped out though because I was staring straight at him and he just mumbled something like 'you're a lecturer in English literature'." Ben laughed, then realized he had just outed himself to his new temporary boss. Not that it was an issue. Being gay was as much a part of him as his love for Brönte or Cadbury's chocolate. He never really held back. Hell, half of Hollywood was gay, right? Chancing a quick look at Cory, he saw a faint smile on Cory's face but no shock or horror. That was a good thing.

"He sounds like a judgmental idiot," Cory commented.

"Totally."

"Do you mind if we stop for something to eat? There wasn't anything decent on the plane and I am so hungry." Cory was so polite. He gestured to a sign that they were passing indicating services ten miles ahead.

"That's fine." Ben resolved to try not to talk for the next ten miles and he almost managed it apart from the odd comment about road signs or other drivers. The rest of the time he spent looking through the glove box and playing with dials on the stereo.

The location company had rented a car for each of their reps, and although it was only a small Ford, it was new and in much better condition than Ben's ancient Toyota. The stereo worked, which in Ben's mind was a good thing. Music stopped the need he had to talk. Music, however, was not enough to get Cory to stop answering calls on his handsfree about everything from accounts to actors to studios. Apparently a location scout spoke to some pretty high-up people in films, like directors and producers, and had way more than one role just finding the right place for filming.

The last call had been met with a stern response, a litany of harsh summing up interspersed with a couple of curse words. Apparently, no, Cory's company did not work for free, and no, there was no way Cory was dropping his pants for an asshole. Whoever was on the end of the phone needed to 'look elsewhere for support' from 'someone who gave an actual shit'. It appeared as soon as the call had finished Cory relaxed. From the tight grip of his fingers on the steering wheel to the deep brackets of tension around his gorgeous mouth, every inch of him instantly became looser. Perhaps stressy-Cory was just a result of him dealing with shit. Maybe he was just a nice guy under pressure. Ben hoped so.

They stopped at a service station on the M1 and decided independently on sandwiches that Cory paid for with a shiny red credit card.

"Expenses," he explained. Ben couldn't take his eyes off Cory's lips as they moved to form words. They really were perfect lips. Full on the bottom, thinner on top, and he had the most incredible white teeth. There was something Ben recognized about him and he wondered if perhaps he had seen Cory in a film somewhere. Something about the tilt of his head and the width of his grin was so familiar.

"Did you ever do any acting?" Ben asked. Sandwiches finished, they were drinking coffee to extend the driving break for Cory. That seemed like a fairly safe question to throw at his companion.

"No way," Cory said. He laughed quickly and Ben didn't doubt the sincerity of Cory's words. He sounded completely adamant like that was the last thing on his mind. "My brother is the actor; I'm happier behind the scenes."

"Your brother is an actor?"

"He's the one that inherited the acting talent from mom. She was an actress; Josh is doing better than her though." Suddenly Ben put two and two together. No wonder Cory was so damn gorgeous and familiar if his brother was…

"Josh Vasilyev? Your brother is Josh clothes-off-in-every-scene-action-hero Vasilyev?"

Cory took his concentration off his coffee and instead looked directly at Ben. There was something in his eyes that Ben had trouble identifying. Accusation? Disbelief? The flush of red on Cory's cheeks indicated anger perhaps?

"My younger brother," Cory qualified. "He's a good actor."

Ben thought back to the last two films he had been to see where Josh Vasilyev was the lead. Neither was an awe-inspiring, Oscar-winning masterpiece but both were big-budget, action-filled numbers with guns and monsters. Oh yes, and a shirtless Josh Vasilyev front and center, killing the monsters and bagging the girls. Both films were huge and Ben had loved every single second of the blood and sweat that had made them such great adventures.

"I think he's bloody awesome," Ben said. He didn't add that he had lusted after the gorgeous blond actor in the way a teenager liked a boy-band member. Josh Vasilyev was right up there with Jude Law and Chris Evans. Evidently Ben had said the right thing though, as Cory nodded in acceptance. Ben wondered if there was any jealousy between the brothers. He imagined Josh was in the very rich, verging on obscenely rich, category. Cory could well have been reading his mind when he spoke.

"I am very proud of him, but I wouldn't swap his life for mine." Cory leaned in to exchange the confidence and Ben found himself echoing the move until they were only a few inches apart and Ben could see flecks of amber in Cory's eyes. He didn't think for a minute that Cory spoke about his brother to just anyone. Who knew what could be passed on to a tabloid paper or magazine. He wondered why Cory was apparently going to confide something. What was it about Ben that invited any confidences? Cory leaned back and after a second Ben copied.

"I love his films." Ben wasn't lying.

Cory smiled. "He is the perfect actor for the roles he is given and he backs it all up with women drooling all over him. He loves it."

And drooling men, like me, Ben added silently.

"Shall we move on?" Cory finally said. He balled his napkin and threw it into the trash, followed by his cardboard coffee container. "Another couple of hours yet."

"Where are we going first when we get there?" Ben really had no idea where he was going or what he would be doing when he got there. Whatever. *Have debit card and mobile, will travel.*

Cory pulled out his mobile and checked something on the screen. "A place called Griffin Wood Hotel; it's about ten miles outside of Haworth." Cory looked at him expectantly.

"Close to Haworth is a good start," Ben offered. He only said it because he felt as if he should be saying something. The smile Cory gave him was hesitant but it lit up his face. Maybe Cory wasn't an idiot film guy who didn't read. Maybe he was just shy or something?

They were back in the Focus as dusk began to crawl across the sky. Ben knew it would be dark before they reached the hotel, and they wouldn't have much chance to breathe in the beauty of the moors on the way up. The change after the built-up Halifax area was absolutely stunning and sudden: from city to the Brontes' wild and windy moors. Shame they would be missing it tonight, but he supposed they would see enough in the morning.

"Would you like me to do some of the driving?" Ben asked as Cory started the engine.

"I'm fine," Cory replied. After buckling himself in and checking mirrors, Cory pulled out of the services and onto the slip road to the motorway, and they soon joined the snake of traffic north. Ben didn't press the subject of assisting with driving. In fact, he attempted to stay quiet for much of what was left of the journey as it was daunting for a foreign driver to be navigating new road and Cory really needed to concentrate.

Chapter Two

*C*ory was thankful he had the driving to keep himself occupied. There was no time to think about anything else when he was concentrating so damn hard on these roads. To be fair, this motorway was straight and as long as he remembered *keep left, keep left, keep left,* he should be okay. Ben had asked at the beginning if he could help with driving, but the car was insured for Cory and he didn't know what the insurance laws were like over here. Ben had subsided into silence and was looking out of his side window after their stop at the service station. Cory wasn't sure what he wanted, to have the peace or to hear Ben's voice. His voice was all gentle tones far removed from Hugh Grant and more redolent of Ewan McGregor when he was pretending to have the same voice as Sir Alec Guinness.

Ben was intriguing and all dark broody gorgeousness with his soulful brown eyes and near-black hair that curled and flicked around his face as if it had never seen a comb.

He was taller than Cory by at least a couple of inches. Cory was fascinated by the Englishman and his inability to sit still and be quiet. His company had definitely sent the packs out to the four lecturers but part of him was so pleased that it had been he who got to tell Ben what film they were scouting for. Ben was like a kid at Christmas. His brown eyes sparkled with enthusiasm and hell, the guy even quoted from the book. Cory liked that enthusiasm in a person.

The ex who had just phoned pleading for money, Tony Abney, never had that enthusiasm. He just thought everything was given to him on a platter and he never loved his project. He had gone full speed ahead making a film and then made Cory's fledgling company go through hell before refusing to pay for time taken when the film fell through due to lack of funding. Cory didn't care about the business or the money; he did care that Tony was now an ex-lover after selling a story about Josh Vasilyev's gay brother to the *National Enquirer* just to raise funds. The fucker. Luckily, if anything, it left Josh smelling of roses as the actor with what the blogs called, 'a really cute older brother'.

His cell vibrated and he touched his earpiece to take it hands free. Speak of the devil and he appears.

"Don't tell anyone, but I got the part." His brother's voice was clear and excited.

"Wow, Josh, that's freaking awesome," Cory answered immediately. He couldn't be prouder of his brother at this moment. The part Josh was talking about was in the steampunk murder mystery that Ben had mentioned set in London. Not a huge film in terms of budget or script, but it had Sony Pictures as a backer, and following on from the Sherlock Holmes films, Tinseltown was ripe for this kind of movie. The setting was faultless and Josh would be perfect in the role. He sensed Ben looking at him as soon as he mentioned the name Josh. He wasn't entirely sure why he had shared that Josh was his brother with someone he hardly knew. Hell, whenever he met anyone new he deliberately mumbled his surname. Vasilyev was too much of a freaky obvious household name now. There was just something about the slim, dark-haired lecturer with his serious eyes that screamed trustworthy. Not only that but he seemed like a genuinely nice guy, if a little excitable.

"Filming starts in three months," Josh continued. "Who is on the locations?"

"Not me this time."

"I was hoping it would be you." Josh didn't sound disappointed; he was just making an observation. It didn't matter if Cory was the one to scout or someone else. At the end of the day, Cory's people would find the right places. "There's all these abandoned Underground stations and I think they want to find one where Winston Churchill worked in the War. Winston-freaking-Churchill, bro."

Cory laughed. In a way his brother's enthusiasm reminded him a little of Ben. "I'm heading north to the costume drama," he said.

Josh groaned. "Who did they stick you with this time as your support?"

Cory chuckled. On his last scouting job he had ended up with this reclusive fisherman in Alaska who didn't actually speak to him for twenty days out of the three weeks. He and Josh had discussed it at length over beers.

Thing was, Cory wasn't ready to share Ben with his brother at this moment in time. He didn't analyze why. He simply forged ahead with explanation.

"We're staying in a small hotel," Cory said. Changing the subject was a good thing.

"He or she is with you, isn't he?" Josh was chuckling.

"Yes, in the car," Cory answered with his own laugh. He glanced down at the panel on the wheel and found the switch for full headlights. The evening was closing in but the satellite navigation system was showing they only had another fifty miles to go.

"He or she?" Josh pushed.

"Yes." Cory felt a smirk twist his lips. Fucking brother and his insistence on knowing every part of Cory's life.

"Oh," Josh said. "It's a guy. Is he gay? Hell, is he cute?"

Cory glanced at Ben, who was focusing on his own phone in his hands. Strong, capable hands on a guy who was probably a few inches taller than him, a curl in soft hair that fell in disarray around his face, and gorgeous kissable lips. Gay? Cute? Cory knew he could answer both questions very succinctly.

"He said so and hell yes."

"Nice," Josh chuckled. "Maybe he can help you decide whether you are opening the UK office at Pinewood."

"Ass." Cory smiled.

"Later." Josh ended the call.

Ben glanced across at him. Cory could see the move in his peripheral vision but Ben didn't say anything and for that, Cory was pleased. He wasn't able to share his brother's news and as to the cute thing? Ben really was very cute in a slim and wild and messy way. Very nice. This next short time could be quite interesting if Ben was up for some fun. And if meeting cute guys like Ben made it easier to decide on opening the new office then that could only be a good thing.

Chapter Three

The hotel was just what Ben expected. Built in the eighteen hundreds and made of local stone, it actually looked as if it had been part of the landscape since the dawn of time. The stones had weathered and the trees had crept close enough to touch. Beautiful. The structure was set back from the road and had parking for maybe ten cars to the front. This led Ben to believe that even with the wide frontage the place didn't spread that far back, something that was verified when the owners showed them to rooms four and five, Ben didn't see much past room seven.

When they were left outside the door of each room, it was Cory who immediately latched on to breakfast, which was available early in the morning. One perk of being away were the frankly awesome breakfasts and the time to actually sit and enjoy them. Too often back home Ben was racing out of the door on just orange juice and toast.

"So meet you in the breakfast room at seven?" Cory said expectantly.

"Seven?" Ben had been hoping for a lie-in given he was on his summer break.

"Sooner we start, sooner we finish," Cory said.

"I'm not sure we need to rush. Three weeks is a long time to explore."

"Three weeks at the outside." Cory frowned. "Hopefully this whole thing will take nothing more than a few days and we can both go home."

A few days? Ben saw his house deposit dwindle before his eyes.

"Don't worry though," Cory continued. "You'll still get paid for the three weeks. It's in all of our interests to get this thing done quickly. I am on a deadline."

Ben pushed down the disappointment. He had been looking forward to showing Cory the real moors, the real Wuthering Heights, and that would take more than a few days.

"Anyway, night." And with that Cory was in his room and Ben was looking at a shut door. Sighing, he let himself into his own room and flicked on the light. The area was cozy bordering on small, the main space was taken up by a huge king-sized bed in chunky oak. Thick dark drapes framed small-paned windows and he crossed to look out of them. He and Cory had been given rooms at the back of the hotel, but there was no view as such as the hotel was surrounded by trees on the three sides facing away from the road. Hugging his arms across his chest, he leaned his forehead against the window and allowed himself a moment to contemplate what was beyond those trees. Moors that stretched unending to the horizon, outcrops of limestone, and steps of rocks that dominated the otherwise green areas of pasture and the purple and brown heather of moorland. The carpet of heathers crept across the startlingly empty space that stretched to the horizon and braved every force that nature could throw at them. Tiny and tenacious, they clung to this place like Heathcliff had clung to his Catherine.

Chiding himself for wasting time, he unpacked the clothes he had crammed in the large wheeled case and eyed the items on the shelves. He had wondered why Cory's bag had been so small—nothing more than a carry-on and an extra sports-type bag. No wonder he had such a small amount of luggage if he was only expecting a few days scouting for the locations as opposed to the prearranged twenty-one.

For a minute Ben wondered if the hotel was paid up for the full three weeks. He could do with a proper holiday; he hadn't had one for a few years—not since university and his last hurrah with his uni friends for a whole week in Rome. Resolving to ask Cory in the morning, he prowled from one end of his small room to the other, from trouser press to kettle and tea bags. There wasn't really enough room to prowl though and briefly he considered going for a walk in the woods until he realized the windows were wet with the start of late evening rain.

Restless, he turned on his TV; it was coming up to ten pm and he had a choice between the news and a rerun of EastEnders. He couldn't face either so he turned off the TV and instead flopped back on his bed and stared up at the ceiling. He needed to get over the disappointment floating in his head. Somehow during the journey up here he had wound this story in his head where the two of them spent the entire three weeks immersed in Wuthering Heights and the dramatic scenery of Yorkshire. In this daydream Cory turned out to be gay and he and Cory had some kind of awesome-hot-sexy holiday fling. He'd never been with an American before. Come to think of it, he had never slept with anyone farther afield than the aptly named Patrick Reilly who was in his prose and poetry classes at college and came all the way from Southern Ireland.

Oh well. Given the three weeks had now been nixed to a few days it was probably equally as unlikely the gorgeous man in the next room was gay or even remotely bi-curious. His brother was the poster sex god for women everywhere, and if Cory was anything like his brother, then he was hetero city and had a parade of beauties passing through a revolving door. That was what Hollywood was like if Ben was to believe everything he read.

He had saved room in his case by not packing anything to sleep in. Boxers would do fine and after stripping the rest of his clothes, he climbed under the heavy quilt. It was only as he lay down that he realized he had left the light on. With a sigh, he climbed back out, but as he reached for the light switch, there was a knock on his door. He peered into the softly lit hallway to see a concerned, grumpy Cory in a T-shirt with his legs bare.

"It's probably something really simple but I can't figure out the TV, could you just… you know…"

Ben looked down at his boxers and bare chest and then up. Being half-naked wasn't normally an issue and Cory's intense gaze was focused most definitely above Ben's neck. Still, a small frisson of excitement insinuated itself into Ben's thoughts. Was the request nothing more than an excuse to get him into Cory's room? Glancing up and down the empty hall, he checked for anyone who would be offended by a man in his underwear and then with a bold grin he grabbed his key card and shut his door behind him.

Cory's room was very similar to his although the bed was a lighter wood and Cory's bag sat in the middle of it still full of clothes. Maybe he wasn't unpacking given the whole only-a-few-days thing.

"I tried to get it to turn on but I couldn't." Cory sounded frustrated and he slumped down on to the bed. Ben was not looking at the edge of underwear he could see under the T-shirt nor the adorably grumpy face that was probably inwardly cursing all things English.

Ben leaned over the TV and followed the lead to the socket where the plug was pushed in. The whole thing was turned off at the wall. After flicking the switch the theme tune to EastEnders filled the room and he dove quickly for the control to dim the sound. Well that was an easy fix and needed none of his expertise at coaxing old TVs to work. Didn't American TV plugs need to be turned on at the wall?

"There. It was just not switched on at the wall," Ben explained. He turned to face Cory and almost swallowed his tongue. Cory had decided to remove his T-shirt, revealing acres of toned, tanned skin with a soft furring of chest hair and a treasure trail that led to all kinds of imaginable sin. Coughing to cover his embarrassment and hoping to hell he could leave before his erection joined them in the room, he handed the control over to Cory.

Cory was clearly having nothing of Ben's escape and instead launched into talking.

"Sorry if I was a bit short with you in the car. I have an ex who is an asshole and I haven't stopped the last few weeks. I think it's caught up with me." Yawning behind his other hand, he stretched.

"No worries," Ben said. A stretching, sleepy, mostly naked guy was sending heat to his groin quicker than a Roger Bannister mile. Quickly he headed for the door and expected a thank you and a goodnight. Instead he got something very different. Questions.

"What is this EastEnders about? I've seen it sometimes on BBC America, some kind of soap opera? Or is it one those real-life fly-on-the-wall things?"

"It's a soap set in London—kind of famous here."

"I like it. Maybe if I watch it I will learn something about living in London," Cory said finally. Ben realized he still stood in boxers in front of his employer with a semi-erect dick. He could feel the blush rising from his toes.

"Night then," Ben offered.

Cory slithered up the bed in small sinuous movements, the pull of the sheets on his jockeys revealing more toned skin. "Thank you, Ben. Goodnight."

Ben opened the door and looked back at Cory who had leaned back on a selection of puffed up pillows and kept his eyes fixated to the screen. One of his hands had come to rest on his stomach and was splayed invitingly with the small finger pointing the way to heaven. Ben groaned to himself at the view and then shut the door. Back in his room and under the quilt he thought he had never really seen anything as oddly erotic and yet cute as a half-naked

Cory Vasilyev watching a soap opera. Endearing and cute wasn't supposed to make you hard. Cute was just that— sweet. It wasn't sexy or hot or anything guaranteed to give Ben a hard-on. Clearly his dick was focusing on the eroticism of that splayed hand on bare skin.

Typical.

Chapter Four

*C*ory pushed his bag to the floor with an irritated huff as soon as Ben shut the door. The bag was so tightly packed with scripts and notebooks that nothing fell out. He genuinely hadn't been able to get the damn TV to work but he hadn't really needed to call Ben in. Cory had his phone, he had his iPad, he could have used either of those. After all, the hotel did display a sign for WiFi. What the hell had possessed him to call in his companion for anything as stupid as a TV? Attraction. That is what it was. Ben was all flicky curly-haired geeky guy and Cory loved that kind of man. Fun to be with. Intelligent. And in Ben's case, hot. Tony had been the ex from hell, and that was the last time Cory was entering into a long-term relationship based on beauty. Boy had Tony been a pretty one, but behind the wide, white-teeth smile had been a vast empty nothingness. Ben was gorgeous as well but in a rough and unsettling way and he had a brain. Cory found himself spending more time looking into brown eyes than focusing south of the man's belt. That was certainly a new one.

Part of him had hoped Ben would be ready for bed and that plenty of that long body would be on show. By the look of what was in Ben's underwear it would seem Ben was ready for more than bed. Cory wondered if it was him that had done that or had Ben been in his room choking the chicken. The guy was hot. Not solid with made-for-movie muscles but lithe and compact and covered in all that cool, pale skin holding together a bundle of unrestrained energy.

Unbidden Cory's hand was on his own dick, slowly bringing his hard-on to full strength while watching someone with ginger hair shout at some older guy. When he came over his hand it was a mere minute after the end of the show. He hadn't wanted to interrupt the story, which had been interesting, and he'd always been good at timing things.

Maybe he should have admitted he was gay and they could have taken it from there. Ben could be laid out next to him at this very moment. Why wasn't he? Cory groaned. He was a freaking idiot. So how to go about this? All he had to do was flash some more flesh, make it obvious he was interested, oh and of course just tell Ben he was gay and available for fun.

On most location journeys, he found someone to be with and here was Ben *actually* gay and *actually* interested if his dick was any guide, so Cory didn't even have to go looking for a fuck. Easy, no-complications sex was available in the next room.

A few days here with maybe some random casual sex with the irrepressible Ben Hyland was something Cory could sign up for but the British man would be the last one. Casual no-holds sex was awesome when you were in your twenties, but he was thirty-one now and spontaneous fucking was starting to wear him down. It was time to do what his brother kept saying he should. Get back to America and organize himself.

Just because he was gay didn't mean there wasn't a life partner somewhere for him. His brother kept saying that. Cory's reply was always 'hell, not every gay in Tinseltown was Neil Patrick Harris.'

He told Josh that but all Josh could say was that he should stop with the casual sex in foreign countries and find a good hot and available American that he could build a life with. Someone who worked in the backrooms of film maybe, a producer, a director, or hell, even a guy who had nothing to do with film but was one hundred percent patient with Cory jetting off to other countries on location searches. There had to be someone like this out there for him. Quick hookups were starting to bore him and Ben, if indeed anything happened with Ben, would have to be his last if he was to stay sane.

He wanted someone special who wouldn't stamp all over him or only want in his pants because of who his brother was.

When he got home it was time for the search to begin.

Chapter Five

"So tell me a bit about other locations you scout so I know what I need to show you," Ben said. Breakfast was finished and they were both nursing coffee in the empty dining room.

"Our company maybe does ten or so overseas locations and only for the big budget studios like Sony."

"What do the smaller studios do then? Do they have scouts?"

"In Hollywood itself there is a wealth of places that can be used to stand in for anything a script requires. Desert, mountains, high-plains grassland, small-town New England, Paris, downtown New York, London, it's pretty much all there."

"I'm not imagining there's the Eiffel tower sitting under the sign."

"No, no Eiffel Tower as such, or your Big Ben, but when you film against green screen you can add enough details to existing Studio City locations to make it seem like you are filming in Paris or London."

"So why are you even here if, as you say, most of the film could be captured using green screen?"

"Sony wants authenticity and they're big enough to be able to afford it. They're not saying that the actors will be brought over here, just that test film would provide enough to build the movie around."

"That's kind of sad."

"How so?"

"Imagine the churchyard where Catherine is buried—"

"I told you I haven't read the book—"

"You said. But… look, have you not even read cheat notes?" Ben couldn't believe Cory had no idea of the story he was looking at.

"I skimmed the script." Cory looked hopeful but Ben wasn't reinforcing that lame attempt at knowing the story.

"But you will read the script in full?"

"I'll read the parts looking for location."

"That's not right." Ben wished he could retract his heated statement as Cory looked over the rim of his coffee cup and raised his eyebrow in question. For a few seconds Ben contemplated sitting back in his chair and being quiet. Then the academic in him, the one who loved *Wuthering Heights* with all of its passion and life, jumped to the fore like a kid high on candy.

"*It was dug on a green slope in a corner of the kirk-yard, where the wall was so low that the heath and bilberry-plants have climbed over it from the moor…*" he quoted. "That is the place where Catherine is buried in the book. She had chosen a spot where she could be close to the wild moors of her youth, but her heart was at Wuthering Heights. Unless you have read that passage, if indeed there is any notation of it in the script, then how can you know what you are looking for?"

Cory leaned over the table and very deliberately said, "This is what we pay you for, you show me what I need to know." His voice held a note of affection in that low growl, and the hint of a smile ghosted his lips.

"Haworth first," Ben stated simply. "We need to get you a copy of the book, or at least a cheat's overview, and I need to read the script."

Cory stood and stretched, covering a yawn with his hand.

"Let's go then."

Haworth wasn't that far from the hotel, and in the space of an hour the two men sat in a cozy tea room on the corner of the high street with tea for Ben, coffee for Cory, and a selection of cakes on a plate. The time may well have been nearing eleven but Ben could not face more food so the cake samples on his plate remained untouched. Cory however was digging in and for a moment Ben wondered where the guy put it. Then he imagined that in LA Cory probably ate some faddy Hollywood diet and this was the first real nutritionally valueless food he had eaten in his life. When Cory grinned with a mouthful of chocolate fudge cake Ben decided he so was not sharing that observation with Cory. Not when what he really wanted to do was lick into that mouth and taste the chocolate inside. It didn't help when Cory's tongue darted out to lick a stray crumb. Jesus, he wished the guy would stop doing that.

Cory, for his part, looked down with one hand on cake

and the other turning pages in a full copy of *Wuthering Heights*. His forehead was creased in a frown. The older English language was sometimes not easy to break into but persevering always helped. Ben had the script lying unopened in front of him. God how he hoped that the movie wasn't going to screw with the story. He hoped that this was going to be a film that choked him and held him in the same thrall as the book, but to open the script and see page one was terrifying him. The front of it was emblazoned with several warnings about sharing and Cory had underlined these when he handed it over. While not a big blockbuster, any details leaked could be costly for the studio.

Sipping on hot tea, Ben finally opened page one and groaned.

[Ext.] sweeping shot of moors. Some heather. A crumbling house.

[voiceover] {In the year of our Lord...}

Someone had scribbled 'James Earl Jones or same' in the margin on page one. James Earl Jones? Wasn't he the voice of that Lion? And Darth Vader? Ben did not for one minute associate the guy with Wuthering Heights. Oh well. Surely it had to get better.

Chapter Six

*C*ory was lost. Chapter one and two passed in a blur of information but it was chapter three that was pulling him in. When Ben spoke all Cory felt was irritation at being interrupted.

"The script is a good interpretation given the restrictions of film and time," Ben was saying.

"Good," Cory replied then buried his head back in the book.

"Where you up to?"

"The ghost bit. Shhh."

After that Ben seemed to get the hint and Cory managed to get to the part where the book started to focus on Heathcliff.

"Here," he announced. He stopped reading and poked at the text with his finger. "I want to see what you think Thrushcross Grange looks like. And Wuthering Heights."

"All in one day?" Ben asked.

Cory bit back his sarcastic reply as Ben looked genuinely confused at the question.

"As much as we can," Cory replied. He could always tack on an extra day to his 'few days' he was staying. Tucking his copy of the book into his backpack, he stood, shouldered the bag, and waited. Ben got the hint, scrabbling to pick up the script and the notes and the pencils. Finally both of them were in the car and Cory, following Ben's instructions, pointed it out of Haworth and into the moors.

The landscape changed even more if that was possible. Haworth itself was softer than the wilds outside of it. From tearooms and B&Bs the road twisted higher and almost back on itself for miles before Ben finally said they should stop. The images in Cory's head, of a ghostly hand grabbing through a broken window, and the description of Thrushcross Grange and the Heights itself were lodged firmly in his mind, and as he stood outside the car and the wind blew a dance around him it felt as if the story was around him as well as inside him. The wind was cold and insistent and for a second Cory paused and just inhaled the cool English air. Where Ben had told him to stop, some kind of viewpoint off the side of the road, had stunning views from the top of the moors and spreading downwards to the horizon.

"Want to walk?" Ben asked.

"Where?"

"I don't know if it's still there, but when I was studying this book for my degree I found this place. It's about half an hour walk out from here."

Cory agreed and Ben pulled his backpack from the rear of the car. Both men already wore decent footwear so just pulled on jackets.

"The weather isn't predictable on the moors," Ben had said back at the hotel. In his rucksack Cory had another jacket, water, food, and various other items Ben had deemed important. Hell, it wasn't like they were mountain climbing but Cory didn't argue. Local knowledge was what they paid these guys for.

Ben led the way, which gave Cory an interesting view of his guide's ass in form-hugging jeans. He could watch the play of muscles as the man pushed up the incline and jumped the small and numerous running rivulets of water carving into the peaty soil. The farther they climbed and dipped the more remote everything appeared. Apart from a few sheep and some tire tracks there was little to mark humanity of any kind. After what must have been half an hour, Ben stopped and stood for a while scanning the options for where to go next. Decisively he led Cory over another peak until finally he indicated an outcrop of stone as they passed it.

"Just past here is this awesome old place that I think would have made a perfect Wuthering Heights," Ben said and then quickened his pace.

A thrill of anticipation buzzed inside Cory and he wasn't disappointed.

A large and mostly derelict house lay nestled between another granite outcrop and a steeply climbing, roughly grassed area. Probably the environment it sat in was the one thing that had protected it somewhat from destruction by storm and snow. Stones upon stones tumbled and piled around what was definitely the remains of a house, Cory was sure. He pulled out his camera. There was no way in hell a camera crew could film anything here but the inspiration for the house would be perfect. Making a note of the longitude and latitude of the place, he began to take photos, following Ben as they skirted the remains and moved out the back. Behind the house the ground leveled out for a while before sweeping down to where Cory knew the road lay.

"This could be the kitchen," Ben said enthusiastically.

Cory looked up at him; Ben was standing on a step of stones, which put him a head higher. There was desire in the guy's eyes. From what he had read so far, this place was pretty damn perfect for Wuthering Heights itself. What was in Ben wasn't pretend and green screen, it was pure passion for what was here and it was real.

It was sexy and all kinds of hot.

Jeez. He hadn't even had the whole 'I'm gay' conversation with Ben yet nor issued the standard disclaimer of wanting nothing more than a few days of hot and heavy sex.

"I'm gay," Cory blurted out. "Too," he added as an afterthought.

"Okay," Ben replied and then he jumped down the small step to move off. Cory grabbed without aim and managed to snag Ben's arm. With slow, deliberate intent he pulled Ben closer, and for his part Ben wasn't arguing. Long expectant seconds passed. Finally they were so close that even with the sound of the wind outside their small oasis of calm Cory swore he could hear Ben breathing.

"Just a few days," Cory whispered. There, he'd said what needed to be said. Thing is, even he wasn't sure what he meant. A few days to kiss and make love or a few days since they met and *jeez fuck what the hell is going on*?

Ben initiated the kiss and it was heat and fire and Cory whimpered as he parted his lips and returned the open kiss with equal desire. The taste of Ben was intoxicating, his skin cold to touch but his lips hot. The kiss deepened, both men tilting their heads and gripping jackets to hold each other upright. The first spit of rain landed on Cory's forehead and he ignored it. The sensations inside him just from a simple kiss were intense, and he needed so much more of Ben. He wanted to climb inside him and hold him close. Rain didn't matter. Nothing mattered. Ben pulled back with a huff and Cory chased for the kiss. He didn't want to stop.

"It's raining," Ben protested. "Shelter here or go back to the car?"

Cory contemplated the options with his hands still gripping Ben's coat.

"Stay here," he murmured then closed in for another kiss. Evidently his body had decided the taste of Ben was addictive and Cory could not get enough.

Ben was obviously the one thinking straight as, still kissing, he backed them up to the overhanging granite. The rain ceased its spattering marks the moment they were under the shelter. Madness splintered inside Cory as Ben held him and then turned them so it was Cory who was pushed back against the rock. Ben cushioned the press of his back with one hand but Cory didn't want that, he wanted to feel being trapped between rock and Ben. He released the grip on Ben's jacket material and instead crossed his hands around the Ben's back, pulling him that much closer. A small shift from the taller Ben and suddenly they were as close as you could be without removing your clothes. Cory released the kiss and tilted his head back to the rock to breathe the cold, rain-tinged air. Ben didn't stop though, he simply took the opportunity to trace a pattern of need with tongue and lips from Cory's chin to his pulse and back. Pushing aside the Cory's collar, Ben tasted skin. It felt so right to Cory, then Ben's free hand was up and under Cory's jacket.

"Jesus. Fuck," Cory exclaimed at the icy touch of cold hands to warm skin. Ben made to move back with a chuckle low in his throat.

"It's warmer if we take this back to our rooms," Ben whispered against his skin.

"I don't want to move," Cory said. "I like it here. Kissing you."

"I want to do more than kissing," Ben said. Cory looked up into dark brown eyes and a face framed with dark curls and was blown away. The anxiety built in the pit of his stomach at the same rate lust was rising. This wasn't how he normally felt. With casual hookups he normally entertained a few days interlude of satisfying sex. The intensity in Ben's expression, so dark and stormy and penetrating, was too much. Too serious.

"We shouldn't," he said. Clumsily he extricated himself from Ben's hold, and breathing heavily, he took a step to the side and away from Ben's reach. The rain was thick, a curtain that separated the real world of the moors from their hideaway under the rock.

"Shouldn't what?" Ben asked. He looked confused and Cory didn't blame the guy.

"I don't want to," Cory stated with finality.

"Okay," Ben answered. He shrugged and moved away to stand just one step from the rain. "No worries."

They stood in silence for a while and Ben pulled his jacket hood up. He turned to face Cory.

"Let's go," he said with a wide grin. Then with a few steps he had moved out into the rain.

The sheeting water had slowed a little and there was even some blue sky showing at the edges of the storm clouds. The air smelled of rain and Cory simply pulled his hood around his face and trudged back to the car in the wake of Ben's footsteps. He stumbled a few times before he realized he wasn't concentrating at all on the path Ben was taking. This way he'd be lucky if he didn't end up with a broken leg or something equally dire. Hurrying his steps a little, he caught up with Ben, who looked at him briefly with another of his intriguing smiles.

Ben didn't appear pissed with him although he had every right to be. What kind of guy leads another man on and then pushes him away with something as crass as 'I don't want to'. *I'm a fucking idiot is what I am.* They made it back to the car much faster than the climb up the hill and it was only when they had shucked jackets and clambered into the small Ford with the doors shut that Cory knew he could talk.

Cory went to start the engine but then stopped and touched Ben gently on the knee.

"I'm sorry." He imbued his words with as much meaning as he could but wished it could be more.

"No biggie," Ben said softly. "Honestly. Let's get back to the hotel and get showers then compare notes."

"I need to read some more," Cory said. He really

wanted to get further into this book and find out more about the ghost of Cathy and how the moors fitted the story. That would surely give the brain in his pants time to convince the brain in his head it was more than okay to just have a short fling with the sexy Brit sitting next to him.

The journey back to the hotel was quiet but comfortable, and when they separated to go into their own rooms Cory had more or less convinced himself that he could pull his head out of his ass and enjoy fun times with Ben. After his shower. After he had read more of *Wuthering Heights*. After dinner.

Chapter Seven

*B*en was disappointed. Way past that, actually. Cory was hot and Ben had been convinced that there was going to be a coming together of momentous proportions. He had never, and he meant never, kissed anyone like that before. Like it consumed them from the inside and there was no need for breath. Ben still had the taste of the man on his tongue, warm skin and the touch of rain. He wasn't sure what to do with all the emotions and need rolling around inside him. So he did what he did best, stiff upper lip and all that bloody nonsense and then had a wank in the shower. It took the edge off the need and the lust but it didn't clear his head of the strange glimpses of emotion in Cory's eyes. Cutting them dead with a simple 'I don't want to' was enough to throw a bucket of ice water over Ben's head, and he wished he could understand where he had gone wrong.

Maybe he'd come across as a bit pushy? Should he have been polite and not initiated moving Cory back against the wall? Ben was a definite switch but maybe Cory wasn't. Hell. That was probably it.

Satisfied with his summing up of the whole crap situation, he dressed in clean, dry jeans and pulled on a shirt. Buttoning it up as he looked in the mirror, he paused as he fiddled with the top buttons. Eyes drawn to the juncture of neck and shoulder he recalled where he had kissed and tasted Cory's skin. Groaning, he remembered the taste and texture. Fuck. This was never going to leave him, was it?

"Bloody hell," he snapped at his reflection. "Pull yourself the hell together, man. Not everyone wants a string-bean English lecturer."

The talking-to helped, and straightening his spine, he began to open the door. Distracted by the sudden thought that he didn't have his key card, he was caught off guard as Cory barreled into his room and slammed the door shut behind him. Wild-eyed he stood with his back to the door and his palms flat against the wood.

"You okay?" Ben asked concerned. "What's wrong?"

"This book doesn't end well, does it? I saw things unraveling so I read the last chapter."

"No, it doesn't end well."

"And the script ends the same?"

"Yes."

"Fuck." Cory slumped a little against the door and Ben took a step forward. Crazy Yank was clearly having some kind of mental breakdown.

"Cory—"

"Don't talk," Cory said. "Let me talk for a bit."

Ben nodded and took a few steps back so he could sit

on the side of the bed. Emotions snapped on Cory's face and Ben couldn't even begin to identify a single one.

"I'm genuinely sorry about what happened on the moors today," Cory began.

"It's fine." It wasn't but Ben didn't like to make people think he was upset about anything.

"No, it's not fine. Look, I had this partner. Started off the same as you. Just a short break fuck in a foreign country." Ben tried not to let the words hurt, but let's face it, they'd only known each other two days, what did Ben expect? Declarations of forever were not thrown about after two days. What they were starting today was really going to be nothing more than just a few days together to ease the itch of need. "He was an asshole."

"Who?"

"The ex. Met him in Canada and he followed me back to LA. He was in films. Jeez. It's a long story. He was my possibly forever guy, or at least my next-few-years guy. Cut a long story short, what he was financing went south and he sold some shit about me and my brother to the *National Enquirer*. I don't give a damn about me but he pulled Josh into it and made a couple hundred thousand out of it all."

"Oh, that's not good," Ben said. He wanted to say more, but relationships were difficult to talk about at the best of times. "No wonder you didn't want to get involved with anyone. I am so sorry he broke your heart like that."

Cory snorted.

"Broke my heart? I hadn't given him that much power. More like made me think anything more than casual sex was dangerous."

"You didn't love him?"

"No."

"I'm not really following all this," Ben said. He rubbed his temples with his fingers. Cory was making absolutely no sense.

"It's all Josh's fault." Cory stepped away from the door and stalked towards the bed. He moved into Ben's space and in response Ben leaned back. A well-placed shove from Cory and he was flat on his back with his feet on the floor. Cory clambered to straddle his lap, and wasn't that all kinds of fucking brilliant? "He said I should start looking for a forever guy, you know, start a family, settle down, actually open an office at Pinewood to expand the whole company."

"You're getting an office here?" Ben couldn't keep the shock out of his voice. Pinewood was no more than thirty minutes from where he lived. That fact held much more promise than an ocean separating them.

"It makes sense, because a lot of the films I scout for end up filming at Pinewood, and it wouldn't hurt to have a European office," he said. Crouching over, he ground himself down on Ben and suddenly Ben was under no illusion that Cory didn't want him. He was hard and ready and Ben was too. "So I find this guy and I start to plan a future, a place here, a place in LA, and then he turns out to be a complete asshole. There was no way he could be anything special for me and I resign myself to the fact that I'm going to be doing this alone. Then I meet *you*."

Cory stopped moving, and suddenly as still as a statue, he simply stared down at Ben.

"Not once did Tony-I-want-your-brother's-money-

Abney make me feel the way you make me feel," he began. "Not once did he make me think I wanted to stand in the rain and wind in the middle of Yorkshire and kiss until there was no air left in my lungs. Not once did he make me imagine that there was anything other than sex at the end of it all." He paused and his gaze skimmed Ben's face. "You see, I don't want sex with you."

Ben wriggled under Cory. If Cory didn't want sex then he was surely going about this the wrong way. Ben didn't want sex either but he meant it in an entirely different way. He wanted to make love and kiss until there was nothing left but the two of them. So sue him if he was the intense type of guy.

"I want to make love to you," Cory said. His voice was a whisper. His lips hovered over Ben's and the small puffs of breath smelled of peppermint toothpaste. "And kiss you until we forget where we are."

"I just said that," Ben offered weakly.

"When?" Cory looked a little confused as he placed a gentle kiss to Ben's lips, a whisper of a touch and nothing more.

"In my head," Ben answered.

"In your head, see, that's why I like you."

"Because I have conversations in my head?"

"Because what you say, what comes out of your mouth, is real." Cory deepened the kiss and for a few minutes Ben got with the plan and simply enjoyed the taste and the touch. When the kisses grew heated Ben wasn't even sure whose hands were where, as jeans and underwear hit the floor and then his shirt and Cory's. Finally he was naked and under Cory—exactly where he wanted to be right at this moment. With muttered curses and whispered commands, they learned what they wanted, and when Cory wanted more Ben was so very ready.

"I don't normally do this," he said. "Not after just two days—" Cory kissed a path to his heavy dick and teased him, biting marks of possession into Ben's hips. Ben suddenly lost the ability to form a coherent sentence when a hot mouth closed over the end of his dick and a lubed finger circled him and pressed and teased. Everything was over embarrassingly quickly for Ben but when Cory fell onto his back he had evidently come just while giving Ben a blow job.

"More," Cory said. He rolled on his side and stole a kiss. "More reading *Wuthering Heights*, more walking on the moors, more kissing and making love, more of you."

"I can go with that," Ben said.

"Three weeks," Cory said gently. He laid his head on Ben's chest. "Let's see how much we can fall in love in three weeks."

"You're staying the whole three weeks?" Ben asked. Hope flared inside him that the man in his arms would be around a lot longer.

"We could finish here then maybe scout some places for the company?"

"I'd like that," Ben replied.

Cory chuckled. "After all, tell me why I would ever think of leaving my maybe-forever guy?"

Ben had so many questions but he could only focus on one. "You think I could be that to you, already?"

"Don't you think that about me?" Cory asked the

question softly and there was determination in his expression.

Ben did. Ben felt a connection with this man that he had never felt before. Strong, unbreakable, full of promise, and very new. Forget the practicalities of who lived where and did what with whomever. This felt right and he wanted to try for more. So much more.

"I do. My maybe-forever guy. I like that. It sounds right." Ben said. He slid a hand between them until it closed around Cory's hard length. "Ready for round two?"

"As long as we never reach the final round I'm happy, Ben. Let's do this thing."

THE END

Valentine 2525

Max never wanted a Companion, but his family and society leave him no choice.

Samekh Taw designation #65572—aka "Sam"—is the Companion created in a laboratory, to Max's specifications.

Working and then falling in love with Sam is easy, but when it becomes clear that Sam believes he is flawed, it's up to Max to convince him to hold their secrets close.

And more importantly, to show Sam that love is never just for one day.

Chapter 1

"*W*hen will you sort your life out? There is no point in going back and looking at all this old information."

Max Absolom raised his gaze from the papers that were crumbled and torn, sitting in the archive fluid for regeneration. He didn't want to have this conversation again, and he sighed, noisily.

"There is *always* a point in a record of history, Senator."

"Will you ever just call me Dad?"

Max wrinkled his nose and glanced around his laboratory absently, blinking at the false daylight that poured in from the floor-to-ceiling holograms, wondering when Aston, the station computer, had decided to switch from night to day.

"It's morning?"

Max was a space rat. He'd been born aboard a freighter on its way from Berris Major to New Earth. His daily life was dictated by the onboard computer's idea of time. To

Max, it seemed there was no rhyme or reason behind the system of hours. It certainly didn't seem to follow a typical day on his home planet. "It wasn't morning when I started work," he muttered, raking his fingers through his hair that desperately needed cutting.

His dad sighed.

"Son, it's *been* morning, and now it's the afternoon."

"I was in the middle of a translation," Max said, defending his lack of time awareness, and then frowned. *Why has Dad come to the lab again? Oh yes. Telling me there's no point in history. Hasn't he done that already this year?*

"We learn from the past," Max finally blurted out, trying to pull the conversation back to his passion and away from whatever the Senator really wanted that made him trek all this way to visit his son. His dad waved off the comment. It was no more than Max expected. The Senator was firmly entrenched with both feet in the present and looking to the future. He wasn't precisely dismissive about Max and his research; after all, he relied on what history had taught him to make reasoned decisions for the future. No, the Senator had a history that he accepted, and he didn't want to hear what he said were the fairy tales of an ancient world.

"Maybe the recent past, but learning about the twenty-first century tells us nothing new."

"I disagree."

"I'm not here to discuss this, you're twenty-five now, and it's getting close to the Day of Choosing, son. Your mother says I need to address the issue of obtaining a

Companion with you as you have not chosen a mate for yourself."

Max winced inwardly. He knew it was a difficult situation for his parents and many a heated debate focused on the subject. To Max's mind Companions existed solely to sustain the human population. Since he wasn't interested in either females or breeding, there didn't seem a point in finding a partner in any natural way, or in ordering a Companion to his specifications. He braced himself for another reasoned discussion, his defense firmly established in his mind.

His da, with a concerned look on his face, handed him a chip labeled with the Companion Program insignia.

"You will need this for the Day of Choosing."

"I was hoping to avoid that altogether," he offered carefully, but his father just shook his head.

"Your mother worries about you being on your own. Just choose one. You can always exchange whatever you order for another if you don't like the first one."

"I don't want—"

"I got you dispensation for a male." Silence. Max blinked and stared at his dad. Dispensations for human same-gender matching were rarer than the missing moons that used to circle Berris Minor. Procreation would always be the dominant theme in all Companion matching.

Max reached for the card, flicking it over in his palm as the words hovered above it, suspended in midair. *Companion Choice from Absolom Labs.* He should have known.

"I didn't know our Labs had invested in the Companion Program." His suspicious nature immediately questioned the sudden presence of Absolom Labs' hand in that particular pie.

"We didn't. We do now. Hence the dispensation." Max stared down at it for a short while, then looked up to tell his father that he really didn't need a Companion. To his dismay, the Senator had left, and once again, Max sat alone in his section of the laboratory complex. He flicked at one side of the card, and a softly modulated voice enquired after his day. He ignored the voice and instead spoke his key code, then waited until his saved search was retrieved. He had visited the Companion Lab once before, a visit his mom and dad had guilted him into, and he had entered his dreams onto the tiny chip that would record them for eternity. A soft, feminine voice repeated back his preselected requests.

"*Male. Twenty-seven New Earth years of age. Hair dark, curls, eyes blue. Characteristics: compassion and an interest in Origin Earth history. Sexual orientation: homosexual (status male)*." The voice stopped. A warning —a blue holographic triangle—flashed before him, and the voice issued an addendum. "*I regret to inform that chosen module, Origin Earth history, is not available at this time. As alternatives, Absolom Labs is pleased to offer you a choice between the popular Advanced Plutonic Physics Module or the renowned Medical Assistance Module*." The voice paused, apparently waiting for a response, and Max considered the two options available to him. Plutonic *freaking* physics or medical assistance? Who the hell wanted either of those? He required someone who would sit and talk Origin Earth history with him, not bore him to death or bandage a paper cut.

"Other alternatives?" he questioned, listening as one by one the options scrolled by in the same calm voice. None of them jumped out at him, so he took the best of the bad. "I'll take Sentient Science." It was the only arm of science that he was remotely interested in, the part of Origin Earth science that had led to the genetics war in 2213.

"Your choice has been logged. Please ensure you forward the authorization code to arrange collection of your companion."

And that was that. The single string of characters and a few numbers were the stamp of his Companion.

Samekh Taw #65572.

Chapter 2

"I'm calling you Sam," Max said as they descended the stairs from Absolom Labs to the subterranean transport. Picking up his order had been straightforward. There were forms to be signed, instructions on bonding to the Companions internal chip, and that was it, he was good to go.

"Sam? I like that," his Companion, now Sam, responded in a deep, carefully modulated voice, as they were jostled by a group of technicians climbing the other way, Max cursed under his breath. This was not the image of rich-guy-who-had-everything he wanted to portray to his new Companion.

"Damn it; I should have organized transport to avoid using the public system."

Sam stopped suddenly, pulling on Max's sleeve to stop him. The Companion had one foot on step twelve, one on thirteen; it put him at eye level with Max. It amazed Max that not one person on their way down the stairs complained that he was in the way. Sam was a formidable figure, and Max could rattle off the statistics of height, weight, eye color, and hair type as a list. What he couldn't have told anyone was that all of those attributes wrapped up in this package were so overwhelming to the senses. He had seen a few other *Samekh Taw* Companions when he went to collect his, a couple of females and another male. The females, to him, were pale, slim and waif like, but he guessed whoever had ordered them considered them to be stunningly beautiful. He had no valid opinion on females when it came down to it, so he kept quiet.

As for the other men there, they'd been created shorter than Sam and were all blond with brown eyes, and whoever had requested them had a different idea of the beauty of the male form.

Then there was *his* Samekh Taw—stunning, sexy, stubbled, a hint of danger, just what Max had erotic dreams about. Someone strong. His Sam had all of this, as people sidled around him with glances that varied from appreciation to apprehension. Nothing marked him outwardly as a Companion; the ownership mark was hidden below his dark jacket. Still, Max didn't want to bring too much attention to his new purchase.

Sam touched him gently on the arm.

"Please, Max, don't worry about me. I know all about this transport system, and I am excited to be here."

"You have excitement?" Max hissed under his breath. He was confused; he hadn't requested that emotion.

"I have the basics. We all do," Sam's tone inferred that Max should have known.

"I didn't know."

"Did you not read the manual?" Sam looked so damn

serious, and all of a sudden, Max felt the embarrassment rise. He should have been more prepared.

"You come with a manual?" he finally choked out. Sam smirked and punched Max gently on the arm.

"Of course not." He smiled and then started to walk again. Max began to following slowly behind, finally having to scurry to catch up.

"Wait, I never ordered a sense of humor." Sam stopped again and looked down at Max, that damn infuriating smile still carved deep into his beautiful face.

"You make me smile," Sam said, then tilted his head to one side, clearly considering Max before leaning towards him and placing a gentle kiss to his lips. Max stepped back and away, glancing around at anyone who may have seen it. No one would be bothered about two grown human men kissing on a community concourse, but he wasn't used to public displays of affection, and it unnerved him, even if no one could tell Sam was a Companion.

"That was highly inappropriate in a civic place," he muttered, pressing his fingers against his lips and pushing down the wave of lust that coursed through his body. He snapped back from staring at the advertisement for the new Samekh Taw line, debating whether his Sam could be identified in the moving images.

"Oh" was all Sam said. The smile disappeared from his face. His lips were a tight line, and his shoulders slumped as he turned and made for the gates to the subway. Max waited, stunned that his big strong man had become a visibly hurt, sad, and reflective mess.

Well, I sure as hell never ordered sulking.

Chapter 3

*T*he journey back to his home on the floating city-ship *Ark Royal* was made in silence. Max wasn't sure what he should be saying to his new Companion. He was painfully lacking in experience and had no reference points.

His new mate spent the time sat upright in his seat observing his surroundings, apparently enamored with both the shuttle flight and the frankly sexual entertainment provided by the newly matched couple in the places across from them.

"Do you have any questions?" Max asked carefully.

"About?" Sam turned to him with an interested expression on his face.

"Your new life on the ship maybe?"

"Yes. I should ask some questions."

"Okay." Max waited expectantly, imagining the questions his companion might have.

"You will require sex, I assume?"

Max spat his water all over the back of the chair in front of him and blinked at Sam, wide-eyed.

"Erm…" Max cleared his throat with a cough. *Wasn't that the reason they were together?*

"It's fine." Sam waved the reaction away. "I'm human; I will need sex too."

"Fine," Max repeated weakly, his breathing still a little ragged. He sipped cautiously on the water again, hoping Sam was finished speaking with such blunt honesty. The thing is, he hadn't finished talking. Not at all.

"I don't mind switching, so whatever way you decide." Sam was thoughtful, even going so far as to pat Max on the knee.

"Do you—can you—are you—" Max tried so damn hard to form a sentence. Really hard. Sam just quirked an eyebrow and half smiled.

"Who becomes the dominant partner is not a decision you need to make now," Sam finally offered. "I'm just throwing it out there, so we are clear."

"Thank you." He stared into Sam's eyes, and something niggled at the back of his mind. When he'd ordered blue eyes, he hadn't ordered any particular strength of blue. He had just asked for blue. Normal, everyday blue. The cerulean sheen, as blue as the oceans, changeable, sparking with intensity, was a gift he hadn't expected. He was a firm believer that the truth of people shone in their eyes. Not the color of them, of course, but the way gazes would tilt away in shyness or guile or engage you directly in anger or honesty. Sam's beautiful eyes were a nice touch for which he would send a thank you to the Labs.

They docked just before the sleep phase, that time where the *Ark Royal* existed in gathering darkness, mimicking dusk, and the corridors of steel were only this side of softened in the dwindling light. By the time Max had Sam in his quarters, fake darkness had started to descend, and he felt ready for relaxation.

With no small amount of pride, he showed Sam the sleep chambers. He had three interconnected spaces, one of the perks of being the ship's Historian and damn rich to boot. Of course, chamber three, the largest of the rooms, was more of an office, given over to the tumble and confusion of artifacts, books, and papers spread everywhere.

Sam stopped at the threshold, and Max could feel himself blushing because of the mess.

"I work in here," he finally muttered, attempting to excuse the mess.

"What is it you do? They told me you were a historian." Sam crossed to a pile of jumbled wires and held up a long length of white wire with a square end. "I thought historians studied books."

Max gently removed the wire from Sam's careful grasp and laid it reverently back on the desk.

"I am a historian, but I specialize in pre-war Earth history."

"New Earth?"

"No, Origin Earth, our home planet. This is part of a consignment that was found on a mining ship in the back end of nowhere on Berris Minor. I was lucky to obtain it."

"What is it exactly?" Sam sounded curious. Max felt suddenly excited and a little wary. Perhaps it didn't matter that his Companion hadn't been preloaded with Earth History. Maybe he was interested all on his own?

"I don't exactly know." He sifted through the pile gently and pulled out a square device. "All I've been able to do is match it to this device. I think it is from way before the genetic wars, and from what I researched on the symbol, it would appear it is a storage appliance. See"—he carefully inserted the long white length into the base of the item—"it fits in here, but I'm waiting until tomorrow to record this. It is an important artifact and needs to be cataloged properly." He knew he sounded excited; he couldn't help it. The black device with the white circle on it was his version of heaven. A puzzle. He had been more excited about the box filled with ancient Earth objects that had arrived yesterday than he had been about getting a Companion.

"What does the symbol mean? I assume it is some kind of maker's mark?" Sam traced the round symbol with the small part missing from its side.

"I think it may be some version of a *franapple*."

"A *citroen*?"

"Sweeter, I think. This *franapple* mark was one used by the first companies that used genetic imprints. Imagine what may be on there. Writing. Sound. Actual era footage."

"I want to read about these things that interest you." Sam reached over to a pile of reading chips. "Which one should I start with?"

Max was genuinely startled by Sam's statement. It appeared Sam was either genuinely interested, or the comment was the result of the imprint from Max's wishes in the selection process. Either way, the thought of sharing the information was thrilling to him.

"I have some reading on Sentient Science as well." It felt like he should offer these to his new Companion; after all, it was that subject that Sam had been preloaded with after Max had chosen it from the list. Max himself had spent a good week reading up on the matter so that he could at least converse somewhat intelligently about the material.

Sam looked at the new chip being held out to him and then down at the pile of chips carefully organized in rows of twelve.

"I don't need to know any more about Sentience. I want to know what *you* know about history." He was firm on his choice, but it wasn't what Max had been expecting.

Flustered, Max handed him some of his higher learning essays, examples from his student papers. Everything that was in print on the bare-bones basics of old Earth history was on those readers. He guessed it was as good a place for Sam to start as any.

Sam grasped the chip in one hand and then he held out the other.

"Show me our bed."

$\mathcal{M}$ax had done his best with the room he had. The chamber was, by its very nature, sterile, as were all cabins on the *Royal*. However, it possessed a wide sleeping area, and he had layered soft covers to make it appealing. He didn't know exactly why he felt the desire to make things look nice. Max didn't usually worry about the look of where he slept as long as the space served his purpose. He realized suddenly, something inside him wanted this to be more than owning a Companion and enjoying the associated sexual gratification.

Max wanted *more*. A Companion could be *more* if the person who purchased them put effort into the ownership. But he hadn't been expecting much from his Companion. His father arranging for a same-gender purchase was in no way a guarantee that Max would enjoy this new man that had been matched to him. He could always return him. A refund or exchange was always offered on lightly used Companions.

He knew a little about what he'd done when he bought Sam.

Companions were matched to the person who chose them after a series of genetic tests—arranged to be emotionally, physically, and sexually compatible, all based on the genetic fingerprint from the buyer and also the buyer's sexual history.

He was aware these Companions were no more than genetic manipulations with a shelf life at the owner's discretion. He was probably one of the few who had studied the full history of genetic options, beginning with the first genetic wars and continuing to the political persuasion of the Companion Rights Movement. He had studied the social problems and knew of the hidden groups who helped Companions escape from what they perceived as servitude.

He saw both sides; he always did. Max's curse was his level-headedness. Companions wouldn't have been created in the first place if people didn't buy them. For most people, the ethics of these creations were lost in the mists of time. Most of the Companions were treated well—his Samekh model would be treated very well—but some were neglected. On the inner worlds, laws prevented such mistreatment.

Some were ordered for work, some for procreation, but most, as with Sam, were purchased for sexual compatibility.

Max didn't have much experience in the matter of sex. He preferred to spend his hours learning history, and his pursuit of that took up much of his time. That wasn't to say that he didn't have the natural impulses of other men. However, very early on, he had decided he was destined to be with males and so took himself out of the accepted mating rituals. This meant he never benefited from the sexual education and procreation seminars at Learning. Nor had he received any higher teaching on the subject when he was at the Academy for Extended Education.

He had made use of simulations, used his right hand, and that had been enough. He had once picked up a streetwalker on a visit home, but all that involved was noise and sweat and grunting, and had been a nightmare.

Max wasn't sure what to expect from someone he had purchased— an acknowledged expert in the arena of sex. Still, he wanted to make Sam feel welcome and comfortable and adding soft covers to the bed was the extent of what he knew to do.

Sudden doubt assailed him as Sam removed his jacket and started to slip off his black top. He revealed honey-toned skin, a faint dusting of hair on a broad chest, and a treasure trail that dipped below dark pants.

"Uhmm" was all Max could say. His head couldn't seem to catch up with his body as he hardened in his pants, his cock pressing against the soft material. Sam shimmied —and that was the right word—sinuously, sexily, sliding his pants down off sharp hips and stepping out of them. Ultimately, he stood completely naked and looked up at Max.

"Is this what you ordered?"

Max frowned. He hadn't been expecting the uncertainty that threaded Sam's voice, as if he was expecting Max to say no. Uncertainty, without a doubt, wasn't something he had wanted in a Companion. Hell, he had enough self-esteem issues himself, and he resolved to check the records of exactly what he *had* ordered. Maybe he had entered the wrong verbal code or something. As coolly as he could, considering he was so turned on, he assessed Sam's features—blue eyes, dark wavy hair, slim, muscled, tall, male. His eyes flicked to the ownership mark enhanced with ink on Sam's chest. All checked out fine.

"Yes, exactly."

"What about this?" Sam looked down, and Max followed his gaze. Sam was holding the most gorgeous cock that Max had ever seen, cosmetically, holographically, or otherwise. It was thick, long, and fully erect at the moment. Sam had one large hand holding it, sliding up and down. Max was mesmerized at the movement.

"That is… more than fine." Max cringed inwardly. Fine. Who called an erection like that just *fine*? The answer seemed to satisfy Sam though, and he continued to move his hand, feeling the length of himself and narrowing his eyes.

"You need to undress."

Max opened and closed his mouth a few times, then decided to get with the program, ripping clothes off between one breath and the next until he was naked as the day he was born.

He was embarrassingly hard and dropped his hands in front of himself at the visible reaction. He couldn't help himself. A living breathing man was standing in front of him, so completely different to sex with holographic hookers

"You are gorgeous," Sam stated, his head tilted to one side and his eyes considering.

"No. No, I'm not," Max said, quick to protest, but as Sam moved that single step towards him, rational thought fled his mind. Max had to look up at Sam. He was a head taller, and his shoulders were broader. His hands were firm and warm on Max's biceps. Sam dipped to kiss Max first on one eyelid then the other gently.

"What do you want now?" the Companion asked, so low that Max had to lean into him. Sam's body radiated heat, and his scent was intoxicating.

"Want?" Max asked, bemused. He wanted sex. Surely that was what Sam was here for? To service him? Was he maybe not being obvious enough about this? He had never done it before, but surely the professional must know.

"What do you want me to do?" Sam tilted his head to one side, frowning briefly.

"*Do?*" Max thought about what he was being asked.

"I am fully conversant with all types of intercourse." Insistent in his line of questioning, Sam's lips were mere inches from Max's. Hell, when had he moved so close? Max reached out and touched Sam's muscled chest, stroking the crisp hair, wondering at the sensation of actual skin against the tips of his fingers.

"I just need sex." *What other answer was Sam looking for?* "I want *you* to fuck *me*," Max finally said.

Sam grasped Max's hand. Curling his huge hand around it in a sure grip, he tugged Max towards the bed, tumbling him back on the thick covers and pillows that were nested in piles.

"Low lights," Max managed to say as he fell back. The room control lowered the main illumination, casting surreal shadows around them. It was only when the clinical white of the light diminished that the heat in Max started to manifest in a tangle of worry and fear. *What if—*

"Stop thinking," Sam commanded.

"I can't help it."

Sam pulled and arranged Max on the covers, seemingly to some preordained order that was apparently in Sam's head. Max was confused. What did he do now? This was so not him. He turned his head to look at the handsome man who leaned over him, and suddenly Max stopped panicking. All conscious thought flew from his mind as this man proceeded to palm Max's erection.

Sam paused and stared at him, and Max was humiliated to know that his nerves had shone through. "I haven't done this before."

"You're a real-mate virgin?" Sam asked. There was no criticism in his voice, and Max felt like he should tell the truth.

"I don't know what I want, Sam. I don't even know where to start. I mean, I know what I like, but what can you do? I need you to show me."

Sam captured a kiss, Max chasing him as he pulled back. "Do you want me to lead this?"

"You mean you take charge?" Max wasn't sure he could get any more embarrassed, but he nodded. "Yes, please."

"You want me to take you?" Sam whispered into Max's ear.

"Don't hurt me. But. Yes. I want—" Sam stole the words with a kiss and gripped Max's cock just this side of too hard. He began to move his hand, twisting on the upstroke and sliding his thumb through the wet collecting at the head.

"I can do that."

Sam's voice was like silk, smooth and soft, and his kisses were gentle. Max was caught up in the erotic push-pull of his Companion's touch, feeling as if he could come there and then. He didn't know what to do with his hands, what he could touch, what he couldn't, what he had paid for, what he hadn't. Finally, he settled for grasping at the covers under his head, his knuckles white with tension.

Sam was talking with every curl of his hand. *Beautiful, sexy, want, need.* Max didn't know what he expected, but he hadn't planned the talking, and it wasn't like Sam was stopping any time soon. His voice was dripping sex into Max's ear, a litany of praise, using his free hand to tilt Max's chin, so they were eye to eye, demanding honesty.

"Did you always want to match with a man?"

Max was lost in Sam's words, but he reacted instantly.

"Always a man." He must have managed to say something articulate as Sam looked into his eyes with something akin to pleasure.

"Do you mind that I talk, Max?" Sam lowered his lips to the pulse at the base of Max's neck, his tongue laving at the flickering point, before traveling with lips and teeth to first one side of Max's chest and then the other, his hand still stripping the length of his cock.

"Gah!" Max was pleased he even managed to get that one incoherent noise out.

"I will keep talking," Sam finally said. "You like that." He leaned his body weight into Max from thigh to hip and used the fingers of his free hand to twist the hard nub of Max's left nipple. Each twist and tug sent waves of want to his cock, and Max couldn't help the noises he made. He was hot under this professional's hands, begging for more with every word of need that his Companion threw at him.

"I will make it easy," Sam whispered against kiss-damp skin, and Max froze as Sam took a container of slick from the unit next to the bed and pumped a generous amount into his hand, smoothing it up and around his cock.

"You want to come here and now, Max? I can make you orgasm now. Or I could go the whole way and fuck you until you can't feel anything but me. You want me to show you how it's done?" He brushed his own erection against Max, who was harder than he'd been for a long time with this stunning, forceful man taking him to the edge. Sam chuckled darkly, lowering his mouth to the shell of Max's ear. "Are you ready?"

Max could only nod and whimper, "Yes, all the way. I need." He cursed under his breath. His words were jumbled, incoherent, and staccato short. He was in Sam's hands, a man so fucking gorgeous, so pretty, so hard, so in control, it blew his mind. Sam shoved Max back, twisting his fingers over the tip of Max's hard length again, unrelenting, bending his head to bite a mark into the base of Max's neck.

"Doing so well," Sam reassured firmly. "You can come, Max." A final twist of his hand was enough to send

Max hurtling into orgasm. There was no stopping, no let-up. Even as the orgasm was still causing his cock to twitch, Sam manhandled Max onto all fours, facing him sideways on the bed, and he reached for more slick. Max could hear himself, the harsh breathing of a man who had just exercised to excess, breath catching and heaving from his mouth. Sam wasn't going to stop and used enough slick to ease his finger into Max, a second finger catching on the first.

Max focused on the obscene slip-slide of wet on fingers, trying not to concentrate on any pain or discomfort. Sam began twisting his fingers, scissoring, mouthing a trail of small nips and bites up and down Max's spine. With another curl of the fingers, he sent Max too high too fast.

Sam didn't wait, just pulled his fingers out and then pushed his hard length deep into Max, his hands bruising and gripping Max's thighs as he pressed and rutted.

He was marking Max with bruises, and all Max could focus on was the keen edge of pain against the growing lust that Sam was creating in him.

"More, Sam, harder," Max begged, and Sam buried a hand in Max's hair, twisting fingers in it, pulling his head to the left with a hard tug. Sam leaned over him and grabbed a bruising kiss, and Max came again without a single touch to his cock. Then and only then did Sam seemingly allow himself to come deep inside Max, losing it with a shout of completion and triumph.

It was Sam who moved first, cleaning them, lying back on the covers, a half smile on his face. Max touched the smile.

"What are you smiling about?"

"I like that you want me to tell you what to do," Sam said, moving his head subtly to capture the finger with a quick suck and a kiss. Max blushed.

"Me too," he said sleepily, turning on his side and not even questioning when his new Companion spooned him from behind.

It just seemed right.

Chapter 5

*I*f possible, the sex got better as the weeks went on. It was an addiction, one that Max was happy to indulge in, and Sam was glad to supply. They fell into a routine and learned more of each other every day. They were a short way from the first inspection; the Labs would be sending out a tech to ascertain whether Max was pleased with his match. The proposed visit didn't even concern Max. He had nothing to complain about. Sam and he were matched well.

Sam had already been educated to a level equal to Max. A similar level of learning had been one of Max's requirements. Besides, Sam had developed a deep interest in Old Earth history, and he was a willing pupil to Max's ramblings.

Max was working on a translation, pulling apart delicate papers from an obscure ancient book and individually logging the information in his journal. Sam occupied his time gently sorting through the white lengths of wiring that lay on one side of the work area.

The device they still sat in the box—a thin rectangle of translucent black that reflected the light in the room. Sam had already scanned the interior. He turned it over, running a single finger over the image of the *franapple*, white with a bite taken out of one side. Max watched him, but bowed his head back to his work before Sam could catch him staring.

"Do you think it communicates or archives?" Sam wondered out loud, and Max lifted his gaze, focusing on the other man and shaking his head.

"I don't know. It doesn't have an obvious power source, so I'm guessing we are missing that part."

"I know some electronics."

"You do? I don't remember selecting that skill." Max could have cut his tongue out as Sam suddenly looked sad. "Sorry, I know you are learning more about things that interest you." Sam's frown disappeared as quickly as it had started.

"I am. I read up on electronics and looked in your archives. They used something that I think they called *wattings*. It might be like our modern *Menschellian Measurement*. We could maybe…" Max tuned out Sam's talking about all the technical details and just stared at the perfect man that had turned his life upside down.

Sam was Max's purchased Companion. Genetically engineered and programmed to match him, of course, he was going to be perfect. Still, as Sam sat muttering over the wires, cursing as tangles defeated his large hands, Max wanted to blurt out what had been building inside of him so long. He wanted to tell this man that he loved him, that he blessed the day that they met and that he couldn't be happier.

The problem was, however, that no owner did that. Companions knew their place, and that place was not one where love figured into the equation. That was part of the law. Companions were not allowed the emotion of love, and owners were discouraged from offering love. It just made the deletion or rejection of the Companion too messy.

How could he even think of burdening Sam with his thoughts? It wasn't fair.

Sam's soft voice interrupted Max's thoughts. "I've nearly got a connection. I just maybe need some other items you don't have here."

"Items?" Max blinked himself back to the discussion.

"I have a list." He flicked his fingers, and the list bumped from his pod to Max's. Max glanced down and then up. Damn.

"I'll go get them now." So much passed between them that was unspoken. Companions had only a certain amount of freedom on the Station, although rules on the *Ark Royal* were somewhat less restrictive than those planet side. However, despite the obscene levels of money Max possessed, he still had to abide by ship rules. Companions were not allowed access to certain areas, including the main emporium at the Center. Max didn't understand why the law existed, but he wanted a quiet life and wasn't one to balk at established regulations.

"I'll stay here and keep working on this," Sam said.

Max hated the segregation, the arbitrary rules that

existed as far as Companions were concerned. The creation of the Companions, including the genetic engineering involved in creating those aspects of Companion-life, was encouraged. Not allowing a Companion to handle money? Requiring them to stay out of shops? Utterly ridiculous.

"I won't be long." Max didn't stop to say anymore, taking the long way down to the Zeta deck where the main provisions area was.

People didn't need to buy much on the *Ark Royal*. Most life requirements were provided, but there was a thriving economy of barter in the bowels of the ship for the somewhat-transient population of the floating city. Max hated bartering and would much rather just hand over real, hard currency than haggle. Taking a deep breath, he ventured onto the central area and focused intently. He would complete his trades and return home quickly. Fortunately, Max easily located and traded for the things on Sam's list, despite it taking more time than he wanted it to. Eager to return to his lover, he retraced his steps to the exit.

"Someone's on the gantry." The urgent call was taken up among the groups of people milling around the concourse, and unwillingly Max was swept backward and away from the exit.

"What is he doing?"

"It's not a he; it's a companion. They scanned it."

"Is it trying to end itself?"

A Companion? Max peered upwards. Why was a Companion standing on the gantry? It was dangerous there, a network of pipes and shafts that fed the sewage and other extra materials out into the darkness of space.

Many a suicide had taken place off that gantry, and people gawked and shoved and pushed for front-row seats.

"There's nothing to worry about; it's only a Companion."

"A Samekh or a Theta line?"

"Some owner is not going to be happy. Those things are expensive."

Max heard snatches of shouts. He had lost his purchases, wrenched away by the moving sea of people. Gripping his pod, he stumbled along as part of the irresistible force heading to the gantry. He wanted to get back to his rooms and Sam.

Then silence, sudden and chilling, the crowd melting away from him, leaving space all around him.

"Yours," someone said. Were they talking to him?

"Your Companion... Max... yours."

---

*M*ax edged carefully along the gantry perimeter, not looking down at the endless pit that opened and closed with air cushions every hour on the hour. It was a complicated web of structure, evil, dark, twisted, and in the center, at the very point overhanging the pit, sat Sam. His Sam. Cross-legged, crying and rocking with his arms tight around his chest.

Maybe it wasn't his Sam. Was it possible another Samekh Taw had been created like his Sam? Did Companions cry? He'd never seen Sam cry.

"Hello?" He kept his voice low, and as the Samekh Taw lifted his eyes, Max knew. They were eyes so blue they showed the ocean in the tears. It was Sam.

"I'm sorry, Max, so sorry." Sam blurted.

"Sam, talk to me."

"I can't do this anymore," Sam half whispered his voice heavy with grief, fresh tears tracking down his smooth skin. Max watched as his lover released the hold he had on himself and collected the tears with fingertips. He stared at them as if they didn't make any sense to him.

"Sam, please." Max wasn't sure what he was pleading for, apart from the obvious about getting the hell off the gantry.

"I can't stop leaking like this, Max." Sam sounded like a small child, looking in wonder at the tears on his hands and bringing a clenched fist up to rest against his chest over his heart.

"You're crying Sam; I didn't know you could cry... please talk to me, Sam."

"Samekh Taw. It's Samekh Taw designation #65572," Sam said, sadly.

"But I call you Sam," Max offered softly, affection in his voice.

"You have no right to do that; it isn't my label," Sam snapped back quickly, then immediately started to rock again, his head bowed.

"If you don't want me to call you Sam, I can stop," Max offered as he picked carefully over coiled tubing, stumbling and catching himself on a railing. He was only a few paces away Sam who lifted his gaze to Max, so much pain in his eyes.

"No, I want to be Sam." His voice was thick with emotion. "I want to be your Sam, but next week, when they visit for the check? They won't like it."

"Because?" Max began. None of this was making sense. "What's wrong, Sam? Why are you here? Who won't like it?"

Shakily, Sam reached into his shirt, the filmy white material clinging to his damp skin, and pulled out the device he had been working on. "I got it to work for a while."

"Okay…?"

"I looked for a word. I didn't know what else to look for. I don't know why I did."

"And?"

"It worked for just short of seventeen and five, almost as soon as you left… And… I saw."

"Saw what, Sam?"

"I looked for the word Valentine. I wanted to know if the program for Companions was even a thought in someone's head back then. But all I saw were images. Pictures for each story on the object, and there was one picture—two men, like us—kissing. The man… He was with another man, but people were so angry, saying it wasn't right."

"Oh, Sam, you can't let this upset you. Some of what I translate says the same things. There hasn't always been the tolerance for same-gender relations that we have now." There, problem solved. "No one is going to take you from me just because we are both males. My father had special dispensation." Max could tell Sam not to worry, and he would stop with all this. Only Sam didn't stop. If anything, he became more agitated, which just seemed so wrong in such a strong man. But Sam wouldn't leave it.

"They were together and so happy on the photos, and one man had made food, had candles. It was the celebration day of a God. They called the God Valentine, and they loved each other with hearts and words. Everything was red." Sam wasn't making a lot of sense.

"What was the story called, Sam?" Max needed to get

a handle on this so that maybe he could understand. He might be able to translate this story if he could see it.

"I didn't see a title. It is only a small part. It was war and Valentine. I saw it was war. One of the men had a mark on him. Like mine." He paused and traced a single finger in the dirt and oil on the metal, forming a six-pointed star. "People hated him because he was different and he had the mark. I don't know what that means but I know I have a mark that makes me different."

He reached one hand to touch the blue possession mark on his chest. Max winced. He hadn't wanted his Companion marked as his, not really, but he'd had no choice. All Companions were branded to avoid people thinking they were pure humans. Sam started to rock again, and Max cautiously edged closer, sliding down the railing until he sat next to Sam, not touching, but close enough that he could feel the heat of his lover.

"It's a story, Sam. Just a story. There were so many wars on old Earth and as much hate and prejudice as there is today."

"People in uniforms took this marked man in the story. The man with the star. They said he wasn't pure, wasn't real enough. I don't know why, but that is why he had the mark. The other man was considered pure, but he couldn't save his lover; he had to let him go. This other man couldn't even cry. He had to pretend he didn't want his lover or else he would die also. His lover told him to stay quiet."

"Sam—"

"Would you stay quiet so I could stay? Or would you

send me away when you tired of me because I am not pure human?"

Max hated that Sam doubted him. Why hadn't he been honest with Sam before leaving for the market this morning? "Sam, this story might not even be real. Everything was so long ago."

"But the people who made me can take me back as soon as they see I have all these extra emotions in me that they didn't mean to put there. You could tell me that you don't want me at any time."

"I wouldn't do that to you, Sam. Please."

Max waited. Sam looked sideways at him, his eyes bright, his face flushed.

"But I'm wrong. I'm not pure; I have the mark. They could take me."

"No one can take you, Sam. You are with me."

"Only"—Sam's voice thickened, his head bowed—"until they take me when they find I am wrong."

"Sam? You are not wrong. You are perfect."

"I'm not perfect. We both know I have attributes I shouldn't. Like lust and guilt and the pain I that I feel for you." Blindly, Sam reached out a hand, and Max gripped it tightly, curling their fingers together.

"You are nothing but perfect," Max reassured Sam.

"Temper. Envy. Sadness. Tears. I shouldn't have these things. You didn't ask for them."

In a flurry of motion, Sam stood, tugging his hand out of Max's hold, and before Max could say *Stop!*, Sam was swaying at the edge, looking down into the big nothing.

"No, Sam!" Max scrambled to his feet, grabbing at the

white material of his lover's shirt and pulling him back a tiny bit, anchoring him to the here and now.

Sam shouted the next words over the noise of rushing wind. "When they come to check, you will have to admit what I am, that I am not perfect. You will have no choice but to send me back for elimination. I don't want you to have to make that choice. I don't want to be rejected and sent back."

A gust of wind curled around them as they stood as still as carved statues. The wind reeked of oil and dirt and the very bowels of the ship. It wasn't the most romantic of places, it was evil and dark and dank, but Max had things he needed to say.

"No one will take you away from me."

Sam wasn't listening.

"They have rejects, you know," Sam snapped back. "I saw them, back at the Labs, Companions who are wrong. Their matched owners don't want them."

"Well, that won't happen. I want you. I will always want you."

"You won't have a choice, Max," Sam pointed out sadly. "When they see what I have, that I am not perfect and I have more emotions than I should, and it makes me wrong, they'll want me recycled."

"You say that. But I won't let them. I'll tell them…" Max couldn't form the words, and Sam looked at him with pain imprinted onto his features.

"Tell them what?" Sam had never sounded hopeless and so utterly defeated.

"That I love you so much that it would kill me to lose you." It was so simple to say at last, so much the truth that

Max couldn't keep it inside any longer. Brief hope passed across Sam's face, but Max had to grab at him as the flow of air grew stronger and scattered debris around them, and the hope slid off Sam's expression.

"You love me?"

"I have since almost day one."

"You just love the image you chose." Sam gestured at himself, dismissing what Max was saying so quickly, and suddenly, Max regretted never saying what he felt before.

"I didn't get an image though, Sam. I got *you*. Special. Different. Mine." He cupped his free hand to Sam's cheek, swept away a tear, and smiled as Sam leaned into the caress with half-closed eyes. "You, with your temper and your laughter and your fears, all the things you have that I never realized I wanted."

"Max, none of that matters anymore. I can't hide my emotions all the time. When someone sees what I am, when I slip up—"

"So we'll go somewhere where no one will see you. We'll buy a means of transport and go far away. I have more money than I know what to do with. We'll go and explore. Just you and me."

Sam hesitated and then took a deliberate step back away from the rim.

"Just you and me?" There was hope in Sam's voice. "Away from anyone that can see I am imperfect?"

Max pulled the other man to him, into the tightest hug, the fear at standing so close to the edge beating hard in his chest. He wasn't lying to Sam. Max didn't need other people; he needed exploration, learning, and history. But most of all he needed Sam. He had the rest of their lives to prove to Sam that he *was* perfect.

"Just us."

"It hurts me when we are apart, Max." Sam pulled back and touched his chest. "It hurts in here, tight… whenever you leave, when you are sad or angry."

"That's what you said it was, Sam. Love."

"Why can I understand all the things they gave me, but not see love?"

"You can't order love for a Companion. You can't create it out of a bottle. It has to grow on its own."

Sam looked at him with hope in his eyes. "I read about love days in your translations, red and hearts and a special day. Is that what love can be?"

"I don't know, Sam, but we don't need red and hearts and a special day to know we are in love."

"Can you maybe teach me how I should use how I feel on the special day?"

Carefully, Max led his lover from the gantry, passing the gawking mass of humanity that stared waiting for Sam, and possibly Max, to fall to their deaths. He led him back to their chambers, closing and then locking the entrance until it was just them.

Sam stood uncertainly by the door. Max grabbed onto his hands and then stepped in closer to kiss his lover. When they parted, Max considered what Sam had said about using love on the special day like the people in the photos.

"Every day we are together, Sam?"

"Yes?"

"We use love on every one of them. In the way we kiss and touch and make love and talk and learn."

"Why don't we have a special day that I can use to tell you I love you?"

"Trust me, Sam; we don't need a special day for that."

THE END

Three

Mark is finding his way in life after six years in the army. He's always wanted to write scripts for TV, and for one show, in particular, Tomorrow's Game.

Half in lust already with the lead actor Zach, he is shocked when he ends up in Zach's bed. Not just that, but Zach's co-star Rob is part of the package.

Is this just hot sex or can two become three?

Want

In the desert, on his knees, with his hands crossed behind his head and an enemy rifle pointed at his temple, Mark Gatlin had an epiphany of sorts.

I'm not going to die. I won't let this happen. I have things I want to do.

Dreams.

That conviction lasted way past his getting out of the situation alive. It was still there when he booked the flights to LA, and it remained right up to the moment he got on the plane this morning. However, as the aircraft approached LAX Airport, Mark's stomach churned with nerves and fear. Maybe he should have stuck to finding a job in the security sector. Given his experience, he'd already be working and earning good money. Hell, he'd had five offers from his first five interviews. The promise he'd made himself in the sandbox was that he would present the screenplay he'd written and at least try to make some headway. He just didn't know how he'd ever thought he could pull this off.

And so he sat in a window seat, 23A, his script in his carry-on bag, and the address of the film set in his head. This was possibly his only shot at getting his work seen, maybe even getting the creator of the show to read his words. He could be holding the next big hit filmed in LA in his hands, but he'd never know unless he tried.

His script was the story of a gay man, secret organizations, life in a small town, and the tragic death of a lover all rolled into one; it was edgy and new and his nerves twisted in his stomach as the plane touched down. Maybe it was pushing it too far; maybe the world wasn't ready for a gay hero but, unless he handed the script to the director or writers of the current rating winner, *Tomorrow's Game,* he would never know.

Finding an address for the production office was the first step, an easy one as it turned out. A few carefully placed questions on various Internet communities brought forward a raft of information; not just the production HQ for *Tomorrow's Game*, but the bars that technicians and stars frequented, and even a home address or two. Mark wasn't ill-mannered; he was a well-brought-up Southern gentleman, and the thought of approaching someone in his home was not on his to-do list. So production office it would be and, after a quiet night in the LAX Days Inn and a breakfast of bacon and pancakes, he felt he could handle anything.

He delayed a little, psyching himself in front of the bathroom mirror, as he pulled at his blond hair, trying to get it to stay spiked, his gray-blue eyes gazing back from what he considered a very average face. He wondered what it would be like to meet the people behind *Tomorrow's Game*.

What were the writers like? Would they laugh at him and think his ideas were nothing? He sighed, slipping on his jacket and straightening his tie.

"This is going to be easy," he told his reflection. "I can do this. I've survived enemy fire; I've been in situations some people wouldn't believe."

Of course, he hadn't completely counted on the security on set being as tight as it was. He watched as some fifty girls of various ages hovered at the gate. It was close to 8:00 a.m., and he assumed that they were there already waiting for the arrival of Zach Cassidy or Rob Kelly, the leading stars of the much-lauded time travel show. He smiled at the thought of maybe catching sight of them; after all, there wasn't that much of a call for a *Tomorrow's Game* convention in North Carolina, so he'd never get to meet them face to face.

Getting to San Diego Comic-Con was on his bucket list, but ex-Army guys didn't get paid enough to cover rent and at the same time enjoy luxuries like vacations with no purpose. He stood back, behind the girls and a few boys with the photos and autograph books. While catching sight of Zach Cassidy, in his opinion one of *the* most gorgeous men on the planet, would be a bonus, it was the director or the scriptwriters he was here to see.

There was a buzz in the group; a black truck had been spotted approaching the main gate, and the sudden surge of excited girls pushed Mark, forcing him to step backward straight into the path of the oncoming truck. Twisting to avoid being crushed, he fell in the puddles caused by early morning sprinklers at the side of the road, the script in his hand flying under the wheels of the sliding truck. In slow motion, he saw his work ruined by water and mud. The truck stopped inches from his outspread fingers as he reached for the loose papers. He heard, rather than saw, the people around him gasp in horror. Then a door slammed, he heard heated words, and a man crouched and pulled him one-handed to his feet. He was tall, strong, with a shaved head and a snarl. He smelled of cigarette smoke, and snapped out an irritated "What the fuck, man?"

Mark didn't know what to say. He felt like his whole life had just been stomped on, and yes, he knew he was overreacting, but the script was ruined. Of course, he had a copy on his laptop, but the ruined script was bound professionally and had his notations on it, ideas in pencil he had added on the flight that he would never recover. Still, he nodded that he was okay; his elbow hurt like a bitch where he'd landed on solid asphalt but, other than that; he was just fine; shaky and shocked, but fine.

"Nick, is he okay?" a voice said from behind the tinted windows, and the girls swarmed, all shouting the same things: *Zach, it's Zach, OH MY GOD, Zach, Zach.* The man holding Mark swore, pushing the girls back and pulling at Mark, even as he tried to reach for his script, torn and trampled under fifty pairs of shoes. Without ceremony he was pushed into the truck, sprawling onto the floorboard, the huge workhorse of a bodyguard following him and shutting the door behind him, locking all doors in seconds. He felt other hands pulling at him, helping him from the floor.

"Jeez, are you okay? Did we hit you?"

Blinking, Mark looked at the man helping him up onto the seat. *Freaking Zach Cassidy.* Six foot of muscled limbs and athletic build, short dark brown, nearly black hair, concerned blue eyes, and that body with his broad chest and muscles. Mark knew his jaw dropped, and he also knew he looked like a dork, soaked to the skin, his elbow throbbing, and his hair damp and curling round his face. It didn't help that he didn't know what to say. He was sitting in the same space as Zach *freaking* Cassidy, whose face at this moment was screwed up in a concerned expression.

Finally, he found words. "No, no you didn't, you didn't hit me that is. I just got pushed by them," Mark managed to force out past the shaking in his voice, focusing his gaze on gorgeous eyes, at the high cheekbones and, not for the first time, lusting after the completely straight actor. He instinctively placed a hand on his chest over the dog tags hanging under his shirt, something he'd picked up in the sandbox whenever he'd avoided getting hurt. A gesture of good luck. Some men made the sign of the cross on their chest; he touched the symbol of the trust he put in his team and the fact that he was still alive.

"We'll get the on-site medic to check you out," the man of his fantasies said quickly. "Is it your chest? Are you having a heart attack?"

"No, I don't need a doctor," Mark said. The last thing he needed was to see a medic, poking at him and making him talk about his time in the army.

"Yes to a medic. She'll look at you, fix you up." The truck came to a stop, and Zach jumped lithely to the ground, holding out his hand to Mark, who grasped it without thought, climbing out of the truck and standing next to Zach. Nothing he'd experienced in his life so far had prepared him for this.

"Stay here," Zach murmured. "I'll get someone."

"Zach, I'll have to deal with it, they need you in makeup," the bodyguard—Nick, Mark assumed—said swiftly, moving to stand between his charge and Mark, who knew he looked like a muddy mess. He was the idiot who had jumped in front of their car, hopeless, pathetic. Not someone who had lived an entire life of action and purpose up until now.

Concern crossed Zach's face. He turned to Mark. "Stick with Nick and get yourself checked out."

"Okay," was all Mark could say. Where was his gift for conversation, his sparkling wit, his grasp of language? Gone, just gone.

Nick mumbled something under his breath; it sounded suspiciously like a line of swear words and "fanboy." Mark tried to ignore it, thinking that perhaps he hadn't heard right; surely Nick wasn't lumping him with the girls screaming at the gate.

"I wasn't here to scream," Mark said stubbornly, and Nick stopped. His face was tight with sudden suspicion.

"What the hell were you doing here then?" he asked, big beefy arms crossed over his broad chest.

Mark swallowed, he needed to defend himself. "I had a script to give to the writers."

Nick snorted. Mark knew at that point that Nick, as bodyguard to Zach, would have heard all kinds of excuses as to why people should be allowed near Rob and Zach, and that his reason probably sounded feeble. "So you thought throwing yourself under my truck would get you an in?"

"I was pushed," Mark protested, righteous indignation straightening his spine. He blushed as Nick doubled over with laughter. "What?"

"What kind of army man can't handle a group of fans? You know your buddies find out and you will never live that down." Mark's lips twitched, he supposed it *was* funny.

Still, how did Nick know he was an Army man? "How did you know I was in the military?"

Nick shrugged, a shadow of something passing over his face. "Let's just say, I had a brother who was in Kuwait; I know the look of a grunt." He peered closer. "Or were you the officer type?"

"I was… I don't…"

"Look, whatever. Let's take you to the doc and maybe we can drop off this script of yours at the office."

"I don't have it," Mark whispered. Regret knifed through him, and instant suspicion crossed Nick's face. "No," Mark defended again. "I did have it, but what's left of it is in the water from the sprinklers at the front gate, covered with boot and tire marks."

"Okay, here's what we do then, just write down some stuff and I'll put it on the main desk," Nick offered with a shrug.

Yeah. Great idea, just write down in five minutes what had taken him months to achieve. Shit.

That was not the solution that Mark hoped for. He didn't argue, though; Nick wasn't interested in what he had to say, not really.

The beer was cold and, as far as Mark was concerned; that was the start of a good night. He had finally been escorted back to his hotel by an overcompensating Nick, who, on the instructions of someone, was told to take Mark back to his motel, settle the bill, and pass over some signed pictures.

Mark had them in his room. Rob Kelly in a classic villain pose, pouty and fuckable, his dark eyes serious, and Zach Cassidy, hands crossed over his chest, a T-shirt pulled tight over his muscles, his "come on try it" hero poses giving Mark an instant erection. Fuck. That photo was so bloody hot. Ever since it had hit his inbox from a friend it had given him the shivers, and he imagined just falling to his knees and sucking Zach off. Didn't matter there was not a single hint Zach was gay or even bi; that didn't stop Mark imagining the taste of the man.

"Hey." Someone knocked his arm, and he winced. The team had been looking at him a little suspiciously, and he imagined that they liked their privacy, not happy to have a stranger sitting in their midst. He looked up with a carefully blank expression on his face to find the man of his lustful wishful thinking standing next to him. Zach Cassidy, with beers in hand, and his ball cap pulled low over his eyes.

Sitting at an acknowledged crew bar was his last-ditch attempt at maybe passing a newly printed copy of the script over to one of the scriptwriters. He never thought for one minute, the stars of the show would go to the same bar.

He couldn't even see their bodyguard guy, and assumed that someone else was watching them discreetly.

He knew it could look like he was a stalker, but he was on a mission, and he hadn't failed an operation yet. He'd just never expected to see Zach again.

"Hey." Great conversation starter. And then his brain stopped.

"How are you? Did the medic look you over?" Zach looked interested. Like it might be significant for him to find out what had happened to the idiot who tried to kill himself earlier on in the day.

"Yeah, just bruises to the pride, thanks." Mark was ridiculously proud of his response, at not dribbling and slurring his words in embarrassment.

"Sit with us, man. Let me get you a beer, by way of apologizing for the screaming fan girls who tried to kill you."

"You don't need to; I'm all right. I—"

"No argument. Come on, meet Rob."

"Rob?" Jeez, Rob *hottest-bad-guy-on-TV* Kelly? That Rob?

Zach frowned. "Rob, Rob Kelly. I mean, you are a fan of TG? Or maybe you were here for something else?"

"No, I know who he is, I mean, I…" Then his voice trailed away, and he shrugged, aware he was probably bright red.

Zach chuckled. "Come on, bring your beer." He nodded to a tall, broad man leaning back against the bar. Some silent communication must have passed between Zach and the guy because the man in cliché-black relaxed from his tense watchful position. This man was clearly the shift bodyguard.

"Sorry, the problem with coming out to an average bar is that the network worries about us."

"I bet," Mark answered.

Zach started moving through the people around the bar, who for the most part ignored him. Mark followed, and they ended up at a table in the shadowed corner. Mark slid in opposite a sleepy Rob Kelly, who had his head laid back against the wall, his eyes closed, Zach slid in next to his costar, placing beers in front of them. Rob mumbled something, his head sliding to rest on Zach's shoulder, turning his face slightly and touching his lips to the bare skin of Zach's neck.

Mark watched in fascination as Zach chuckled and moved his shoulder, pushing Rob awake.

"Company," he said.

Rob sat upright, blinking. Mark was lost for words; Rob Kelly was damn sexy. Warm-toned skin, long eyelashes, gorgeous pouting lips, and eyes so dark brown they reminded Mark of melted chocolate. But, even with Rob sitting there looking all perfect, it was still Zach that Mark found himself unconsciously staring at. Zach wasn't perfect; he was *interesting*, quirky, laughing, sexy, strong, just the very man of Mark's fantasies. Mark caught Rob smirking at his preoccupation, and then he leaned back against Zach again.

"I'm a bit tired tonight, Zach," Rob said. Zach let out a low laugh, and Mark caught himself staring at the man's broad chest as it moved.

"Rob, he's not here for that, dude. This is um…" Zach waved a hand. They hadn't been introduced.

"Mark," Mark inserted helpfully, lifting his beer to his lips to cover the nerves he knew would be apparent in his voice.

"Yeah, this is Mark, the guy I almost killed this morning."

"Hey Mark," Rob said, his voice rough and tired.

Zach chuckled again, leaning forward to place both elbows on the scarred wooden table. "Forgive Rob, he's been on set since five this morning, and he is on a major caffeine diet trying to stay awake." Zach elbowed Rob in the side for emphasis.

Mark nodded, actually relieved that he only had to make conversation with one of them.

Several beers later and the conversation flowed like he and Zach had known each other for a long time. There was no shortage of things to talk about: Zach, an actor, Mark, a wannabe screenwriter, Rob, mostly just offering incoherent grunting as he dozed on Zach's shoulder.

When the offer came to continue the smooth, comfortable conversation back at Zach's house, where Rob had a room, it was a natural progression of their evening. Zach was such an easy person to talk to, and Mark's gaydar was in confusion mode. As they talked about all kinds of things, from the show to Hollywood, to Mark's time in the Army, there had been some flirting, Mark was sure of it, but he couldn't understand why. Zach was the poster boy for heterosexual alpha male, but he was inserting suggestive remarks into everything they talked about and didn't bat an eyelid when Mark talked about staying the closet in the Army.

Anyway, if this was Zach flirting, why would he be flirting with Mark?

Mark had never rated his looks; he kept himself fit, his hair was short, and he had a naturally muscled body from years of physical exercise, but he was surely not in the league of Zach Cassidy, be he gay or otherwise.

It wasn't as if Mark had heard anything about the twenty-six-year-old actor being interested in anyone other than the guest star actresses he was seen out with. Rumor had it he was dating one of the girls who had appeared in a few episodes in season one, a short redhead with a thing for murder.

The thing was, it seemed like maybe, in Zach's eyes, Mark was a little bit better than ordinary, as Zach pushed him up against the wall inside the front door.

Zach was close; his lips close from Mark's. "Tell me I'm not wrong. Tell me I can kiss you?"

So much for not being gay.

Mark didn't even answer. He reached up and twisted his fingers, as best he could, into Zach's short hair, pulling him toward him, mumbling "Not wrong" as he opened his mouth under Zach's.

It was overwhelmingly hot, tongues searching out the taste of beer, kisses so deep and hard they curled Mark's toes and left him short of breath. Zach pulled back to grab Mark's hands, pushing them above his head and holding them in place, just holding him there for a long while, leaning into him, hard and heavy and needy up against him. Before Zach began tracing a path of open-mouthed kisses from temple to ear, stopping to caress the shell of Mark's ear with the tip of his tongue, it seemed to Mark that breathing was almost impossible.

Whining deep in his throat, he moved restlessly under the onslaught, impossibly hard and desperate for friction, grinding up against Zach to relieve the pressure. Finally, Zach moved his lips lower, focusing all his attention on the fluttering pulse point in Mark's neck as Mark just gave in and leaned his head back against the wall, helpless against Zach's exploring mouth. He wanted to say something, anything, but couldn't.

It didn't enter his head to think where Rob had gone until another mouth touched his lips even as Zach was marking the skin pulled taut at his neck. He opened his eyes to find liquid-chocolate-colored eyes inches from his. He must have looked startled; Rob blinked once, twisting his fingers into Mark's hair and pulling his head further back to give Zach free rein on his neck, taking Mark's lips in a heated kiss then trailing fiery touches over Mark's high cheekbones to his ear.

"Zach wants you… I want to watch," Rob said in his sleep-deprived growly voice. Accompanied by him sliding his hand under the blue shirt Mark had changed into after consigning his ruined sweatshirt to the trash. Unerringly, Rob located Mark's sensitive nipples, not pulling or twisting, but gently tracing around the left nipple, and over it, with practiced ease. It was all Mark could do to remain standing as his knees started to buckle at the onslaught against his senses and Zach chuckled into his other ear.

"Vanity, or for real?" Rob asked, as he gripped and tugged at Mark's dog tags. The question didn't make sense at first; then Mark realized what he was asking. He'd clearly slept through the whole discussion on Mark being in the US Army.

"Real, former Army," he managed to force out between kisses.

Rob groaned. "An honest to God hero. That is so fucking hot."

"Uh-huh" was all Mark could say as Zach began pulling him along the corridor, continually kissing, stripping clothes as they went through a door at the end, into a dimly lit room dominated by an enormous bed. Rob moved to one side, still dressed, his belt loose, and dropped fluidly into a chair positioned directly at the end of the bed, like Rob and Zach had had this scenario played out in this room before, and the chair was placed there just in case.

Mark whimpered as Zach concentrated on tasting every part of Mark's tightly muscled chest, focusing on touch and taste, gently guiding Mark closer to the bed until his knees hit it and he started to topple. Zach followed him down, pushing and pulling until Mark lay fully on the bed, his cock hard and heavy with need, his body arching up into the pleasure-pain of tiny sucks and bites marking his body.

He was muttering almost incoherently at the extremes of pleasure winding through his body, as hot as fire, as Zach concentrated those tiny sucking bites and kitten licks on each nipple, in turn, moving his hard body over Mark with an insistent push and sinuous twists. Mark moved his hands until they naturally rested on Zach's hard biceps, and he realized he was feeling the muscles move under the skin as Zach forced his upper body up and away to move his mouth further down.

Zach kissed a trail to the spur of Mark's hips, sucking small marks into each, his breath hot on sensitive skin, avoiding the one place Mark wanted that made-for-sin mouth. Mark keened for the touch but a single command from Rob, *not yet*, made Zach avoid it, using his hand instead, circling Mark's hard cock firmly, moving up and over him, smoothing a thumb through the precome that collected at the tip, humming in appreciation as Mark started to beg. He moved to the left, biting and sucking at Mark's inner thigh, and Mark moved his head to see Rob, to find out what the man with the careful gaze was doing. Rob was sitting back in the chair, blissed out, his hand on his cock moving in slow, steady strokes from root to tip, his eyes focused on the journey Zach's mouth was taking. Mark turned back to Zach.

"Please, please…"

And then Rob's soft voice, a growl, a hissed command.

"Zach, suck him."

Zach was there in seconds, swallowing Mark down as far as his circled hand. He moved slowly, then faster, alternating sucking and pulling. He took each ball into his mouth, rolling the sacs gently with his tongue, moving again slowly. Mark could see Zach's mouth stretch obscenely wide around his cock, and he writhed at the touch. He half-sobbed the plea for more, for harder, for faster, looking away from Zach's lips to Rob's hand, each image more erotic every time he moved his focus. Mark could feel the orgasm rising in him with incredible speed, and he moved his hand, pulling hard at Zach's hair, a moan in his mouth.

"I'm coming." He wanted to give Zach time to pull off. All Zach did was suck deeper, and Mark lost it hot and deep in Zach's mouth, incoherent words at the release, arching and then falling back onto the covers. Zach climbed back up, laying open-mouthed kisses on hot skin, capturing Mark's lips in a kiss, with the taste and texture of his come shared in a messy heated exchange of air.

So fucking hot.

Zach reached across him, pulling out a tube and condoms and gesturing for Mark's acceptance. Mark nodded simply, pleading in his eyes, and he heard Rob groan.

"You gonna come again for me, Mark?" Zach whispered soft and low in Mark's ear.

"Fuck" was all Mark could say, his headspace in the most erotic place it had ever been, visions of what Zach was going to do to him, with him, blowing his mind, and then he felt the wet, the slick, as Zach massaged and pushed and started to prepare him. Tonight was the hottest one-night stand of his entire life, and that was saying something given the kind of life he'd had so far.

"So fucking tight." Zach moaned into Mark's neck.

Mark pushed back on his fingers and then forward into the circle of the tight hold.

"More."

Three fingers and Zach pressed them inside Mark, searching out the sweet spot, rubbing the swollen area gently, insistently, all the time whispering words of encouragement into Mark's heated skin until Mark was an incoherent mess of want and need.

Mark sensed Rob standing, coming to stand in front of him, crouching down, so his eyes were on the same level as Mark's, reaching his hand to cup Mark's balls, pull at his cock, his movement's jerky.

"Now Zach," Rob said. "Mark's ready; I can see it in his eyes. He wants you inside him. Fucking him," Rob whispered all of this from his crouched position. In one move Zach pushed inside, and then inch by inch eased further until he was so far in, so big, Mark had never felt anything like it.

The burn was intense, and he moaned his pleasure-pain even as the burn started to subside, and he felt so full and fucking close. Zach began to move, the sting exquisite and akin to ecstasy, Mark's name a litany from Zach's mouth as he pushed into Mark's body, steady and strong. Mark started to move with Zach, one hand locked to the headboard to steady himself as Zach progressively and slowly built the pressure, his hand turning and twisting on Mark's hot cock.

Rob moved, knelt up to capture his lips in a desperate kiss, little more than an exchange of tangled tongues, and Zach leaned over him, biting down on the corded muscles of Mark's neck. This time, the orgasm had built so slowly, it seemed to catch every nerve ending on fire, and when Mark finally lost it, bowing his back, curling in on himself, hot and wet and so heavy across Zach's hand, he heard himself whimper. Rob stumbled to stand and gave a guttural groan for his completion, ribbons of come painting Mark's neck, profanity slipping from his full lips as he shut his eyes and lost himself in the sensation.

Zach moved harder into him once, twice, before losing it inside him, Mark's name a gasp, and then falling heavily on the shorter man, mumbling an apology for his weight. Mark winced as Zach's still half-hard cock brushed over his sensitized prostate. Zach slumped down and held out a hand to a still-dressed Rob, encouraging him onto the bed on the other side of Mark.

"He is fucking gorgeous, Rob; I want him to stay tonight," Mark heard Zach murmur.

"So do I," Rob agreed quickly, a smile in his voice like he could never refuse his lover anything.

Mark slipped into sleep, curled up against Zach's broad back; his body was spent, his mind dead to the world, not even thinking about the next morning, or exactly what the hell he had just done.

Tomorrow could wait.

Tomorrow

———————

Mark experienced a moment of disorientation when he woke. He certainly wasn't in his motel room. The light was different, there was a warm body next to him, and he blinked trying to get his bearings. He pushed himself to a seated position, looking down at the length of Zach Cassidy next to him. None of this seemed real as he rolled off the bed, no Rob in sight, and padded to the bathroom, taking a piss, and then washing his hands before he grabbed a new toothbrush from the cabinet.

His mouth tasted like a bar floor, and he wanted to meet the morning, at least, looking fresh and awake, even if he wasn't. As he rinsed his mouth, he felt Zach brush against him, carrying out the same morning routine. He hovered at the door, unsure of his next move. They probably wanted him to leave; it had just been the beer that had ended up with him being here. Zach brushed past again; this time, his hand grabbed at Mark, and he found himself being pulled back to the bed, slipping and sliding and squirming under the still-heated sheets.

"We have a late start today," Zach supplied helpfully. "Come back to bed?"

Mark didn't think twice. He wasn't stupid enough to turn down skin on skin with Zach. In fact, he was no sooner in the bed than Zach had his hands on him, smoothing them up and down his chest, stopping every so often to discover the details of muscle and skin, gently kissing each mark Mark knew adorned his neck. Mark relaxed into the touches; his morning wood very interested in the journey of Zach's huge hands. Zach pulled the covers up over them, guiding Mark's face to his, exchanging slow mint-fresh morning kisses, punctuated with small words, *morning, hot, hello* and breathless moans of pleasure.

Mark lay half on and half off Zach, his cock hard against Zach's hip.

"Beautiful," Zach said against Mark's mouth, nibbling softly on Mark's full lower lip, his tongue touching briefly, open-mouthed kisses that had no purpose other than to taste and to learn.

Mark pulled back, "Stop saying things like that," he murmured.

"Why?" Zach asked.

"Because I'm hard, and scarred, and it's not a fair description."

He wondered why he'd thought it a good idea to say anything at all when Zach frowned at him.

Zach kissed him gently. "You are beautiful, and every scar is a badge of honor."

Mark smiled at Zach and kissed him back. He kissed

the corners of his eyes that held such strength of emotion, and on his dark hair tousled from sleep.

"No. You're the beautiful one," Mark replied softly, smiling.

Zach tugged the dog tags, and then pressed his hand to Mark's chest, on the scars from a near miss with an IED. They hadn't talked about the injuries; they didn't need to. "So brave."

Mark leaned forward to pull Zach in for more kissing, more touching, the warmth of the covers around them isolating them from the rest of the world. Mark wasn't going to come from this, but it was new, and he was just enjoying every spark. His mind, though, was desperate for the next step, for Zach to force him down onto the bed, and kiss and push and make Mark feel every inch of him. God, he wanted that so much. He sighed into the kiss, unconsciously winding a leg with Zach's, and their cocks aligned, the hardness enough to send a shiver down Mark's spine. Hands, he needed Zach's hands, but they stubbornly remained buried in Mark's hair, cradling his head for breathless soul-touching kisses from ear to throat and back.

"No time for that. The car for the set is here; you have twenty minutes," Rob said, and pulled back the covers. Mark felt immediately exposed and shy. Stupid when he considered what they had done last night.

With a moan, Zach rolled and climbed off the bed. "My shower first, then you," he said, looking back at a thoroughly relaxed Mark.

"Come to the lot with us," Rob suggested.

"Bring your script," Zach added with a smile, finishing Rob's sentence and then disappearing into the bathroom.

Jemima freaking Cunningham.

I'm in the same room as Jemima Cunningham, creator of the number one show on cable TV, and I have the audacity to bring her a script?

What am I thinking?

"Sit, sit, Zach has got you ten minutes, so lay it on me," Jemima said brusquely, her eyes on the clock, a pencil in her hand and a script in front of her covered in penciled annotations.

Mark sat, his own script curled in hot sweaty hands, and cleared his throat.

"The whole story is based on a man, who loses his lover and realizes he was born with powers that he didn't know he had. A man who has this whole normal family life, but comes to learn he has these powers—"

"Powers?" The director-producer-writer-creator looked skeptical. Powers were nothing new.

"Yeah, he can control, um… thoughts, other people's ideas, well not control, but suggest, suggest emotions, and when he does this, unconsciously, at first, he learns that when he does this, it is as if he was stronger."

"Uh–huh." Jemima had, at least, looked up from what Mark assumed was a *Tomorrow's Game* script.

"Well, turns out his family, or the people whom he thinks are his family, are not. His mother is human, but his father is from the future which makes it all kinds of fucked up."

They talked way past ten minutes. Jemima stood and paced, moving to a whiteboard and scrawling words and lines and small doodles. Mark gave up any pretense of politeness and grabbed a pen, standing next to Jemima adding lines and characters and doodles of his own.

"Gay. Hmmm, a gay hero," she mused. "That would be interesting, but he'd need a hetero sidekick, we'd have to balance it. I'm not sure prime time is ready for a gay hero just yet, at least not one that isn't balanced with some straight-ass hero. No, wait." She scribbled more. "Fuck it, let's do this."

"Really?" Mark couldn't keep the surprise out of his tone.

Jemima slumped down into her chair, looking thoughtfully at the board. "Do you have a title yet, a working title even?"

"I called it *The Mind Outside*, but that was just…" How did he finish that line? She didn't look overly impressed.

"That might need some work," she finally offered. "Maybe some kind of… I don't know… three letters… like CSI… maybe, or two words."

"Okay."

"And I guess you have some casting ideas?"

"Yeah. I mean, from the pool of studio talent I suppose, as I assume it would be to this studio I am pitching through you?" Mark handed a list over, suggested alternative names and Jemima nodded as she dragged the tip of her pencil down the page.

"And for the gay lead? Do you know who you had in your head when you wrote?"

Mark just sat. Of course he did, but would telling Jemima just make her laugh? "Zach Cassidy," he almost whispered. "I wrote it for Zach's acting range, even though he's not what people would think of as gay."

Jemima snorted, then composed herself. "Interesting choice," she said, nodding, not dismissing the idea out of hand. "Look, this is kind of a big deal, this whole idea. I need to sit with it, then maybe we could get some of the *Tomorrow's Game* writers in, have a chat, get some ideas going, and then present it to the powers that be."

"You would do that? For me? Introduce the idea?"

"You would be doing the presenting; it is your idea. I would be... I don't know... a mentor. I'll make suggestions, and push you along."

"Well damn."

They took a break and, after two hours with Jemima, Mark found himself at craft services standing in line with a raft of extras covered in fake blood, and the two leading men themselves.

"Did it go okay?" Rob asked, indicating the papers under Mark's arm.

"More than. Jemima wants to run with it, maybe get some of the *Tomorrow's Game* writers in, present to the studio."

"I knew it would happen. Rob said it was good." Zach nodded, and Mark just looked at him in surprise. Had Rob read it? When? This morning when Mark was in the middle of a lazy make-out session with Zach?

"We need to celebrate," Zach said, grabbing three cans of drink and his food and wandering off in the direction of his trailer, Rob following, pulling at Mark's jacket.

"You too, Shakespeare," he said.

When they reached Zach's trailer, food seemed to be forgotten. Rob left it on one side and slumped back on the bed, his feet on the floor. It seemed maybe the food wasn't exactly what the three men were in the trailer for.

"My turn," Rob murmured. "I want your mouth on me," he added, looking directly at Mark, who still stood at the door, his food in his hands. Mark looked at Zach, uncertainty in his eyes, but Zach only reached around him and locked the door to the trailer, tilting the one blind and throwing the van into shadow.

"He wants your mouth on him," Zach repeated Rob's words softly, pulling Mark away from the door and toward the bed. "You want that? Both of us?" he added, pulling open the belt on Mark's jeans and helping to push them down before moving back to pull his clothes off layer by layer.

Mark wanted it more than his next breath. He was mesmerized. Rob still lay on the bed, fully clothed, his eyes wide as he watched Zach strip. In seconds, Mark had pulled off his boots, his jeans, and the rest of his clothes, his cock so hard it was painful and, without real conscious thought, he fell to his knees in front of Rob's spread legs, his hands immediately on his own painfully hard cock.

"No hands," Rob said, his tone leaving no room for argument. "Not your hands on you and not your hands on me, just your mouth." Mark dropped his hands immediately, cursing at the loss of their touch on his cock, as he and Zach started to strip Rob, a layer at a time, each item pulled from Rob's body with confident searching hands. When Zach finally pulled off Rob's boxers and all three of them were naked, it was impossible to tell who was hardest.

Zach guided Mark until his mouth was inches from Rob, and Mark watched as Rob unconsciously tilted his hips, and then Mark moved forward. He closed his mouth over the tip of Rob, licking gently at precome, the taste of it intoxicating. He heard Rob's sharp intake of breath and Mark felt his hands instinctively move toward Rob. He wanted to hold, but Zach stopped him, pulling his hands behind Mark's back and then exchanging a two-handed hold for one, restraining Mark.

"He said no hands, sexy, just your mouth. Let me…"

Zach was there, caressing Mark's face, feeling the hardness that was Rob inside, his hand slipping up Rob's length, circling the base, moving his grip, so it touched Mark's lips, obscenely stretched around Rob's cock, encouraging with words.

"Tighter, Mark, harder, shit, fuck, doing so well, so gorgeous, Rob you should see this..."

Mark felt he could come just from this, Rob writhing beneath him, Zach guiding and pulling and touching Rob inside Mark's mouth.

"Suck me lower," Rob gasped. Zach must have known what he meant because he sank his free hand into Mark's hair and pulled him back and off Rob's hard length. He guided Mark to Rob's balls, moving his fingers to open

Mark's mouth around them, Zach's fingers inside his mouth, touching Rob.

Jesus, fuck, shit, more.

Zach moved his whole body behind Mark, releasing Mark's hands, using his body to trap them where they were and lifting his now free hand to bury itself in Mark's hair, holding his head still.

"Fuck Mark's mouth, Rob," Zach begged hoarsely. He guided Rob's cock back into Mark's mouth, holding Mark still, allowing Rob to set the rhythm. Meanwhile, he pushed his cock between Mark's legs, pushing up and against Mark, forcing him on each move to rub against the side of the bed and the loose sheets. The friction was both intense and so sweet.

Rob moved his hands down, feeling Zach holding Mark, feeling Mark's mouth on him, and arched off the bed, losing it, hot and hard down Mark's throat, apparently no time to even warn, falling back on the bed with a muttered curse. Zach didn't let Mark move, only closing his hand around Mark's length, creating a tightness that held Mark still, and whispering in his ear.

"C'mon, Mark, show me."

Mark came, his orgasm intense, powerful, concentrated, Zach not far behind, hot and wet between them.

"You give good head," Rob said, yanking at Mark and stealing a kiss, a tangle of tongues and taste, and, this time, Zach was the one watching.

"We want you to stay," Zach finally said, moving in to kiss Rob hard before kissing Mark.

"You do?" Mark asked. His headspace was still fucked

out, and those kisses were unlike anything he'd ever tasted before. Forbidden, deep, and demanding.

"Three is a good number," Rob said.

Didn't matter to Mark if he was used as a spare third; he liked being used, and he wanted more.

Dressed, they left the trailer, Zach and Rob to go back to the set, Mark, on a complete high, on his way back home, his mind buzzing with what Zach and Rob had just said.

He could be a third; fuck, he had so many fantasies that he wanted to be part of. He wanted Rob to fuck him, push him down and fuck him so hard while Zach sucked his cock; he wanted to be the middle man in that scene.

I'm so hard.

Something to show you

Mark couldn't believe it. He was here, in a room with Jemima Cunningham and the queen of science fiction herself, Anna McKendricks, and they were talking to him.

To him.

Not only that but they liked his idea, wanted to run with it, wanted to push it to studio heads, wanted to get funding for it. They even wanted to approach Zach for the lead if he wanted to move away from *Tomorrow's Game* at the end of the next season. Zach just said he'd always wanted to leave when the show was on a high. Zach *fucking* Cassidy. It just blew Mark's mind; he didn't know what to say, what to do, just thanking them over and over.

The only sticking point was that they wanted an Army slant; they wanted to pick Mark's memories dry and use them in the show.

He wasn't ready to do that, and they'd understood, said he should think about it.

Nevertheless, he was on a high, and it was on this same high, this same utterly shocked level, that he arrived back at Zach's house, some hours after Zach and Rob had left the set. It was dark, almost midnight, and the house was curiously silent. Nothing. Maybe they'd gone out; maybe they were already in bed? They didn't owe Mark an explanation after all. He was only really a house guest at the end of the day; the spare third.

He dumped keys and his cell on the hall table, hung his jacket on the hook, and pushed his boots off next to Zach's near the door, moving into the kitchen, not bothering with the lights, opening the fridge and looking for a late-night snack before bed.

"I've got something to show you." Rob's voice echoed in the large kitchen from behind him, making Mark jump and clutch at his chest, spinning to face Rob, who stood there in sweats, no shirt, his face flushed.

"Jeez, fuck, you scared the shit outta me," Mark said, panting heavily, and leaned on the open fridge door.

"I've got something to show you," Rob repeated carefully, holding out a hand. Mark hesitated for all of two seconds before shutting the fridge door and grasping Rob's offered hand, following him down the hall and into the main bedroom. There were no lights on in the room, the only real sources of light the one in the hallway and the low hazy moonlight through the single window. At first, it was difficult to see, but as his eyes became more accustomed to the dark, he could make out Zach's figure lying on the bed. His hands were tied beautifully with silken rope to the headboard, his legs spread and fastened to the base with the same intricately tied ropes, his eyes covered with a blindfold.

"Mark is home," Rob murmured. "Are you ready for

my present?" He kneeled next to the bound man, his lips a breath away from Zach's ear, Zach twisting to capture a taste of skin, murmuring something Mark couldn't hear. Mark just focused on Rob's deep chuckle, the noise going straight to his cock, watching as Rob straightened.

"He loves this, you know, loves being tied up and left, unable to see, wondering what I'm gonna do to him. I can leave him for hours, come back, push him so close, so near, and then back off. It's been three times tonight where I got him close, just using my hands, feeling him, stroking, coming on him. Only, this time, I promised him *you*. I promised I'd show *you* what he likes so that we can do this together." Mark couldn't think of a word to say. The filtered moonlight cast a silvery sheen to the sweat on Zach's smooth muscled body, and Mark's cock was hard against his zipper.

Rob moved to stand in front of him, palming him through the soft worn denim. He pushed Mark back against the wall, laying kisses up from throat to lips, biting into the skin, each mark dragging heated moans from Mark. Carefully he opened Mark's zipper, his hands reaching past denim to soft cotton.

"Moan for me so he can hear," he whispered in Mark's ear. "I need you to be loud and show Rob what I'm doing to you." Mark had no option, given permission to release his pleasure in a long, drawn-out moan for more. It wasn't going to take much, just the erotic sight of a near-whimpering Zach arching up on the bed, his leaking cock hard and heavy against his stomach.

"He won't ask us, he won't say a word," Rob said confidently. "Doesn't matter how much you moan, he will never force himself to ask us for a thing." Pushing Mark's jeans down over bare hips, Rob's lips started a journey south. He teased and tasted the muscled expanse of Mark's chest, focusing on nipples, biting trails down to the revealed spur of the hip. He sucked a bruising mark on the taut skin there, then pushed back and climbed with insistent kisses to Mark's open panting mouth. "Do you want me to suck you, Mark? Do you want me to fall on my knees and close my mouth around you, suck you down? Do you want to put your hand there, hold me still, and fuck my mouth?" It was too much, too many words, the picture of a wanton Zach burned on his retinas, Rob's words, quiet and unrelenting, creating images guaranteed to push Mark to the edge.

Not saying anything, no words, just sighs, and moans and Rob's hand, he lost it, coming over his stomach, his jeans, Rob. Rob, who scooped the come from his stomach, pulled Mark with his other hand until they stood over a keening Zach, taking his hand and gently encouraging Zach to open his mouth, putting his come-covered fingers inside. "You want to know the taste of him again?"

Freaking, holy, what the fuck?

Zach lifted his head to suck at Rob's hand, the muscles in his neck straining against the restraint of his bonds. It was an obscene sound, licking and tasting and pulling Rob's hand into his mouth, Rob murmuring words of promise against his hooded eyes.

"Mark, you got to see this, see him tasting you, fucking taste you in him."

It was all Mark could do to scramble out of his boxers, pulling his shirt over his head and leaning over Zach, his lips joining Rob's hand, knowing himself then in the dark taste of Zach's mouth. Zach whimpered, an honest-to-god whine, and Mark could feel himself hardening against Zach's thigh.

"So gorgeous," Rob whispered. He guided Mark to lie down to one side of Zach, his hands exploring Zach's toned muscled physique, taking the time to learn the curves and the lines of Mark against Zach. They fit so well together. And then there were no more words, just guided touches. Rob followed Mark's hand with his own, and between them they forced gasps of pleasure and want from their tied lover, concentrating on biting and sucking, one, and then both, stopping to kiss each other as their journey down Zach's body met with heat and lust.

They stopped at Zach's hips; his cock hard and leaking, lying thick against his skin. Mark reached for Rob's cock instead, swallowing him down, and listening to Rob tell him to slow down, that he was going to come. Mark tightened his hand at the base of Rob's cock, glancing up to see the ecstasy on Rob's face as he was close, so near, the dark eyes hard and half-lidded with passion. He shook his head.

"Don't let me come. For Zach, I need to hold back…"

Mark stopped his movement on Rob, removing his hands and instead focusing on Zach, who by now was whimpering low in his throat. Rob leaned in to whisper in Zach's ear, detailing every movement.

"Do you want Mark to suck you off, do you want him to use his fingers inside you, where you're still loose? Maybe move his hands inside you?"

Zach said nothing, just pushed his hips, lost in the

sensation of the slick on Mark's hands, of his fingers as they pushed inside him. He was still loose from Rob, still slick with Rob's come, from the second or third time he had taken him to the edge.

"Do you want Mark to fuck you, hmmm, shall I untie your feet and turn you over and just let him fuck you?"

Mark closed his lips over Zach's cock, his fingers, three, four, twisting inside, finding the sweet spot wired straight to Zach's brain, sending him higher, his other hand tight around the base of Zach's cock, holding him on the edge.

"I should just get Mark to fuck you on the bed so that you can hump the covers."

Mark looked up at Rob's face, at the obvious love and passion he saw there for Zach. He almost came again, edging so close to coming he nearly lost control. He released the pressure on Zach's cock and swallowed him down in one smooth move, sucking and releasing, his head moving, and his hands twisting, Rob pulling at Zach's hard nipples, mirroring the same insistent movement as Mark.

"Fuck him," Rob ordered. Mark scrambled back, grabbed more lube and a condom, and in short order had his fingers curling inside Zach. Then he was there, his blunt head breaching, pushing inside, and waiting until Zach's body sucked at him, pulled him, held him in a vise of need.

"Jesus. Fuck," Mark said, words scrambling around in his head.

Rob murmured soft words as he kissed down Zach's body, sucking Zach's cock into his mouth then moving again. Zach instinctively pulled out a little and Rob kissed

Zach's balls, sucking them, tugging them, Zach groaning and writhing. Then his tongue touched the rim, running along the length of Mark and sucking on Zach's taut skin.

Mark had to think about anything to stop himself coming.

"I can't," he groaned, warning Rob, who scooted up a little and swallowed Zach down.

Zach couldn't hold it, his back arching, coming with a muffled shout, hard and long, Rob pulled back, swallowed, taking as much as he could, some escaping his mouth, slipping his hands up and down his cock, watching as Rob came in his hand.

"Finish," Rob said, and Mark pushed deep, his rhythm harsh and stuttering, coming deep into a still-squirming, heaving Zach. Both Rob and Mark fell to either side of Zach, breathing erratically and loud.

"See?" Rob finally said. "Told you I had something to show you."

Sharing

Zach and Rob were due back home after lunch, and Mark knew that when they got back, they would be exhausted; it was always the same way when *Tomorrow's Game* was filming at night. Rob had pinned the schedule of shoots to the fridge with a magnet and had scrawled a big black SLEEP across the afternoon for today. An action that had made Zach laugh, even as he snaked his hand into Mark's jeans and pulled him closer for a thorough kiss, giving Rob the show he needed as he sat at the table eating pizza.

"No sleeping," Zach said confidently. "More fucking."

"Need sleep," Mark heard Rob mutter at the table. "Lots of sleep."

Zach and Mark exchanged concerned looks; it wasn't just rest Rob needed. He wasn't sleeping, and something was on his mind that he wasn't sharing. The three of them had lived in this heaven for six weeks now, and Mark never wanted it to end. So much so he'd sublet his small apartment to an Army buddy and wasn't planning on going home anytime soon.

The sex they had, the three of them, it sometimes scared Mark to see the depth of passion in Rob's eyes when he watched Zach and Mark together. Was it scaring Rob to the point he was shutting down?

Rob being so quiet, and not sleeping, terrified Mark. What if Rob was worrying how to tell Mark that he wanted to end this complicated three-way connection they had? When Rob watched them, his hand on his cock, arching his spine, wringing an orgasm that forced a guttural moan from his mouth, Mark was sure he could see the end every time.

Mark didn't mention that to Zach, didn't raise it as a concern, his fear that Zach would just turn around and say, *well Mark, he has a point, you are outstaying your welcome.* So he kept it inside, his anxiety, his fear they were going to call time on this. It would be easy if Mark weren't in love.

Not in lust. Love.

Love with all its complements, like worry, and fear, and plans for the future, and he couldn't help it. Call it commitment issues, call it not being able to do casual sex like this, call it need, but whatever, he had found himself falling in love with Zach almost immediately. What was not to love? So intense, yet relaxed and accepting of his focus, steady and precise; wearing his heart on his sleeve for everyone to see. If it was love to want to be with Zach all the time, outside the sex, outside the bedroom, wanting to talk to Zach, learn Zach, map every bump in his life, every point that made him the man he was today, then yes, Mark was in love.

Not to mention Rob. Affection and sex was turning to

more, but he didn't even think about it. Rob wasn't interested in more with him, just wanted Mark on the edge of things. Rob was in love with Zach, and he was only interested in Rob. So Mark stayed quiet about it all.

He didn't show it, wouldn't show it, tried to stay casual, attempted to accept his place in this strange circle of lust he found himself connected to, but he swore Rob knew he loved Zach. He was convinced he could see it in Rob's eyes.

Worrying thoughts like those meant he could not settle to write, an itch in his skin that he needed to work his way through. He was used to using physical work to relax, to using his hands, finding peace in mending and solving, in creating, and in manual labor that made his muscles ache and his skin wet with sweat. This same itch sent him to the garage gym, wondering, not for the first time, if the guys had anything in the way of tools, feeling the push inside to get some physical labor behind him, work off some of the fear.

Rummaging behind closed doors he only found more sports stuff, weights, bars, and it was enough for the wannabe carpenter in him to rage at the lack of equipment here to repair anything, sending him out in Rob's truck to the nearest trade suppliers for what he needed. He had a porch roof to mend, and it was nice to slip back into his hobby, focused and intent on that one thing. He loaded everything in the truck, tools, lumber, the extension ladder, everything he thought he needed and a few bits more, for when he left so that the guys could be more self-sufficient.

Some three hundred dollars on his credit card later, he arrived back at Zach's house. It always surprised him to see just how ordinary the area around it was; houses all similar in size, detached, with well-tended gardens and evidence of families with children everywhere, dogs in the yards, and barbecues on the weekend. Zach had bought the very last house on the back of the cul de sac, away and up into the wooded area behind, and well back from the other houses, buying up some of the land behind it, so he had complete privacy. It wasn't a secure gated community; Zach hadn't wanted that. He just kept his privacy and stayed friendly with his neighbors.

Mark reversed the truck onto the drive and climbed out, emptied the contents of the truck bed, and walked through to the garden. He piled everything carefully in the corner on the back porch that needed fixing, still not entirely sure whether maybe he was overstepping the mark by touching Zach's house, and grabbed a bottle of water from the fridge before he started working. The day wasn't exceptionally hot, but the heat that did linger around the house was enough to make Mark stop for another water and to pull off his T-shirt, wiping his face with it before dropping it just outside the back door.

He tightened the tool belt; the leather snug against his hips as his jeans rode low. Then he climbed the ladder to reach the break he wanted to start working on. He found familiar peace in the repetition of wood and nail, satisfaction at the physical work that he was doing, turning up the music on his iPod and losing himself in his thoughts.

Noise below him had him lowering the volume on the music, and he half-turned on the ladder to look down. Rob was home.

"I followed the noise of hammering," Rob said.

"Yeah, sorry, just needed fixing and I couldn't settle to write."

Even to his ears, it sounded like he was apologizing for something he didn't need to.

"Zach's been kept back for a redo on a scene."

"Shit. Really?" Mark contemplated climbing down the ladder. Rob seemed distracted, and he thought maybe he could be a sounding board if he wanted to talk.

"I'm tired, grumpy, and need something, anything," Rob said, the words snapped and peppered with exhaustion, not making sense.

Mark tensed. Was Rob spoiling for a fight maybe? Or was this the point where Rob said it was all finished, that he wanted Mark to leave.

"Maybe it's just pent-up character aggression from your filming," Mark suggested. He'd heard Rob suggest the same thing.

"Yeah," Rob said noncommittally. Then the tone of his voice changed. "I was hiding on the porch, watching you work."

"Okay." Mark started to move, but Rob stopped him with a hand to Mark's calf.

"Stay."

"Okay."

He looked up at Mark and shook his head as if he thought something inside that didn't make sense. "I know you're Zach's."

"What?"

"Zach lets me play, but when it comes down to it, you are here to be with Zach."

"I don't understand." Mark said the words, but he had a good idea of where Rob was coming from.

"I saw you; no shirt, skin glistening with sweat, jeans low on your hips and a fucking tool belt. Fuck, Mark, how is any of that fair?"

"Rob?"

"I went back into the house; my cock was so hard. I thought I'd do it myself, make myself come to the kinkiest fucking image I could imagine after seeing you, practically naked, in the sun."

"I'm wearing jeans," Mark said. He was becoming steadily more uncertain as Rob talked. It seemed like there was violence in Rob here and Mark didn't know how it was going to end, fuck or fight. He'd seen this kind of thing in the sandbox when tension got to the snapping point, and all that was left was impulsive aggression.

"I tried to get off, you know. I promised I wouldn't touch what is Zach's, not when he isn't here, but it didn't happen. Nothing fucking happened. So I thought I'd find you and maybe even start a reasonable conversation with you." And then he stopped talking, his hand on Mark's thigh.

Rob pulled at the tool belt, unclipping it and letting it fall to the floor, always concentrating on what he was doing, not looking up into Mark's eyes.

"Rob?" Mark questioned tentatively. "What are you doing?"

Rob lifted his gaze to look at Mark. "I want you. I think I'm falling…" He stopped. His voice was rough, the words barely audible. His hands slipped under the top button of Mark's jeans, hot against his skin. "Is all of this we do… is it just about Zach?" he added, closing his eyes briefly and then opening them. The raw emotion in his voice scared him.

"I thought you liked that I made Zach happy," Mark said.

"We're all happy together. Aren't we?" Rob murmured. He'd just revealed that Zach and Mark were not the only ones with an emotional stake in what was happening between the three of them, and it sent a shiver of want and longing through Mark, a moan low in his throat.

Rob lowered his eyes, gesturing for Mark to move back up a step, pushing him to lean back against the rungs, his fingers easing each button on the fly open, the strength in his hands already pressing against Mark.

"Is this okay? Even if Zach isn't here?"

"Fuck…," Mark moaned.

Fire and need curled low in Mark's belly. Finally, all the buttons were undone, the material hanging loose on hip bones. Gently Rob pushed the denim lower, only Mark's thighs stopping it from falling all the way.

Rob pressed at those same hipbones, fingertips pushing into the skin, near enough to Mark's center as to make him keen and push forward. Rob's mouth was at the height of Mark's chest, and he leaned back.

"I fucking love your chest." He reached up and curled the fingers of his left hand around Mark's dog tags, and his right hand circled Mark's cock. Then he bent his head and sucked at Mark's nipples, moving only slightly to pull one nub into his mouth, alternately tonguing and pulling on the hard flesh. He didn't move his hands, kept them still, and he kissed from one nipple to the other, sucking a path of possession across Mark's chest.

"Zach will see this," Rob murmured. "He can follow my marks and know I've been here when we're alone; he wants that so much."

"He does?"

Rob glanced at him. "That surprises you?"

"Yeah, I mean, I don't know what to think."

"He loves you, do you love him?"

Mark thought of a million ways he could coat the truth and make it easier to swallow for Rob. In the end, he could only say one thing. "Yes."

"I think I'm falling in love with you," Rob said. He eased Mark up one more step, and then another, each step accompanied by that same path of taste until his hands on Mark's hips were almost at his head height. He only had to dip his mouth to taste. "This is more than just sex."

"Really?" Mark wanted to ask more than that, but he couldn't get the words right.

"I do, you know, I couldn't imagine not having you here."

"I love you, too," Mark admitted. That was such a scary thing to have out in the open air.

"Thank fuck," Rob murmured. Then he chuckled a little. "You smell of soap and heat," Rob said against Mark's skin and mouthed his cock through the soft cotton.

"God, Rob, more…"

Rob stopped.

"Don't stop," Mark pleaded.

Rob pushed harder into the flesh indenting at the hips and finally eased lips and tongue past material, ran an experimental taste, another trigger to Mark's already overworked senses. Mark, for his part, just tried to hold on, his hands twisted into the ladder above him, desperate to push. The sun was hot on them, not to burn, but enough to throw a net of lust around them.

"Rob, please..."

How could it last long? The sudden switch from outsiders, from strangers to lovers, had been so sudden in the sun-soaked garden. Rob didn't hesitate in his movements, using his mouth to increase the friction, taking Mark as far as he could go, making it as good for him as he could without hands and as far as the bunched material of his boxers would allow him to. Until the desperation in Mark's shaking body seemingly made him relent and he released one hand to push the boxers fully down, grasping Mark from base to mouth and starting a countermovement to his mouth. When Mark lost it, when he shouted his completion into the summer's day, Rob helped Mark slide down each step, biting his way back up to his chest, then higher, capturing his lips in a hot wet messy kiss.

"I love you, I love Zach, please don't make me leave," Mark begged. He hadn't even said it to Zach yet; this was wrong. Then he couldn't think of anything else but the taste of himself in Rob's mouth. He licked into Rob's mouth, tongues battling for taste, exchanging kisses filled with want and need. Mark dropped his hands, pulling at jeans and cotton, finding Rob as hard as he had ever felt, and slick.

"Rob? Mark?" Zach's voice, filled with lust and heat, surprised them both.

Mark's eyes flew open. Had Zach heard what he'd said

to Rob? Mark looked right into Zach's eyes; Zach had to know how Mark felt. "I love you."

"I love you, both," Zach murmured. "And no one is leaving anyone."

And then Zach was there, his hands on Rob's cock, lacing his fingers with Mark's and they moved their hands together. They said nothing, exchanged no words, just held Rob firmly between them, kissing and holding and asking for nothing as Rob keened and came over joined hands, falling back against Zach, his eyes closed, a hitched breath as he settled into Zach's supportive hold.

"Feel better now?" Zach asked Rob softly, leaning around him to pull Mark in for a welcome kiss; a thank you kiss. Rob said nothing, exhaustion settling in him for anyone to see, but Mark hoped his head was clear and empty of worry. Zach just smiled and started to guide them all to the house; he was doubtless exhausted, probably needed sleep, and Mark was happy to doze with his two lovers. Rob's bed was big.

Big enough for the three of them.

THE END

Single Dads

Single

Today

Promise

Single - Book 1 of the Single Dads series

Reeling from the painful rejection of a man he thought he loved, Asher is left holding the baby.

Ash wants a family, and is determined to continue with a

surrogacy he'd begun with his ex. Bringing baby Mia home, he vows that he will be the best father he can be. Nothing in this world matters more to him than caring for his daughter, not even accidentally falling in lust with the doctor next door. Challenged by his growing attraction to Sean, and confronted by painful memories of his family, Ash has to learn that love is all that matters.

When ER doctor Sean moves in with his friends next door to sexy single father Ash, he falls so quickly it takes his breath away. The sex they have is hot, but Ash is adamant his heart is too full with love for his daughter to let anyone else in. Why is Sean the only one who sees how scared Ash is, and how can he prove to his new lover that he desperately wants the three of them to become a family?

Mystery / Murder / Suspense Romance

Lancaster Falls

What Lies Beneath (August 2019)

Without a Trace

All That Remains

What Lies Beneath

In the hottest summer on record, Iron Lake reservoir is emptying, revealing secrets that were intended to stay hidden beneath the water. The tragic story of a missing man is a media sensation, and abruptly the writer and the cop falling in love is just a postscript to horrors neither could have imagined.

Best Selling Horror writer Chris Lassiter struggles for inspiration and he's close to never writing again. His life has become an endless loop of nothing but empty pages, personal appearances, and a marketing machine that is systematically destroying his muse. In a desperate attempt to force Chris to complete unfinished manuscripts his agent rents out a remote cabin for an entire year. All he has to do is write, but it's not that easy and even the solitude and silence can't make stories appear from anything.

Sawyer Wiseman left town for Chicago, chasing the excitement and potential of being a big city cop, rising the ranks, and making his mark. A case gone horribly wrong coincides with a family tragedy and draws him back to Lancaster Falls. Working for the tiny police department in the town he'd been running from, he spends his day's healing, and his nights hoping the nightmares of his last case leave him alone.

Cowboys Ranchers Family - Romance

Cowboys, ranches, family, and love.

Texas

The Heart of Texas | Texas Winter | Texas Heat | Texas Family | Texas Christmas | Texas Fall | Texas Wedding | Texas Gift | Home For Christmas

Legacy (spin-off from Texas series)

Kyle | Gabriel | Daniel

Montana

Crooked Tree Ranch | The Rancher's Son | A Cowboy's Home | Snow In Montana | Second Chance Ranch | Montana Sky

Wyoming

Winter Cowboy | Summer Drifter

Action Adventure Romance

Heroes, Bodyguards, First Responders, SEALs, Marines, Cops

Sanctuary

Guarding Morgan | The Only Easy Day | Face Value | Still Waters | Full Circle | The Journal of Sanctuary 1 | World's Collide | Accidental Hero | Ghost | By The Numbers

A Reason To Stay | Last Marine Standing | Deacon's Law

Bodyguards Inc

Bodyguard to a Sex God | The Ex-Factor | Max and the Prince | Undercover Lovers | Love's Design | Kissing Alex

Standalone

Alpha Delta | Seth & Casey

All The King's Men | Retrograde | Force of Nature

Hockey Romance

Standalone Titles

Secrets | Dallas Christmas | Last Chance

Written with V.L. Locey

Harrisburg Railers

Changing Lines | First Season | Deep Edge | Poke Check| Last Defense | Goal Line | Neutral Zone | Hat Trick | Save the Date

Owatonna U

Ryker | Scott | Benoit

Arizona Raptors

Coast To Coast

Small Town / First Responders Romance

Ellery Mountain

The Fireman and the Cop

The Teacher and the Soldier

The Carpenter and the Actor

The Doctor and the Bad Boy

The Paramedic and the Writer

The Barman and the SEAL

The Agent and the Model

The Sinner and the Saint

Christmas Romance

The Christmas Throwaway

Love Happens Anyway

New York Christmas

The Christmas Collection

Jesse's Christmas

The Road to Frosty Hollow

Christmas Prince

Dallas Christmas

Angel in a Book Shop

Mr Sparkles

Standalone Romance Stories

One Night

Moments

Back Home

Boy Banned

Deefur Dog

Child Of The Storm

Spirit Bear

The Decisions We Make (YA/NA)

The Bucket List

The Summer House

Three (MMM)

How Much For The Whole Night

Single (coming soon)

For a Rainy Afternoon

Snow & Secrets

Co-Authored Romance

with Meredith Russell

Sapphire Cay

Follow the Sun | Under the Sun | Chase The Sun | Christmas In The Sun | Capture The Sun | Forever In The Sun

Boyfriends For Hire

Darcy | Kaden

Standalone

The Art of Words | The Road to Frosty Hollow

with Chris Quinton

Salisbury

Heat | Ice

Paranormal Romance

Standalone Stories

The Gallows Tree | The New Wolf | The Soldier's Tale | Ghost In The Stone (Coming Halloween 2019)

In the Shadow of the Wolf

With Diane Adams

Shattered Secrets | Broken Memories | Splintered Lies

Oracle

Oracle | Book of Secrets | The Oracle Collection

End Street Detective Agency

With Amber Kell

End Street Volume 1 (Cupid Curse / Wicked Wolf)

End Street Volume 2 (Dragon's Dilemma / Sinful Santa)

End Street Volume 3 (Purple Pearl / Guilty Ghost)

Kingdom

Kingdom Volume 1 (Vampire Contract, Guilty Werewolf, Warlock's Secret)

Kingdom Volume 2 (Demon's Blood, Incubus Agenda, Third Kingdom)

Fire

Kian's Hunter | Darach's Cariad | Eoin's Destiny

Meet RJ Scott

RJ is the author of the over one hundred published novels and discovered romance in books at a very young age. She realized that if there wasn't romance on the page, she could create it in her head, and is a lifelong writer.

She lives and works out of her home in the beautiful English countryside, spends her spare time reading, watching films, and enjoying time with her family.

The last time she had a week's break from writing she didn't like it one little bit and has yet to meet a bottle of wine she couldn't defeat.

www.rjscott.co.uk | rj@rjscott.co.uk

facebook.com/author.rjscott

twitter.com/Rjscott_author

instagram.com/rjscott_author

bookbub.com/authors/rj-scott

pinterest.com/rjscottauthor

Printed in Great Britain
by Amazon